Praise for Lina Bengtsdotter's debut thriller, *For The Missing*

'This smash hit Swedish debut breathes new life into a few well-worn det-fic themes to create a thriller that lingers in the memory' – *Sunday Times Crime Club*

'A powerful Scandi Noir debut by a promising new author . . . Atmospheric, evocative and with a heroine who overcomes some of the genre's clichés, this is a first-class procedural with all shades of grey unveiled like onion peel as the narrative progresses. With various parallel story strands deepening the mystery before they all come together in a flurry of unwelcome truths, this makes for an altogether excellent thriller' – *Crime Time*

'This debut novel is intelligent and arresting. And grim' – *Morning Star*

'This debut novel upholds the recent tradition of dark Nordic noir. A girl goes missing on her way home from the party in the forested village of Gullspang. Enter a Stockholm detective with a secret of her own' – *i Newspaper*

'A brilliant, dense crime novel' – *Dagens Nyheter*

'The next big Swedish crime sensation' – *Dagbladet*

'A wonderful debut' – *Dziennik Zachodni*

Lina Bengtsdotter grew up in Gullspång, Sweden. She is a teacher in Swedish and Psychology and has published a number of short stories in various newspapers and magazines in Sweden and the Nordic countries. She has lived in the UK and in Italy and today resides outside of Stockholm with her three children. *For the Missing* is her debut novel.

Agnes Broomé is a literary translator and Preceptor in Scandinavian at Harvard University. With a PhD in Translation Studies, her translations include August Prize winner *The Expedition* by Bea Uusma.

FOR THE MISSING

LINA BENGTSDOTTER

Translated from the Swedish by
AGNES BROOMÉ

ORION

An Orion paperback

First published in Great Britain in 2018
by Orion Books,
This paperback edition published in 2019
by Orion Fiction,
an imprint of The Orion Publishing Group Ltd,
Carmelite House, 50 Victoria Embankment,
London EC4Y 0DZ

An Hachette UK company

1 3 5 7 9 10 8 6 4 2

A CIP catalogue record for this book
is available from the British Library.

ISBN 978 1 4091 7935 1

Typeset by Deltatype Ltd, Birkenhead, Merseyside

Printed in Great Britain by Clays Ltd, Elcograf S.p.A.

MIX
Paper from
responsible sources
FSC® C104740

www.orionbooks.co.uk

It was many and many a year ago,
  In a kingdom by the sea,
That a maiden there lived whom you may know
  By the name of Annabel Lee;
And this maiden she lived with no other thought
  Than to love and be loved by me.

From 'Annabel Lee' by Edgar Allan Poe

That night

Fog had settled across the fields and crickets were chirping from the grass verge. The girl was staggering down the gravel road. There was a throbbing between her legs; something was seeping out of her. She thought to herself she should be crying, but no tears came.

What time was it? Eleven? Twelve? She pulled her phone out of her purse. Almost half twelve. Her mum was going to have a fit. She was going to meet her at the front door, shake her shoulders and furiously demand to know where she had been. Then she would notice the rips, the blood, her torn dress. And how was she going to explain those things?

She was so preoccupied she didn't notice the figure in front of her until he was no more than a few feet away. A yelp escaped her at first, but when she recognised his face, she relaxed.

'Oh, it's just you?' she slurred. 'You scared me half to death.'

I

It was early June and the nights were never truly dark. Fredrik Roos was sitting in his car, gazing out across the misty meadows. He knew Annabelle often cut across them, that she had tramped her own paths through the tall grass. Naturally, Nora had told her she wasn't allowed to walk there at night, but Fredrik knew she did it anyway and he could see why. With Nora's miserly curfews, every minute was precious. He hoped he would see his daughter walking through the tall grass any second now, wearing the thin, blue dress that was apparently missing from Nora's wardrobe. Nora had flown off the handle when she noticed. He thought about his wife for a while, about her fiery temper and anxiety. She had always been unstable, a worrier. When they first met, he had found it somehow fascinating: the way she had been able to build nightmare scenarios out of regular, everyday events. As the years went by, his fascination had been replaced by exasperation. And now, as he sat in the car, sent out by Nora yet again to bring Annabelle home, he realised he was reaching the end of his tether.

You can't protect them against everything, he would tell her, even though he knew nothing irked Nora more. The fact that it was impossible to protect them from everything was not an argument, obviously, for not protecting them whenever you could. The only problem was that they disagreed on where to draw that line. As far as Fredrik was concerned, Annabelle should be allowed to walk home from her friends' houses on her own, even if it was the middle of the night. And he didn't like it that she had to call and tell them where she was if her plans changed. When he was growing up, he had come and gone as he pleased. He would have kicked off big time if someone had tried to control him the way Nora did with Annabelle. No wonder Annabelle had started breaking the rules. Too much free rein is not the issue here, Fredrik mused: it's Nora's enormous need for control that is causing problems.

The building that had once been a village shop was on the other side of town. It had been empty for years and was a long-standing venue for parties thrown by the local youth. Fredrik knew many townspeople wanted the house torn down. He had signed one of the petitions about it himself, but mostly for appearance's sake. He knew very well that tearing the building down would only mean the young people took their partying elsewhere, probably even further from the town centre.

He parked in front of the main entrance. Decades-old yellowed newspaper placards still clung to the big glass window. A deep bassline could be heard all the way to his car. Fredrik picked up his phone to call Nora and ask if Annabelle had come home yet. He wasn't going to crash a teenage party if he didn't have to. Just as he was about to dial, Nora rang. Was he there yet?

'I just pulled up.'

'Is she there?'

'I just stepped out of the car.'

'So go in then.'

'I was just on my way.'

3

The overgrown flowerbeds along the building's facade were littered with beer cans, cigarette butts and bottles. Entering through the main door, he stepped straight into the large space that had once housed the shop. A smell of dereliction hit his nostrils and for a moment he paused to survey the filthy floor, the counter with the old cash register and the long, empty shelves lining the walls. The music was pumping above his head. He walked towards the door he knew led up to the flat above the shop. Locked. He went back outside and around the corner to try the back entrance. A young man was asleep on the veranda with his hand down his trousers. Fredrik had to step over him to reach the door.

A sweet smell hit him in the hallway. He followed the music up a long, winding staircase.

They were in the kitchen, three boys, around a dark wooden table buried under ashtrays, bottles, cans and tobacco pouches. One of them was compulsively stabbing at the table top with a small knife. Their faces looked familiar, but Fredrik couldn't remember their names. They must be a slightly older than Annabelle, otherwise he would have known. None of them noticed him until he was standing right in front of them.

'Hi there!' yelled the one with the knife.

And now Fredrik realised it was that one, the plywood factory owner's son. Wasn't his name Svante, or possibly Dante?

'Have a seat, and a drink!' he bellowed. 'Hey, no need to look so glum,' he continued. 'It's a party. Everyone else pussied out but we're going to keep going till the sun comes up.'

'It's already up, Svante,' the boy next to him laughed. He tapped on the dirty kitchen window. 'In fact, I don't think it ever fucking set.'

'Is Annabelle here?' Fredrik asked.

'Annabelle?' The young men looked at one another.

4

'Annabelle,' Fredrik repeated.

Svante shot him a smile and said he knew Annabelle liked older gents, but that there were limits. 'You're old enough to be her bloody father, mate.'

'I *am* her father,' Fredrik said. He took a few steps towards the table. He suddenly had a violent impulse to wipe the stupid grin off this boy's face.

All three of them stared at him.

'Shit, that's right,' Svante said. 'You actually are.' He kicked at an unoccupied chair and apologised profusely. He hadn't meant ... he didn't mean ... he just hadn't recognised him. They'd had a few too many. 'And with this heat as well, anyone could be excused for feeling parched, no? Get the man a drink, Jonas,' Svante said, nodding to the boy across the table. 'Go mix up something proper fucking strong. Go on then, get up.'

'I don't want a drink,' Fredrik said. 'I just want to know where my daughter is. Have you seen her?'

'There was quite a crowd here earlier,' Svante said. 'Things went a bit mental, if you know what I mean. We were already going at seven, that's why everyone's fucked off already. But yeah, she was here, though I think she left. But some people are still upstairs,' he said, pointing at the ceiling. 'If it were me, I'd go have a look. There's several floors,' he called as Fredrik made his way to the stairs. 'Check all of them because people will lie down anywhere.'

Fredrik climbed a flight of stairs. The music grew louder with every step. There was a big landing on the next floor up. There was an aquarium against one wall. When he moved closer, he discovered a turtle bobbing around in water full of cigarette butts. What are people like, he thought, putting cigarettes out in an aquarium?

Beyond the landing was a living room with ripped, green

plush sofas. A girl with tangled hair was sprawled on one of them. At first, Fredrik thought she was asleep, but on closer inspection he realised her eyes were wide open and staring.

'Are you all right?' he asked.

'Wonderful,' the girl whispered. 'Thanks for asking.' Then she started giggling and waving her hands about. Fredrik figured she had enjoyed something other than just plain alcohol, that maybe he should find out her name and give her a ride home to her parents. He would, he decided, as soon as he had located Annabelle.

The stereo was in the next room. The music was ear-splitting. It took Fredrik a while to find the volume and turn it down. Then he walked on through the house, opening one door after another, but the rest of the rooms on that floor were empty. He ended up in a small hallway with yet another staircase. How many floors are there in this house? he wondered. Does it go on forever? At the top, there were two doors. The left one was locked, but the door on the right opened when Fredrik pushed the handle down.

A window was open in the room; a white curtain billowed in and out on the wind. In a bed sitting in the middle of the room, something was moving rhythmically under a duvet.

'Annabelle?' Fredrik said. 'Is that you?'

'What the fuck!' A boy peered out from under the duvet at the foot of the bed. 'Get out,' he said. 'Are you some kind of pervert, or what? Get the fuck out!'

'I'm looking for my daughter. I just want to know if Annabelle is here.' Fredrik watched for a reaction to the name.

'No. I have no idea where she is.'

'So who's under the duvet then?'

'Rebecka,' the boy said. 'Show him it's you.'

'It's me,' Rebecka said from under the duvet. 'I don't know where Annabelle is. She said she was going home.'

'I thought she was at yours,' Fredrik said. 'Nora told me you were going to be at your house, watching a film.'

'We were,' Rebecka replied, 'but then some stuff came up.'

'When did she leave?'

'I'm not sure. We had a bit too much to drink and Annabelle ... she was ... she was pretty drunk. I'm sorry!' Rebecka called out as Fredrik was leaving the room. 'I would have walked her home, but ...'

'She wasn't up there, was she?' Suddenly Svante was standing right behind him.

'No. Rebecka just told me.'

'Like she'd know.'

'What's behind this door?' Fredrik said, pointing.

'She's not in there. That much I can promise you.'

'How can you be sure?'

'Because,' Svante said, 'I'm the only one with a key to that door.'

'Then maybe you could open it for me?'

'I'd be happy to. Except I've lost the key. I lost it yesterday. That's how I know no one's in there. Do you need help looking for her, by the way? We have a moped downstairs, it's souped up like nothing you've ever seen, we could head out and ...'

Fredrik looked into Svante's big eyes. There was something strange about them. He thought to himself that this was not a person he wanted out on the roads looking for Annabelle; that in this state he would in fact constitute a clear danger to the public.

'Of course we're going to help you look,' Svante pressed on, 'I mean ... I've heard she has to be home pretty early and ...'

Fredrik studied the young face and thought to himself it was true what he had heard them say: the factory owner's son was an unpleasant sort.

When Fredrik returned to the car, he had three missed calls from Nora. He called her back, hoping she just wanted to tell him Annabelle had showed up, but he could instantly tell from her voice that wasn't the case.

'Are you still at the shop?' she asked. And before he could reply: 'Was she there?'

'No,' Fredrik said. 'She's not here.'

'Well then, where is she?'

'I don't know.'

'Go by Rebecka's.'

'Rebecka is here,' Fredrik said. 'Calm down,' he continued, as Nora burst into tears. 'I'm sure she's on her way home. I'll look for her on the way.'

'Just get her home,' Nora said. 'You bloody well get her home right now, Fredrik.'

2

Charlie woke up at seven. She never slept well after a night of drinking, particularly not in a strange bed. She looked over at the man next to her. Martin, was that his name? And what had she told him her name was? Maria? Magdalena? She always lied about her name when she picked up men in bars – her name and her profession. Mostly so they wouldn't try to look her up, but also because nothing was a bigger turn-off than jokes about handcuffs and women in uniform. Being easily bored was one of her many problems.

Anyway, this Martin bloke had come up to her to ask why she was sitting alone at the bar, then without waiting for a reply he had bought her a drink, and then another; and when the place closed they had moved on to his house. Martin was not the type to go home with someone on the first date; he had told her so while fumbling with his front door lock. And Charlie had replied that she was. Martin had laughed and said he really liked women with a sense of humour and Charlie hadn't had the heart to tell him she wasn't kidding.

She got up quietly. Her head was pounding. I need to get home, she thought. I need to find my clothes and then get home.

Her dress was on the floor in the kitchen, she didn't bother looking for her knickers. She had almost made it out when she accidentally stepped on a toy that started playing a loud tune, 'Mary Had a Little Lamb'. 'Fuck,' she whispered. 'Goddamnit.' She could hear Martin moving in the bedroom. She quickly found her way to the front door, grabbed her shoes, opened the door and ran down the stairs.

She was unprepared for the light that hit her as she stepped out onto the street; it took her a moment to sort through her sensory impressions and pin down exactly where she was. Östermalm, Skeppargatan. A taxi would get her home in five minutes. She looked around, but there were no taxis in sight, so she started walking.

When she had walked three blocks, Challe called.

'Out running?' he said.

'Sure, it's important to stay healthy. Are you at work?'

'Yep. After all, if you're going to be up at the crack of dawn, you might as well make yourself useful.'

Charlie smiled. In terms of work ethics, she and her boss were peas in a pod. In other respects there were many differences, but unlike some of the older men on the force Challe didn't seem ever to doubt her professional abilities, at least not privately. It bothered her no end that he wouldn't stand up for her when she took abuse for being young or a woman, but at the same time she couldn't help but find it flattering that, behind closed doors, he called her his star detective.

Charlie had started at the NOD two years earlier. It had been tough at first. During her police training, she had heard horror stories about how the old guard were all chauvinists, but she had never fully realised just how pervasive the sexism really was. The jargon, the jokes, the PMS insinuations whenever she didn't agree about something. Most of her colleagues at the

National Operations Department were middle-aged men who had been looking out for each other for decades. That much had been clear on the very first day; they were far from pleased at having a little girl for a colleague, at least in the job Charlie had. One of them had even told her to her face that the only time he accepted a woman on top was in bed. It made no difference that Charlie was a rising star, that she had completed a BA in psychology before she even started her police training. How had she had the time to do that, one of the men on her team had asked her when she first started. How had she managed to squeeze in a three-year degree, if she was only twenty when she enrolled at the Police Academy?

And Charlie had told him the truth, that she had skipped a grade in school, completed school at seventeen and gone straight to university. Her colleague had frowned and said something about how it wasn't a good idea to go straight from school to university, that it was better to get some life experience, travel and grow as a person. Charlie had almost retorted that she didn't see the point of travelling around, wasting time, just for the sake of it. And as far as life experience went, studying had given her plenty. It's not like life stood still just because you were at university. Her colleague had given her a superior smile as though she was too young and foolish to understand what he meant.

For a long time, Charlie had hoped their disappointing attitude would improve over time, but it was as though their jealousy and suspicion only intensified as she rose through the hierarchy. When she was new, she had defended herself, argued, left the break room in protest and written angry emails to her managers. But then she had done what most of the women who had made it within the police profession had done: lowered her voice and stopped smiling. And after that, she had

had more time and energy to dedicate to what she was paid to do. Lazy, she berated herself sometimes: cowardly and selfish. But if she hadn't done it, she wouldn't have been able to stay, develop, climb – and that drove her more than her desire to fight meatheads who didn't know any better.

Not all men on the force were the same, of course. There were some exceptions, and one of those exceptions was called Anders Bratt and was her closest colleague. He was only a few years older than her, and she had liked him from the first. They came from completely different backgrounds. Anders was a typical upper-class bloke, the kind of person who had enjoyed a stable and well-to-do childhood, sailing camp in the summer and skiing in the Alps in the winter. He could be smug, condescending and annoying, but Charlie forgave him everything because he had the three qualities she appreciated in a person: a good heart, a sense of humour and self-awareness.

Anders would often joke about how much he had enjoyed her joining the group, stirring shit up. There had been talk about her name. On the first day, someone had asked her if she would be okay with being called Charline, just to make things easier, otherwise they would have to add surnames every time they referred to her or the boss. And Charlie had said that she wasn't okay with it. She wanted to be called Charlie and nothing else.

Later on, Anders had told her that everyone had laughed at that, at how the boss had been forced to change his name when she started. How many people could make their boss change their name, just like that?

Charlie missed a step and let out a curse.

'What's happening?' Challe said.

'Nothing.'

'Could you stop by later?' Challe said.

Charlie's chest went cold. Was she on today? Challe telling her to take the day off – had that been a dream?

'I know you're supposed to be off,' Challe continued, 'and I know there's a heatwave and all that, but something's come up. Have you seen the headlines?'

'Headlines?' Charlie realised she hadn't checked the news on her phone.

'A seventeen-year-old girl is missing in Västergötland.'

'Since when?'

'Friday. The hicks down there reckoned at first that she'd run away, so they didn't file a report. But since then things have come to light that suggest suspicious circumstances.'

'Like what?'

'The usual: her phone hasn't been used and her bank account hasn't been touched.'

'Where in Västergötland?' Charlie asked.

'In Gullspång.'

Charlie froze mid-step. Challe carried on talking about the case, but she had stopped listening. The only thing ringing in her ears was the name of the place. Gullspång.

'Charlie?' Challe said. She could hear him lighting a cigarette. 'You still there?'

'Yes.'

'I'm sending you and Anders. It might do you good,' he continued, 'to get away for a bit.'

Charlie couldn't help retorting that if that were true it would be equally good for Hugo to get away. Besides, she had her hands full with other things. But Challe told her he was going to reassign the case she was working on, since the investigation was in its early stages anyway, and, well, of course he could send Hugo just as easily, but Charlie shouldn't think of it as a punishment but rather as a ...

This is it, Charlie thought. This is the time to tell him I can't go.

'Charlie?'

'All right,' she said. 'I'll go.' Is the old police station even still there, she wanted to ask. But instead she heard herself say she would be there in an hour.

After they hung up, she went into the nearest 7-Eleven. Under the headline MISSING, a big-eyed, strawberry-blonde girl started at her from the newspaper placards. She opened her news app and read. The girl was seventeen-year-old Annabelle Roos. The surname sounded familiar, but Charlie couldn't place it. How was she supposed to remember all the families in that place? She hadn't been back for ... she counted the years. Had it really been nineteen years?

3

Charlie was still several blocks from her flat. No taxis had turned up and she never took the underground. There was something about being underground that made her struggle to breathe. Her feet ached in her high-heeled shoes. She stopped and took her shoes off. The asphalt was warm against the soles of her feet. If people saw me now, she mused, they'd be hard-pressed to guess my profession.

When she entered her flat and caught sight of her face in the hallway mirror, she cursed loudly. A cut just above her left eyebrow glowed angrily against her pale skin. She touched the thick scab and realised she wouldn't be able to magic it away with make-up. How the fuck had she cut her forehead? Then it suddenly came back to her: the shower, how she and that Martin bloke had been lathering each other up and how she had slipped and hit ... the shower head? She didn't even know what she had hit.

I'm like a caricature of a detective, she thought to herself, this lonely loser who drinks too much. But then she told herself it was only a periodic thing. Everything always got more dire when summer was approaching or when life messed her about.

She almost regretted not having a man for her colleagues to focus their suspicions on. Now everyone would assume the cut was ... actually, what would they assume? Given their most recent office party, over-indulgence in alcohol would probably be high on the list. Challe would tell her she needed help and she would say she was doing fine, that everything was under control.

But did she even believe that herself?

Self-medication? an earnest therapist had once asked her when she had reluctantly told her about her relationship with alcohol. *Do you drink to reduce your anxiety?*

Charlie had told her it wasn't about that.

So what was it about then?

It was about being able to relax, about calming her nerves, silencing her thoughts; sometimes she just needed a glass or two to feel good.

The therapist had given her a stern look and told her that was the very definition of self-medication.

Charlie went into the living room. Beer cans and an ashtray littered the coffee table. Good work on the smoking, she thought to herself as she went to fetch a plastic bag to put it all in. When she had cleared the worst of it, she sat down on the sofa and looked at her flat: the surfaces, the high ceilings, the wooden floors. It might have been beautiful if not for the dying plants, the piles of clothes and the windows that hadn't been washed in years. Everything pointed to its occupier being someone who didn't care one jot about decorating. In fact Charlie would have liked to have a nice home, but it was as though she was incapable of creating one. Every now and again, on a whim, she would decide to turn her flat into a show home – the kind she saw in pictures in the glossy magazines at her dentist's. She reckoned a completely white flat would make her happier, or at least less unhappy. White walls, white floors and then a few strategically placed antiques, either inherited or brought back from foreign lands … But she had never inherited anything, and as for foreign lands … she never went anywhere. Besides, she knew far too many miserable people who had lovely homes to fall for the ruse.

A single cigarette was sitting on the kitchen counter. She was about to bin it when she changed her mind, lit it instead, sat down under the kitchen fan and smoked it all the way down to the filter. This is when I call, she thought. This is when I call Challe back and tell him I can't go, not to that place … that I have personal reasons. She picked up her phone, then put it back down again. The cigarette had made her feel nauseous, so she stood up and went into the bathroom instead.

In the shower, she turned to face the jet and told herself she was going to behave professionally. So long as she behaved professionally, everything would be fine. Right? She had done what she could to forget and move on. Forget the place, the house, the parties, forget Betty's light and darkness. Sometimes she almost thought she had succeeded, but over the years she had come to learn that it was only ever a temporary respite, that calmer periods were inevitably followed by heavier ones, that the memories could overwhelm her at any moment and hurl her back to that place, that night.

Such an inspiration, that was what a lady from social services in Gullspång had called her when they ran into each other in central Stockholm one day. *A neglected child* who had succeeded against all odds.

And Charlie had looked at her over-enthusiastic face and thought, maybe you should learn to read between the lines.

When she was done in the bathroom, she went to pack her things. The three books she was reading were piled on the bedside table. She dog-eared each one and put them in a bag.

There were almost no clean clothes in the pile in her wardrobe. She grabbed a few dresses, jeans and jumpers from the laundry basket and reflected that what she was going to wear was the least of her problems.

4

'What the fuck happened to your forehead?' was the first thing Anders said when Charlie met him in the lobby of the police headquarters on Polhemsgatan.

'I hit my head.'

'Yeah, I figured, but how?'

'What's it to you?'

'You're going to have another scar.'

'I'm a good healer.'

They walked through the barriers. At the lift, they parted ways. Charlie always took the stairs. She didn't care that her colleagues made fun of her claustrophobia. The worst thing that could happen, they liked to explain to her, was that the elevator got stuck, and all you had to do then was call maintenance. But to Charlie, the thought of being stuck between floors in such a small space was horrifying. She would lose her mind well before help arrived.

'Challe is waiting for you in the conference room,' Anders said, when they met outside the lift on the third floor.

'Where are you going?'

'To get a cup of tea. I had a brutal night.'

And how is tea going to help with that, Charlie thought.

*

'Annabelle Roos,' Challe said when Anders had joined them with his cup of tea and they had sat down on the soft red conference room chairs. 'She disappeared last Friday after a party she did not have permission to attend. From the looks of things, it was a fairly wet event, so the other guests have not been able to provide much in the way of information. At some point during the night, probably between midnight and one a.m., she left the party on her own and since then ... since then she's missing. Her phone has not been found and no money has been withdrawn from her bank account.'

'Four days ago,' Anders said. 'How come they didn't start looking earlier?'

'She's seventeen,' Challe replied, 'and apparently, this isn't the first time she's gone missing. According to the local police, she has a reputation for being ... uninhibited.'

'Uninhibited?' Charlie said. 'What kind of word is that anyway?'

'I'm only telling you what they told me. In any case, they need assistance, that much is obvious. I've emailed you all the information we have. It's almost two hundred miles to Gullspång, so you'll have time to start going over the material on the way.'

Anders disappeared to the bathroom. Charlie pulled out her laptop, logged in, opened her email and started skimming the documents Challe had sent her. It didn't help that the reports were formal and matter-of-fact; for her, it was all in vivid colour.

'You look pale,' Anders said as they walked to the car.

'I'm just a bit tired,' Charlie replied. 'It must be the heat.'

Neither one of them liked riding shotgun, and their trips always started with bickering about who would drive. But today, with breath that reeked of a night out and alcohol, Charlie was not in a position to argue.

Charlie turned down the sun visor and studied her face in the little mirror. Anders was probably right. She was going to have another scar. Just next to her left eye was the white reminder of the incident with the glass bottle. It was shaped like a backwards S. Betty had told her she had been supremely unlucky to have such an unfortunate fall, but lucky nonetheless that her eye was okay. It could have been a lot worse.

'Late night?' Anders looked at her.

Charlie nodded.

'I don't know how you do it. And you never go home either. You always have to close the place when you go out.'

'It actually wasn't that long since you and I used to close those places together.'

Anders heaved a sigh. 'It feels like a whole other lifetime.'

Charlie didn't reply. It bothered her that Anders had changed so much since becoming a father. These past few months, he had been irritable and grumpy most of the time. Charlie knew his wife was keen on gender equality and to her that meant the two of them taking turns staying up nights. It made no difference that she was on maternity leave, Anders liked to gripe, because taking care of a child all day was as much work as a salaried job. He would say things like that to elicit Charlie's sympathy, but Charlie honestly didn't know what she thought about it; she figured it depended on what kind of job it was, what kind of child.

Anders turned the radio up. A country song was playing.

'Don't,' he said when Charlie leaned forward to change the channel. 'Listen – it's about a girl named Annabelle.'

Anders upped the volume even more.

'Eerie for this song to be playing. A dead girl with the same unusual name as the one in our investigation.'

'That's just chance,' Charlie said.

'Aren't you the one who's always saying you don't believe in chance?'

'You have me mixed up with Challe. Fate is what I don't believe in.'

'Isn't that a bit dull, to just believe in chance? Most people I know believe in some form of predestination.'

'That's because they can't tell the difference between fate and chance,' Charlie said, 'that, and a lot of wishful thinking.'

'I suppose most people would like to imagine things happen for a reason.'

'Exactly. That's why they start imagining there's such a thing as fate.' She turned the music back down and wished Anders would stop talking.

5

'Have you read up on where we're going at all?' Anders said.

They had reached the motorway and Charlie was feeling increasingly peevish about his uneven driving. She shook her head and tried to suppress her rising nausea by watching the road and not thinking about all the things she had poured down her throat last night. She had promised herself to stick to beer (most nights began with a promise of that kind). She had met up with a former colleague and everything had started so well: a few pints, memories and shooting the breeze. But around midnight her colleague had called it a night: he had to get up early to travel somewhere. And that was when that Martin bloke had come over and ruined everything. She thought about the sweet cocktails and suppressed a gag reflex. More and more memories of the night before were surfacing. She had spilled a glass of wine all over herself, and that was when Martin had carried her into the shower and in there ... in there he had pressed her up against the shower wall and taken her while the water streamed down on them. Almost like a film, she thought, if they hadn't been so drunk, if she hadn't slipped and hit her head and had needed help to get to the bed and ... bloody hell, why did she never learn from her mistakes?

Anders started telling her what he had read about Gullspång

online. It was a small manufacturing town, six thousand inhabitants, youngest mothers in the country, bad dental health, high unemployment. Sounded like a great place, he chuckled.

'You're such a Stockholmer,' Charlie sighed, 'condescending and sarcastic about anything outside the city limits.'

'Someone's in a right foul mood.'

'How am I supposed to feel when I'm being thrown from one case to another?'

'You don't usually have a problem with that. Aren't you the one who always says you play the position the coach gives you?'

'Not when he's punishing me.'

Anders didn't understand. What did she mean 'punish'? Challe wasn't the kind to hold a grudge. If she was still thinking about the Christmas party, surely that was water under the bridge by now?

He knows, Charlie thought. He knows everything.

'What have you heard?' She turned to him.

'What do you mean? I was mostly thinking about how you got a bit … how you were somewhat inebriated. Why are you staring at me?'

'Because I suddenly have the feeling you know things about me I haven't told you.'

'But you never tell me anything about yourself.'

'Who blabbed?' Charlie said. 'Challe? Hugo?'

'Neither. I saw you once. One time when you probably thought everyone had left. In the conference room …'

Charlie blushed. She thought about how she had told Hugo no, how she had told him they should go back to hers instead. It's not that she was a prude, but her job was everything to her and she had no desire to be caught with her trousers around her ankles on a conference table. She had tried to resist but Hugo had been adamant. He had wanted her right then and there.

And so he had touched her in all the right places until she gave up and forgot where she was. And meanwhile, Anders had still been around, apparently. What had he seen?

'I didn't see much,' Anders said. 'At first, I couldn't tell who it was, but then I realised it had to be the two of you, since everyone else had left.'

'Why didn't you say something?'

'What was I supposed to say?' Anders shot her a look.

'Well, to me, later, that you knew.'

'I guess I reckoned you would tell me yourself if you wanted me to know.'

'It's over now anyway.'

'Good,' Anders said.

'What's good about it?'

'I just reckoned ... I mean, he's obviously married and ...'

'He told me he was unhappy,' Charlie said. Then she had to laugh because it was only just then, as she said it out loud, that she realised how predictable it had been. A married man with a wife who didn't understand him. How was it even possible she had fallen for that?

'And I don't like him either,' Anders said. 'Just between us, he's ... he just thinks far too highly of himself.'

Charlie could only agree. She thought about that time in the archipelago. Hugo and her in bed. He had tried to get her to 'open up' and tell him about her past. How had she grown up and where? For God's sake, he didn't even know where she was from.

Does it matter? Charlie had asked.

No, it didn't matter in the slightest.

There you go then, she had said.

Still, couldn't she ... couldn't she tell him something.

Like what?

Like maybe a secret.

Charlie said she would if he went first.

Hugo had made himself comfortable and with poorly concealed pride told her about how he used to do graffiti when he was young. And then, when she burst out laughing, he had been offended. What was so funny?

And she said that it was nothing. Just that surely all young people did their fair share of vandalism. That it wasn't exactly a mortal sin.

And what had she done that was so bad then, Hugo had wanted to know.

And for a split second she thought she might tell him, *I let a person die once*; but then she got a hold of herself and told him she had never done anything illegal.

Liar, Hugo had said. Everyone has broken the law. He had straddled her and locked her wrist in a one-hand grip. Now tell me.

Nothing illegal, but I've been with quite a few men, she had told him.

How many? His grip had tightened and she had seen the lust spark to life in his eyes.

A few hundred.

And Hugo had laughed. That's why he liked being with her so much. He loved women who could make him laugh.

And she remembered thinking that Hugo was wrong about that thing he always said, that he was great at reading people. Now, when the passion had faded slightly, she could see it clearly, that he was the kind of person she normally didn't have much time for: deluded, devoid of self-awareness and intuition. So why couldn't she just move on?

*

They had been on the road for twenty minutes when Charlie realised she had left her sertraline at home. Had she even taken it this morning? The first thing she would have to do when Anders was out of earshot was call her doctor and sort out a prescription. She had made the mistake of going cold turkey before, thinking the warnings about withdrawal symptoms were exaggerated, but then she had got the sweats and felt nauseous and anxious. It wasn't an experience she was eager to repeat, especially not considering where they were heading. She might even have to up her dosage.

'What do you think about the girl?' Anders asked.

'Too soon to say.'

'Yeah, I realise. But she seems the type who could potentially disappear for a while of her own accord.'

And then Anders started talking about what they had been told about Annabelle. She had a history of running away. Maybe she was the kind of girl you didn't start looking for until some time had passed.

'She hasn't gone missing before,' Charlie said.

'But Challe said ...'

'I went over the file; the report was about her not coming home on time. She was staying over at a friend's house; her mother found her there herself before the next morning. Completely normal.'

'When did you have time to read that?'

'I skimmed it when you were in the bathroom.'

'I can't have been away for more than five minutes.'

'I'm a fast reader.'

'You're fast, period,' Anders said. 'You do everything so bloody fast.'

Charlie thought about how often people commented on how fast she was. She almost never gave it any thought herself. It was only when she had to read together with someone else, or walk next to someone, or when people said she talked too fast, that she realised she was out of sync with the world around her. But that usually only led her to conclude that everyone else was slow.

'Come across anything else of interest?' Anders asked.

'It was not a derelict house. The party. It was in a boarded-up village shop.'

What difference did that make? Anders wanted to know. Did it matter what kind of house it was?

Not to an outsider, Charlie thought, not to someone who hadn't had their first drink there, who hadn't made out there, fallen down the stairs and vomited all over the floor. To someone who had grown up anywhere else in the world, it made no difference. But to her ... every detail was significant.

'Would you mind not driving so fucking unevenly,' she said.

'What do you mean?' Anders looked at her uncomprehendingly.

'I mean that you keep braking and accelerating instead of keeping an even speed.'

'I'm just following the flow of traffic.'

'No, you're not. You always drive like this, even when there's no traffic. That's why I prefer to drive.'

'In that case,' Anders said, 'you might consider trying to stay sober.'

'Lay off, will you.'

'I'm serious.'

They were quiet for several miles. Charlie was thinking that she was tired, that she should be at home, in bed, with sertraline, a couple of aspirin and an oxazepam in her, but instead she was sitting here, feeling sick and shaken, on her way to the one place on earth she had promised herself she would never go back to.

6

They stopped to eat at a roadside restaurant. There was something familiar and attractive about the dark chairs and the tables with their red-and-white checked plastic tablecloths. An older woman took their order. Anders was being indecisive at first, but eventually settled on the same thing Charlie had ordered: a shrimp sandwich.

'Not hungry?' he said, watching her push her shrimp around.

'All right, enough already. I don't need a daddy.'

'Who said you did?'

'I just don't understand why people can't mind their own business. I'm thirty-five. What's the problem if I like to have a drink from time to time?'

'Thirty-three.'

'What?'

'You're thirty-three.'

'Whatever.'

She watched Anders pick all the toppings off his sandwich and discard the bread.

'Why don't you just eat it as is?' she asked.

'Trying to cut carbs.'

'Pretty stupid to order a sandwich then – if you're not eating bread, I mean.'

'There wasn't exactly a superabundance of outstanding options,' Anders said and shoved a lettuce leaf in his mouth.

He started talking about how there was nothing wrong with exercising a bit of caution. We all get just one life, one body, after all. And Charlie said she agreed, which was why only fools would waste their time counting calories, working out and messing about with miracle cures.

'Our brains actually need carbs,' she added.

'There's nothing wrong with the activity level up here,' Anders said, tapping his forehead with his middle finger. 'At least, I haven't noticed a slowdown.'

'Maybe you're just deluded. You do know men tend to over-estimate their abilities, right? I mean, generally speaking.'

'I mean, generally speaking,' Anders mimicked. 'Aren't you the one who hates it when people make generalisations?'

'Only when it's someone else doing it. I suppose it's because I like to think I have facts to back my statements up.'

'Doesn't everyone when they make generalisations? Isn't that the problem?'

'Maybe,' Charlie said. She put her fork down and stood up.

'Where are you going?' Anders said.

'Cigarette.'

'I thought you'd stopped?'

'I started again.'

She went over to the petrol station next door and bought a pack of Blend Menthol, the same ones Betty used to smoke. She stood under the roof in the forecourt, because she was dead certain she would faint if she ventured out into the sunshine.

The taste of mint instantly transported her back in time. She could see Betty sitting at the kitchen table with a cigarette dangling from the corner of her mouth, hear Joplin's raspy voice from the record player in the living room. There had always been music playing at their house. *I can't bear the silence, Charline. Without music, I'd lose my mind.*

And Charlie's forbidden thought: *You've already lost your mind, Mum.*

A memory: dancing with Betty in the garden. The cherry trees in full bloom, the cats slinking about their feet. Betty has thrown the windows open so they can hear the music from outside.

Betty is the man and she is the woman. *Don't forget that the man leads*, Betty says, pretend-sternly.

And when Charlie asks why, Betty shrugs and says she doesn't know, that it's just a silly rule. And what the hell – rules are meant to be broken, so sure, she can lead.

Betty teases her about her feet, saying they are like missiles aimed at her toes. *Relax, you have to relax.*

But Charlie can't. She is stiff and limp in all the wrong places.
You'll never be a dancer, Charline.
You always told me I could be anything I wanted.
Anything except a dancer, sweetheart.

Charlie pulled hard on her cigarette. She was no longer the lanky teenager who left town almost two decades ago. Even her dialect was gone. And yet, she thought – and yet so much remains. She thought about the people who had been in her life back then, about who might still be there and who wouldn't be. She hadn't had too many friends and everyone she had hung out with had agreed they would leave Gullspång at the first opportunity. Because of the tedium, because there was nothing there, because their dreams drew them to the big cities. And then she thought about Susanne, the girl who had been her best friend once, the two of them together in Betty's bedroom window in Lyckebo, their legs dangling against the wood panel, their parents laughing, shouting, cavorting down in the garden.

We're the only grown-ups here, Charlie.

And then, the memory of the two of them on the cliff beneath the falls, their tanned naked bodies, Susanne squinting at the sun, sketchpad in hand. *It really bothers me that I can never draw you the way you look. No, you can't look, I'm not done, stop it!*

Charlie grabs the pad from her.

You've drawn me much more beautiful than I am.

But I wasn't finished!

So finish.

Charlie leans over Susanne's shoulder as she carefully draws the scar next to her eye and adds a dot under it so it looks like a question mark.

You're a riddle, Charline Lager.

Susanne ... Charlie had left her without saying goodbye.

Why?

Because she hated goodbyes.

Charlie closed her eyes, leaned her head against the wall behind her and saw herself in the forest that night, barefoot, screaming, stumbling.

'How many are you going to smoke?' Anders was suddenly standing in front of her. 'And what's with standing so close to the pumps?'

'It's not that close.'

'I was going to get a cup of coffee.'

'I'll be right there,' Charlie said. 'As soon as I'm done.'

Before going back into the petrol station, she pulled her phone out and called her GP. Annoyed, she navigated through all the choices and prayed they would call her back. She really needed her prescription.

'You're quiet,' Anders said. They had brought their coffees back to the car.

'I'm thinking,' Charlie said.

'What about?'

'All kinds of things.' Oh my God, why couldn't he just leave her be?

Her phone rang. Charlie looked at the screen, where an *H* appeared. It bothered her that it still triggered a split second of hope. Love or passion or whatever it was really had a way of making people stupid.

'If you're not going to answer it you could at least turn the sound off,' Anders said.

Charlie turned the sound off. Seconds later, she had a message from her voicemail. She couldn't stop herself from calling to listen to it.

'Hi, it's me. I think we need to talk. It's Anna. She went through my phone and all hell broke loose and I ... I told her it was just a harmless fling, that we're not seeing each other any more, but she doesn't believe me and now she's saying she's going to call you and ... Well, it would be nice if you could call me back as soon as possible.'

Fuck that, Charlie thought and put her phone back in her bag.

'Who was it?' Anders asked.

'What's it to you?'

'I thought it might be about work.'

'If it was, I'd tell you, wouldn't I?'

'I just feel like you're being really secretive,' Anders replied. 'I mean, more than usual.'

'It's the place we're going to,' Charlie said, 'Gullspång. I used to live there.'

'What do you mean?'

'Exactly what I said, that I used to live there.'

'And you're only telling me now?' The look Anders gave her made it clear he thought she was insane.

'It was ages ago.'

'What difference does that make? So is that where you grew up?'

'Yes.'

'And what's it like?'.

'I guess it's like the rest of small-town Sweden,' Charlie said. 'Young mothers, bad dental health, unemployment. I haven't been back in almost twenty years.'

'Why?'

'I guess I didn't feel like it.' She thought to herself that it had been a mistake to tell him, but in case anyone recognised her, unlikely as that seemed, it was probably best to have mentioned it.

'Do you know the girl?' Anders asked.

Charlie shook her head. How could she, when Annabelle hadn't even been born when she left?

'When was it?'

'A long time ago,' Charlie said. 'I was just fourteen.'

'Your family moved to Stockholm?'

'I did,' Charlie said.

'Just you?' Anders looked at her.

'Yes, things weren't great at home. I ended up in foster care. Could you look where you're going, please?' she continued.

'Why haven't you told me this?'

'It's not something I think about, and if you don't mind, I'd rather not talk about it.'

But Anders didn't seem to get it. He wanted to know what her foster family had been like. Because obviously there were a lot of horror stories about teenagers who ended up in foster care.

'I was fine,' Charlie said.

'And so this is the first time you've been back since then?'

'Yes.'

'But what about your parents?'

'It was just my mother and she's not there any more.'

Charlie took a big swig of coffee and thought about the house out in Lyckebo. A few months ago someone had called from the local council, telling her she should consider selling it – coming down to do it up and then putting it on the market. But it was her house and she was free to do what she wanted with it. And so what if she neglected the upkeep? Were the neighbours complaining? Surely that was her problem?

Anders continued his interrogation.

'Are you close, you and your mum?'

'Not particularly,' Charlie said. 'I haven't seen her in a long time.' And that's the truth, she thought. It's the absolute truth. She had no intention of telling Anders about Betty. She had made that mistake with a few old boyfriends a long time ago and it always ended up with them feeling sorry for her.

Anders asked some more questions; she replied increasingly tersely.

'The woman without a past,' Anders said eventually.

'Is that what you people call me?'

'Are you surprised? You never give anything personal away.'

Charlie sighed. She had never understood the point of turning yourself inside out for the people around you. Once, a friend of hers (who had wanted to be more than friends) had said it was the reason she never got close to anybody. No wonder she was alone, he had said, given that she clammed up any time someone wanted to really get to know her.

Depends on who it is, Charlie had replied, and that had ended that relationship.

'So you talk about me?' Charlie said, turning to Anders. 'I thought men didn't gossip about things like that. Isn't that what they say, that male-dominated workplaces are so great because you don't have to deal with gossip and office intrigue?'

'I don't think that's true. Men talk as much as women do. At least that's my experience.'

'Either way, I don't like being too private with work colleagues,' Charlie said. Only when it was already said did she realise what she had left herself open to.

'You seem to have been fairly intimate with some,' Anders said, grinning.

Charlie had to smile. And then she told him how she saw it, that there was a difference between the physical and the emotional. Just because you exchanged bodily fluids didn't mean you actually opened up to someone.

Anders grinned again. Then he turned serious. No one was asking her to reveal her innermost secrets, but it was in fact a bit odd, to his mind, to never speak a word about one's past. They had worked together for almost three years and all he knew about her was what he could see.

'And what do you see?' Charlie asked.

'I see a thirty-three-year-old woman who is afraid of commitment.'

Charlie started laughing. Clichés always made her laugh.

'What's so funny?' Anders wanted to know.

'Nothing. Go on. What else do you see?'

'I see a thirty-three-year-old woman who likes to party, hates small talk but has a phenomenal ability to see the details in the general and the general in the details.'

'Thank you,' Charlie said.

'You're welcome,' Anders said and turned back to the road.

That day

Annabelle woke up at four. She picked up her phone and read the message again.

> This isn't working any more. You have to understand that it's not working.

She had received it last night and her first thought had been to go over to his house and make a scene. But then she had calmed down and stayed in bed, feeling her heart pound in her chest.

> You have to understand that it's not working.

It was exactly what he had told her the day before as well, but reading the words made it feel even more final somehow. She had to understand, but how was she supposed to do that, when only two days ago, he had caressed her clothes off and done it with her in a way that …

She had just drifted off again when her alarm went off. Her first thought was to stay in bed. But then she remembered about the party that evening. She wouldn't be allowed to go anywhere if she was ill, and the last thing she wanted was to spend the weekend at home. She was depressed enough as it was.

She slowly climbed out of bed and put on a pair of shorts. She went over to her closet and stared at her tops for a while. Then she looked down at the T-shirt she had slept in and decided it would do. It was as though every decision, big or small, required superhuman effort. She managed two strokes with the hairbrush before her mother started yelling at her from downstairs about breakfast. She brushed the rest of her hair extra slowly to make the point that she was seventeen, not seven. If there was one thing she was fed up with, it was being treated like a child.

7

'Anders,' Charlie said. 'Pull over.'

'This is a motorway. You'll have to wait until there's an exit.'

'Just pull over anywhere, don't you get that I have to ...'

Anders took the next exit. It had a rest area with plastic tables and little red houses with toilets. Every last one was occupied so Charlie ran around the back, put her hand against the wall and let it all out. I'm going to end up like Betty, she thought. Unless things get easier soon, I'm going to end up just like her.

When she returned to the car, Anders was on the phone. She could hear from his voice that it was his wife. Maria called at least five times a day and Anders always answered.

'I'm not sure how long it'll take,' he said. 'You know there's no way of knowing for sure. A young woman is missing.'

When Charlie climbed in, Anders got out.

'Problem?' she said when he came back.

'She doesn't like it when I'm away. It's not easy being alone with a little one.'

'As far as I recall, she didn't like you going away before either.'

Anders made no reply. He, who fancied himself so open, didn't like discussing his wife's jealousy problem.

'Feeling better?' he said.

Charlie nodded. 'Are we going, or what?'

'I'm just wondering how you're really doing. Weren't you the one who said you were going to ... slow down?'

Charlie opened her mouth to tell him it was none of his business. But suddenly she felt on the verge of tears, so she turned away and stared out of the window. Yellow fields rushed past. Oilseed or turnip rape? Once upon a time she had known things like that.

'You know I'm here if you want to talk,' Anders said.

'What about?'

'I don't know, but it's pretty obvious you're not doing too well.'

'I'm fine,' Charlie said. She sat quietly for a while, thinking about that bloody office party. That was what had made everyone concerned about her drinking, that was what had triggered the unhealthy phase she was now living through.

When Hugo had brought his wife (a tiny woman who was so radiantly beautiful, happy and mild), she had been unprepared for the avalanche of emotion it had set off in her. And she had done what she always did when things got tough: drunk too much too quickly. At eleven, Challe had had enough and put her in a taxi. She didn't remember much from the night of the party, but she would never forget her meeting with Challe the next day. How was it, he had wanted to know, that she felt she should get utterly badgered at a work function?

Charlie had defended herself by saying she hadn't been the only one, and either way it was hardly the first time in history someone had had a bit too much at an office party.

But Challe didn't give a toss about history; he had wanted to know what lay behind this particular case.

Charlie had said she didn't know, that she hadn't had enough to eat, had drunk too quickly. That she was simply a bit ... rusty.

That thing about being rusty hadn't been a complete lie.

During her months with Hugo, she had been too busy to go out at night. They had taken long walks around the island where his summer house was, made love, talked and laughed. She had thought that it might be serious, but had belatedly come to understand that there would never be anything more, that all she had been to Hugo was ... She didn't know what she had been, only that he had no intention of divorcing his wife. In fact, he had told her as much a few months in, as though it were a given.

I'm never going to leave her.

After that, she had avoided him as best she could. She had looked through him at work and not answered her phone when he called. What she had really wanted to do was tell him what a nasty little person he was, but she knew things like that had a tendency to go off the rails. When she was hurting, she was liable to say just about anything. Anders liked to joke about it, that there were reasons why Charlie had slightly too much sympathy for people who committed terrible crimes of passion. If Hugo had only been smart enough to stay away, the whole thing would probably have petered out, but he was not that bright. A few weeks after the Christmas party, he had come into her office, demanding a chance to explain. There had been yelling and shoving and, inevitably, Challe had appeared, asking what the hell was going on. It was of utmost importance, he had said once everyone had calmed down a fraction, that private problems were solved outside work hours.

'This is it,' Charlie said. 'It's this exit.'

'I didn't see a sign.'

'Well, this is it, sign or no sign.'

'What happened there?' Anders pointed to a semi-burnt-out building.

'No idea, but it used to be a pizzeria.'

'Well, there seems to be another one,' Anders said and pointed across the road. 'Happy Salmon Pizzeria.'

Charlie gazed attentively out of the window as they approached the town centre. On the left, she could make out the black river that marked the county boundary.

'Swim across and you're in Värmland,' she said and nodded at the river. 'Bad luck for me I lived on the wrong side.'

'So there's a wrong side?'

'There's always a wrong side.'

'So the slightly more well off live in Värmland?' Anders studied the river.

'No, it wasn't about money,' Charlie said, but then she realised that was exactly what it had been about. She told him about how the school children from Värmland had been given money from a fund each year. There had been an old couple who had donated their fortune to the children of Värmland because ... She didn't really know why. Maybe because the school was in Västergötland. Charlie told him how angry it had made her every year when the Värmland children were given their envelopes in school.

Why had it made her angry? Anders wanted to know.

'Why? Because it was unfair, obviously. Children can't help where they live.'

'Was it a lot of money?'

'Like ten kronor or something,' Charlie replied. 'What?' she added when Anders burst out laughing. 'What's so bloody funny about that?'

'Nothing, but ten kronor, I mean, maybe that's not enough to get upset about.'

'It's not the amount. It's the ... principle.'

'I'm sorry I laughed, but I thought we were talking much

more significant sums.' Anders looked out at the water again. 'Did you really go swimming there?'

'Yes.'

Charlie thought about how she had spent every summer swimming in that river, to Värmland, Västergötland and back to Värmland again, and then even further where the river widened into Lake Skagern, near her house.

When I die, Betty liked to say, *scatter me over Skagern. I've always wanted my ashes to be scattered at sea. Imagine, just drifting on the currents, who knows how far.*

At those times, Charlie would remind Betty that Skagern was just a lake, that everything came to a halt at the inlet gates or the water treatment plant, that it wouldn't take her anywhere.

But eventually, Betty said, *everyone returned to the sea. Sooner or later, we all do.*

'I would never swim there,' Anders said.

'Why not?'

'There's something about black water – well, lakes in general – that I find incredibly unsettling.'

'It's not the water that's black,' Charlie said, 'it's the depth that makes it look that way.'

'Then that's one hell of a deep river.'

'People used to say it was bottomless.'

Anders laughed and said that was typical of a backwater like this, that people still believed all kinds of rubbish. That it was like entering a time warp.

And Charlie said it was remarkable, that he, who never ventured further from Stockholm than the archipelago, knew so much about Sweden's backwater towns.

'But you said so yourself, that people thought it was bottom-less.'

'Whatever,' Charlie said. She had never believed it was bottomless, and neither had Susanne.

Everything ends somewhere.

The two of them would even go swimming in the spot locals called the abyss, where it was said the undertow was so strong it could pull people under even when the inlet gates were closed. It was only after the accident that the lake scared her. She had never gone swimming in Skagern after that.

'Is there a power plant?' Anders said. 'Strong currents and such?'

'Yes, there's a power plant.'

Charlie thought about their death-defying sunbathing by the falls. It was a forbidden place, because at any time the gates could open and the water would snatch up anything not tied down and hurl it out onto the sharp rocks. Sometimes, as she lay there, she had almost wished it would happen.

8

Gullspång town centre looked like a ghost town. Boarded-up shops, broken windows, flapping newspaper placards with Annabelle's face on every lamp post. If it had not been for all the people in yellow vests outside the supermarket, the whole place would have seemed abandoned. The bench outside the supermarket was still there and on it were three tattered men clutching cans of lager. Maybe it was the same group that had used to sit there back then, the ones who would shout after Betty every time they walked by.

Come here and give us a kiss, beautiful Betty!

Shut up, Betty would retort, *stop yelling at me when I'm with my little girl.*

Your daughter, one of them said once, *your daughter looks more like her mother with each passing day.*

That time, Betty had let go of Charlie's hand and walked over to the bench. She had stepped in close to the man who had claimed to see a likeness and hissed that he was going to stay away from her daughter. *Stay the fuck away from my daughter.*

What do you mean, Betty? All I said was …

Just stay away.

Charlie wished she was alone in the car. In all the dreams she had dreamt about returning, she had always come alone. It felt so surreal seeing it all again, seeing the dilapidated facades, the supermarket, the kiosk, the shuttered building that had once housed the café. To an outsider, it might be a sad little town centre, but to her … Her nose started stinging. She closed her eyes and took a deep breath. She thought to herself that she was going to have to pretend this was just like any other small town, that the buildings, the water and the roads were unknown to her, that it was a place she was visiting for the first time. Was that even feasible? A stubborn, well-worn adage started running on a loop through her mind. *You can take the girl out of the village, but not the village out of the girl.*

'They're fast,' Anders said, nodding at the yellow vests.

'Good thing,' Charlie said. 'We need all the help we can get. But a beautiful seventeen-year-old Swedish girl – there's not going to be a shortage of eager volunteers.'

She looked up towards the little town square where journalists with notepads were talking to sobbing 'friends'. She knew the kind of description such interviews inevitably elicited. Missing persons were always amazing, well behaved and wonderful. And no, they had no enemies and were loved by one and all.

'What on earth is that?' Anders said when they passed the hulking old smelter sprawling at the heart of the town centre.

'GEA,' Charlie said.

'GEA?'

'A smelter.'

'Is it active?'

'Doesn't look like it.' Charlie studied the rusty metal facade and the tall smokestacks.

'It looks bloody awful. How can it be allowed to just sit there, and in the middle of town as well? I mean, if it's not even open?'

Charlie looked up at the building and only now realised it really was hideous. Growing up, she had never given it any thought. It had always been there.

'It seems it's being put to different use,' she said. A sign on it read 'Shooting Club,' and a bigger one 'Library'.

The smelter. It had been Betty's workplace for a while. She had detested it.

Why?

Because it was as hot as hell, because the work was so monotonous it could drive the most stable person insane. There was no place in this world she had hated more than the smelter.

And when Charlie had asked why she went back there if it was so awful, Betty had laughed and said she didn't have much of a choice. Later, when GEA closed, Betty had found a job at the plywood factory. She had been happy about it, about trying something new, getting away from the heat, growing her eyelashes back. She really had a good feeling about it. But after her very first day, she came home and complained. It was the heat, she said, the bloody plywood factory was every bit as warm as the smelter had been, and she had scratched her arms too. The smelter had robbed her of her reason and now this bloody factory was going to claim her body. Was it never going to end?

'Since you're from here,' Anders said, 'maybe you know how to get to the hotel?'

'There is no hotel,' Charlie said. 'At least there wasn't when I lived here.'

'But Challe said ...'

'There's a motel,' Charlie said and pointed to a yellow building further down the street.

'What's the difference between a hotel and a motel?'

'I suppose you're about to find out. Turn here.'

Anders looked at the big yellow building. A wooden staircase spiralled its way down from a window on the top floor to the ground.

'Nice fire escape,' he said. 'Assuming it is a fire escape. Really blends in.'

'It serves its purpose,' Charlie said. 'In this case, function might trump aesthetics.'

'Sure, but why can't you have both?'

'Money, possibly. Fuck if I know.'

'You're always your most charming self when you're hungover.'

Anders parked outside the motel and killed the engine.

'What's that smell?' he said as they climbed out of the car.

Charlie took a deep breath, sucking in the smell of ...

'Shit?' Anders said. 'Is it from the fields?'

'No, the paper mill.'

'There's a paper mill as well?'

'No,' Charlie replied. 'It's miles and miles away, but when the wind is right, the smell carries all the way here.'

She had almost forgotten that unique smell, but now she recalled how they hadn't been able to hang laundry outside if there was a strong north wind blowing, and how Betty had always forgotten and how they had had to sleep in sheets that smelled faintly of sewer.

'That's awful,' Anders said, 'stepping outside and being greeted by this.'

'I like it,' Charlie said. 'It smells like ... childhood.'

'What a delightful childhood you must have had.'

'By the way, I'd appreciate if you could keep it to yourself that I'm from here.'

'How come?'

'Because it's irrelevant. And unfortunately, I think it would only make things harder.'

'But won't people recognise you?'

Charlie shook her head. She didn't think so. It was a long time ago. She had changed.

There and then

There's a tap on the window. Alice opens the curtains. Rosa is standing outside in her nightgown.

'Go on, then, open up,' Rosa says through the glass. 'Open up, quick.'

Alice unlatches the window. Without a word, Rosa climbs in, tiptoes across the floor and crawls into Alice's bed.

'You're ice cold,' Alice whispers when Rosa's feet touch her shins. 'You're like an ice cube.'

Rosa doesn't reply. Without saying why she has come, she turns to the wall and falls asleep.

Alice lies awake for a long time, listening to her regular breathing. It's as though she still can't quite believe they're friends, that she, Alice Lo, is friends with Rosa Manner. They live just a few houses from each other, but before that day in the field, they had never spoken a word. Everything had started out in that field. Alice had run into it to get away from the scooter gang. It had been raining for days; the ground had turned to mud and suddenly, she was stuck. She had stood there, knee-deep in mud, and that was when Rosa had spotted her from the road. *At first I thought you were a scarecrow*, Rosa had laughed as she helped free her, *I thought the Larssons had found themselves a living, breathing scarecrow.*

And then: *Don't forget I saved your life. If not for me, you would have sunk. Don't you ever say I didn't save you, Alice.*

Alice moves in closer to Rosa's body and thinks how lucky she is, that from now on, life is going to get better.

9

The man who greeted them in the motel restaurant looked familiar, but it wasn't until he introduced himself as Erik From that Charlie realised he was the son of the man who had run the place when she lived in town. Back then, he had been awkward and nervous, but now his handshake was firm and his gaze steady.

'So you're the constables from Stockholm,' he said when they had introduced themselves.

Charlie had to smile at his choice of words. Yes, they were the constables from Stockholm.

'Olof, our local copper, came around earlier, telling me there would be specialists arriving from Stockholm today. I hope you catch the bastard who took her.'

'Do you know the family?' Charlie asked.

'I suppose in a town this size everyone knows everyone to some extent; it's not like Stockholm. And when things like this happen ... well, it's only natural to want to help as best you can, isn't it? The trouble is we can't help out with the search like we'd want to, the wife and I, because the whole place is booked solid with police, journalists and people who have come to join the search.'

A young man wearing a yellow vest and a headset entered

the room. He was talking loudly about which areas had been searched and which ones were left to cover.

'Missing People,' Erik said, nodding at the man. 'That one's the leader of the whole operation. They arrived yesterday. Before you.' He paused as if he were expecting them to comment. 'I just hope you can find her now,' he then went on.

'We will,' Charlie said.

'How can you be so sure?' a woman's voice said from the kitchen.

'My mother,' Erik said, pointing to the flushed woman coming through the swinging doors behind the bar. 'This is my mother Margareta, who misses nothing.'

'I could hardly help overhearing you when I was standing right behind there,' Margareta said. She came up and shook their hands. First Anders's, then Charlie's.

Was it just her imagination, or did the woman's eyes linger on her for a second? Margareta who missed nothing, did she also forget nothing?'

'We're all glad you've come,' she said. 'The whole town is shaken up. Poor Nora and Fredrik, that's all I have to say. We've sent flowers and food and ... If someone hurt her ... if someone hurt that girl ... I just hope you catch them.'

Charlie nodded.

'We'll do everything we can.'

'At least you can rest assured,' Margareta said, 'that no one, *no one*, in town wanted to harm Annabelle, that whoever this madman was, he had to have come from outside.' She stared at them intently for a long moment. Then she threw a tea towel over her shoulder and disappeared back into the kitchen.

'Jonas,' she said to someone in there. 'Just because I leave doesn't mean you have to get your phone out. You're paid to work.'

'I'll ask Jonas to see to your bags,' Erik said. 'Jonas,' he called in the direction of the kitchen, 'you're all right to take the bags up to their room later, right?'

'Their room?' Anders said. 'I hope you meant rooms.'

'Separate rooms?' Erik walked over to the bar, consulted a ledger and heaved a loud sigh. 'Jonas,' he called again. 'Come out here.'

The young man called Jonas came out, looking confused.

'These people,' Erik said, pointing at Charlie and Anders, 'are police officers from Stockholm. They're here to find Annabelle, not to get married, if that's what you were thinking.'

'Why would I think that?' Jonas said.

'Then why on earth did you put them in the honeymoon suite?'

'I did?' Jonas said.

'Yes, you reserved room 3.' Erik turned to Charlie and Anders. 'After working here for a full year you'd think he'd know what he was doing.'

'I must have misunderstood,' Jonas said. 'There's not a lot of rooms free. People keep calling, journalists and ...'

'It's okay,' Charlie said, because Jonas had gone ashen and looked like he was about to collapse any moment. 'It's just a booking error.'

But then she realised from Anders's expression that he considered it more of a problem than she did.

'You'll have to excuse him,' Erik said, as though Jonas wasn't standing right there next to them. 'I guess we're all a bit shocked by this ... disappearance. We'll get you another room as soon as we can.'

'Tonight?' Anders asked.

'As soon as we can.'

*

'How hard can it be?' Anders said as they walked to the car to drive to their first meeting at the police station.

'Weren't you listening? It's a small town and everyone's upset and they're not exactly used to having so many people travel in at once.'

'But still.'

'I'm not going to throw myself at you, if that's what you're worried about.'

'I didn't think you were.'

'Then what's the problem?' Charlie said, even though she knew very well what the problem was. It was obviously about Maria. Anders's wife had an uncanny ability of sniffing things out. Charlie liked to crack jokes about it, that she would make an excellent detective, that they should recruit her immediately if she ever decided to change careers.

'Has she become ... ?' Charlie didn't know how to finish the sentence. Worse? More controlling?

'It's more now since Sam was born. And I understand her. Of course it's hard being on your own so much with a baby. They can be pretty ... demanding.'

'What would she do if she knew?'

'Knew what?'

'That we're sharing a room?'

'Then we would both be dead presently.'

'Being married sounds dangerous.'

'And you're saying being single is harmless?' Anders pointed to the cut on her forehead.

'Given the statistics on women and murder,' Charlie said, 'single life seems preferable.'

Anders started laughing. Okay, okay, she had him there.

IO

Four days since Annabelle disappeared, but to Fredrik it felt like an eternity. He really had done his best to stay strong, to tell himself that she was staying away of her own free will. It had happened once before. It was only a few months since the night Annabelle didn't come home after a party. Nora had called the police then too, stood there shouting down the line and gone berserk when the police explained that they were not in the habit of opening a missing person case whenever a seventeen-year-old was a few hours late. Taking matters into her own hands, Nora had gone around to every single person Annabelle might be friends with and had finally found her at a classmate's house.

Fredrik lit his pipe. He didn't usually smoke indoors. He didn't usually smoke at all, but this time, he didn't even bother turning on the fan. He looked out at the driveway. He was still hoping to see Annabelle come walking up the gravel path, dishevelled, tired and cold. She would cry, ask for forgiveness, swear never to do it again and he would just hold her, not yell, not scold, just stroke her hair, warm her up and tell he she was home now, that nothing else mattered. For two days, he had been telling himself that was how this story was going to end, not with newspaper headlines, not with maps tracing

Annabelle's last known movements. And then … He thought about all the yellow vests in town, all the people who had come to join the search. At first, he had gone out with them, but it had almost driven him insane to walk with the search party in this heat. It was as though he saw Annabelle everywhere, saw her sprawled on the moss in Nora's dress, saw her red hair under the carpet of spruce needles. In the end, a police officer had told him it might be better if he went home to be with his wife.

Nora neither ate nor slept. She mostly paced around and cried. *Find my daughter!* she would tell the officers who came to ask questions, *you have to get me my daughter!*

And Fredrik said that Annabelle would be back. Over and over again he said it. But the truth was he no longer believed it himself. Increasingly, his impression was that people had stopped looking for a living girl.

II

The police station in Gullspång was housed in a handful of rooms on the ground floor of a block of flats on the high street. Big windows looked out onto the town square. Charlie had been in it once before, when Betty was arrested for being drunk and disorderly.

What about it is so bloody disorderly? Betty had shouted. *What the fuck do you mean 'disorderly'?* And then she had kicked a chair and a police officer had restrained her and explained that if Betty didn't calm down, she would not be allowed to take her daughter home with her. It was actually not particularly appropriate, he felt, for someone in Betty's state to be in charge of a child. They had spent hours at the station that time, because the officer was in no hurry to get home and he was determined to hold off until Betty sobered up. He was not about to send a little girl home with an inebriated and agitated mother.

The man who met them at reception was in uniform. He looked very grave when he shook their hands and introduced himself as Olof Jansson. He had worked at the station for sixteen years and had never handled a case of a missing minor before. In these parts, everyone kept an eye on everyone, he explained.

They found two more officers in a conference room, smoking.

Anders shot Charlie a look that said, *Talk about time warp*.

'Maybe I should introduce myself,' the younger of the two said. 'Adnan Noor.' He shook Charlie's hand. 'I thought we were expecting two men,' he continued, 'just on account of the name; I figured ...'

'I hope you're not disappointed,' Charlie said.

No, he wasn't, Adnan assured her. Why would he be?

His colleague cut them off and introduced himself. His name was Micke Andersson and he had worked in Gullspång since ... Charlie couldn't bring herself to listen to his professional back story. She was just relieved she didn't recognise any of them and that no one had seemed to react to her surname. *Lager ... there used to be a Lager family in town back in the day*. The one thing she wanted was to get started on the case. Olof began talking about his previous experience. He had worked homicide in Gothenburg in the nineties and had no problems staying on as lead investigator. He obviously knew the area as well, so maybe that was the most logical way to proceed.

'Because I'm assuming one of you will take on the role of lead interrogator?' He looked at Charlie.

She nodded. That suited her fine.

'I'm happy to assist Charlie in that role,' Anders said.

Someone had drawn a timeline on a whiteboard. Above it was a picture of Annabelle and below it, photographs and names of the places she had been seen during the hours before her disappearance. First at her best friend Rebecka Gahm's house, then at the party and then ... not a trace.

The coffee was served black. There was no milk, Olof informed them. And no soya milk either. But they had sugar, both cubed and the diabetes kind.

'No thanks,' Anders said. 'No sugar.'

'You're definitely from Stockholm, no mistake,' Micke said.

Anders asked what he meant by that. Micke smiled and said all Stockholmers had trouble adapting, conforming to local custom.

'Surely not all Stockholmers are alike?' Anders protested.

And Micke laughed and said they certainly were, at least the ones he had met.

'Maybe you haven't met that many.'

'I've met enough,' Micke said and put three sugars in his cup.

When everyone had been served, Olof ran through the sequence of events. Annabelle Roos had been to a party at Vall's, the village shop.

'Is that an organised event?' Anders said.

Micke snorted.

'What?' Anders turned to him. 'Did I say something funny?'

Micke shook his head. It was just his choice of words, he said, *organised event*, in the same breath as Vall's village shop.

'I'm trying to build a clearer picture, if you don't mind.'

Olof continued his run-through without acknowledging the verbal sparring. There had been fifteen teenagers there in all. They had all said roughly the same thing, that Annabelle had been very drunk and that she had quarrelled with several of them. She had been louder than usual and drunk more than she normally would. When her dad came to look for his daughter there were six people still in the building. Olof pointed them out on the whiteboard: Svante Linder, Jonas Landell, Noel Karlsson, William Stark, Rebecka Gahm and Sara Larsson. None of them had been able to say with any certainty at what time Annabelle had left the party, but it had likely been some-where between midnight and one. Noel Karlsson, by his own and other people's account, had passed out soon after Annabelle and Rebecka arrived, so he could more or less be excluded from inquiry, both as a potential perpetrator and as a witness.

'Jonas Landell,' Charlie said. 'He works at the motel.'

'Sure,' said Micke. 'What of it?'

'Nothing, I just recognised him.'

Olof cracked his fingers. Then he went through the technicians' findings from the scene. Blood had been discovered on the table in the kitchen. No significant quantities, but they had sent it off for analysis anyway. And no, of course there was no word from the lab yet. Then they had found the remnants of a cannabis plantation in a locked room on the top floor as well. So there was reason, Olof felt, to assume that the teenagers who partied in the derelict shop had things to hide, though that didn't necessarily mean they had anything to do with Annabelle's disappearance.

'Have you requested her phone records?' Charlie said.

Olof nodded. There was a recurring number linked to a pay-as-you-go sim card. They had checked with the other teenagers at the party and many others who were known to move in Annabelle's inner circle, and they were all on pay-monthly contracts. No one had admitted recognising the number in question.

And yes, of course they had tried to call the phone, but the phone was turned off.

'And the messages? The texts?' Charlie clarified when no one said anything.

'We made a mistake,' Olof said. 'We contacted the service provider too late, we ...'

'They couldn't restore the messages?'

'No, the phone had been dead for too long. We didn't think ... we were just focused on finding her. We thought she'd show up any minute.'

'These things happen,' Anders said.

'That her friends have contract phones doesn't necessarily

mean anything,' Charlie said. 'It's possible to own two phones. That's usually the way of it if ... if you have things to hide. And considering the cannabis in the village shop ...'

'The thought obviously occurred to us too,' Olof said. 'Either way, there's not a lot we can do about it at the moment. The point is that Annabelle called and was called from this prepaid phone several times over the last few months. And there was an outgoing call registered on the day she disappeared.'

'We need to find that person,' Charlie said.

'Yeah, don't you think we know that,' Micke said. 'The question is how.'

'Talk to her friends again,' Charlie said. 'Ask them if they know if someone happens to own two phones instead of one.'

'We already did,' Micke retorted.

Charlie didn't bother replying. She looked at the photos of the people who had been at the party in the village shop that night. They all looked very young. 'The quarrels,' she said, turning to Olof. 'What were they about?'

'According to what we were told, there was an element of jealousy. William Stark, the ex-boyfriend,' Olof said, pointing to a picture of a dark-haired boy with a crooked smile. 'He was dumped by Annabelle a few months back and is apparently now seeing Rebecka Gahm, Annabelle's best friend.' Olof moved his hand to a picture of a blonde girl. 'They had a minor dispute about it that Friday at school, and before they got to the party. Annabelle had been a bit upset, but Rebecka says it was nothing serious, that Annabelle was just being a belligerent drunk, so it doesn't seem as though the quarrelling had anything to do with the disappearance.'

'And how do you know that?' Charlie asked.

'I said *seem as though*. It's not been our impression that it has anything to do with the fight or her break-up with William.'

Charlie resisted the impulse to inform him about what the statistics said about murdered women and their ex-boyfriends.

'Tell us more,' Anders said. 'How long had they been seeing each other?'

'According to William Stark, it was a matter of months,' Olof said, 'but the parents, Annabelle's parents, didn't even know they were going out.'

'How come?' Charlie said.

'Well, we don't know. Annabelle has apparently never brought a boy home. The mother is a bit ...' Olof scratched his forehead. 'Well, she's a bit special, if you'll pardon the expression. She had called us once before to report her daughter missing, but that time Annabelle was simply spending the night at a friend's house. Maybe that's why I didn't take this entirely seriously at first.'

'What does she do for a living?' Charlie said. 'The mother?'

'She worked at the home before,' Olof said. 'The nursing home,' he clarified, 'but now she doesn't do anything, I think. Neither she nor Fredrik are locals, they have no family here and mostly keep to themselves, so I don't know much about them. But Fredrik works at Bäckhammar's paper mill.'

'What do their jobs have to do with anything?' Micke demanded.

Charlie shot him a quick glance. He was chewing on a toothpick, looking confrontational.

'I'm just trying to get a picture of the family,' Charlie replied.

'Does William Stark have an alibi?' Anders said.

'Yes,' Olof replied. 'He was with Rebecka Gahm when Annabelle left. They stayed at Vall's until dawn. Fredrik Roos, the father, spoke to them when he was there looking for her.'

'Why have you not managed to get more out of Rebecka Gahm?' Charlie wanted to know.

Olof asked what she meant.

'I mean, she's Annabelle's best friend, she must know more about her than what she's told us so far.'

'You're implying that we're not asking the right questions?' Micke put in. 'She said it herself,' he continued, 'she was practically unconscious, she has big memory lapses from that night.'

'Maybe she remembers more now,' Charlie said. 'Now that she understands how serious this is.'

Olof nodded: she was right. Aside from finding the owner of the prepaid sim card and conducting additional interviews with Annabelle's friends, they didn't have a lot to go on. It could be, he continued, that a lot of them would recall more now that they realised this wasn't a game.

'I would like to know more about Annabelle as well,' Charlie said.

'What don't you know?' Micke said. 'I thought you had had time to study the case file. It's all in there.'

'I want to know more about her as a person,' Charlie replied, 'not just facts about the last hours before she disappeared. I want to know who she is, what she likes to do, her dreams, wishes, fears. What?' Charlie said when she noticed Micke rolling his eyes at Adnan.

'Nothing,' Micke said. 'It just sounds difficult to me, finding all those things out.'

'According to her parents, she's a normal teenager who likes to read and does well in school,' Adnan said.

'Doesn't exactly sound like a normal teenager,' Charlie said.

'All her social media activity confirms that assessment,' Olof said. 'Her Facebook account is full of book recommendations and questions from classmates looking for help with their homework.'

'She could have more than one account,' Charlie said. 'In

fact, a lot of young people have one account they let parents, relatives and employers see, and a hidden one where they can be slightly more ... open.'

'I didn't realise you were an expert on young people as well,' Micke said.

'I'm not,' Charlie replied. 'I'm just telling you that may be the case, that I've seen it before. There's probably a different side to her, one she only shows to a select few.'

'We already know that. I mean it's not exactly her grades people are talking about in town.'

Charlie looked at him, waiting for him to continue.

'She has a bit of a reputation,' Micke continued. 'They say she's a bit ... flirtatious.'

'Who says that?' Charlie asked.

'It's just a rumour, but ...'

'But what?'

'People say she likes the fellas.' Micke looked at Olof. 'Well, it's what they're all saying,' he said as though someone had objected, 'I'm just telling you what I've heard.'

'Do we have names for these fellas she liked so much? Or the names of the people making the claims?' Charlie said.

Micke told her he didn't, that it was just rumours. He simply wanted them to be aware.

'Anything else?' Charlie said. 'A diary?'

Olof shook his head. They hadn't found anything like that when they searched her room.

'So what do you reckon?' Anders said. 'What happened?'

'We don't know,' Olof said. 'How are we supposed to know?'

'But judging from what you know so far, what's your first instinct?'

'I can't help thinking,' Olof said, gathering up a few sheets of paper, 'I can't help thinking she must have run into a lunatic.'

'How often does that happen?' Anders said.

'Not that often, but it does happen. The motorway passes by not too far from here. A lot of people come through town, stop for a pint at the motel and ...'

'And find themselves out by a boarded-up village shop in the middle of the night, kidnapping a seventeen-year-old girl?'

'You asked about my first instinct,' Olof said. 'I'm just telling you what it is.'

Charlie's throat was dry. She excused herself and went out into the tiny kitchen. The disorder in there made her feel unexpectedly relieved: no stern signs about cleaning up after yourself, just dishes, Tupperware containers and glasses full of dirty cutlery. The only clean mug was adorned with the green and white logo of the local football club. Charlie filled it up with water, took a few deep gulps and tasted the familiar taste of Gullspång's tap water. Outsiders always complained about the water quality. There was something not right about the taste: iron, lime, sewage? Only now did she understand what they were on about.

12

The first run-through was done and Olof was showing Anders and Charlie where they could keep their things.

'It hasn't been used in a while,' Olof said as he unlocked the door to a room whose walls were lined with shelves full of black binders. 'These are leftovers from the eighties. We haven't exactly needed the space, put it that way. I'll ask someone to clear up a bit so there's more room.'

'We just need the desks,' Charlie said. She nodded at the two teak desks with green bankers' lamps that stood facing each other by the window.

Olof had a call and disappeared; Anders walked over to the desks and started tugging on the window blinds.

'What are you doing?' Charlie said.

'I figured we could use some light.'

'I'd prefer keeping it dark.'

'Why are you always so contrary?'

'I could ask you the same thing.'

'Most people like light,' Anders said, 'especially now we're finally having some sunny weather.'

'There's nothing more ominous than a clear blue sky.'

Anders burst out laughing. What did she mean by that?

'Ingmar Bergman said it, so at least I'm in good company.'

Charlie unpacked her laptop and plugged her phone in to charge.

'I'm starving,' Anders said. 'Aren't you hungry?'

Charlie shook her head. She wasn't hungry in the slightest. Olof had given them all the interview transcripts and she would prefer going over them to heading out for something to eat.

She flipped through the transcripts, read about ex-boyfriends, love triangles and rumours about flirtations, and thought about what Margareta had said about no one from around here wanting to hurt Annabelle. Maybe it was time to put that statement to the test.

Adnan came in to ask how they were getting on.

'I'd like to speak to the parents,' she said. 'Today, if possible.'

'Just go over there,' Adnan said. He handed her a note with their address. 'The house number is a bit hard to spot, but it's the white house with the green door.'

Charlie let Anders drive. They passed Gullspång town centre again. A group of teenagers on mopeds had gathered in front of the little kiosk.

'Was that where you used to hang out?' Anders asked.

'Sometimes,' Charlie replied. She was watching a blonde girl in her lower teens who was smoking a cigarette. Next to her was an equally young girl with an identical hairdo and in a circle around them a group of guys on mopeds. She remembered all the evenings she had spent there with Susanne. How sometimes they had walked up to the main road and fantasised about hitching a ride somewhere. But the stories about men in white cars, the kind of men who kidnapped girls, killed them and cut up their corpses, had made them keep their hands firmly in their pockets.

But someday soon, Susanne had told her one night when they had had one too many cans of lager, *someday soon, I'm going to risk it. I'm going to get in the first car that stops.*

And if no one stops?

There's always lorries, I guess.

And if no lorries stop?

Maybe I wasn't talking about them stopping.

'I've never understood,' Anders said, 'what people get up to in these small towns. I mean, there's nothing here.'

Charlie thought about summer days in Gullspång, about sunbathing below the falls, the parties.

'There's more,' she said. 'There's so much more than meets the eye.'

That day

Never again. Annabelle had promised herself never to call him again. And yet, here she was, behind the school gym, smoking and dialling his bloody number with her free hand. He picked up straight away.

'Belle,' he whispered. 'I can't talk right now. Can I call you back?'

'What difference does it make?' she said. 'Your message already pretty much said it all.'

'I'll call you in a bit.'

'Don't.' She was on the verge of tears. 'Everything you told me ... was it just ... ?'

'No,' he said. 'It wasn't, but consider my situation. After all, you knew from the start that ...'

'Shut up,' she said as the tears started streaming down her cheeks. 'Fuck off. You're as big of a coward as everyone else.'

Then, before he could trot out any more excuses or lies, she hung up. She tapped out another cigarette with trembling hands and thought about the mistake she had made a few weeks earlier. Maybe it had made him realise what their relationship could cost him. He had told her his wife was out of town and Annabelle had taken it as an invitation. She had no recollection of him saying the children were going be there. If she had known that, she obviously wouldn't have gone over to surprise him.

Swedish class had already started, but how the fuck was she supposed to focus on textual analysis when the world was falling apart?

Her phone dinged. It was from Rebecka.

> Where are you?

> Just walking around, everything's shit, she replied.

> Your mum's not going to let you go to the party tonight if she finds out you're skiving off.

> I'm not allowed to go to parties either way.

> But you won't even be allowed to go to mine. Come here!!!

> Ok.

Annabelle stubbed out her cigarette and entered the school building. She bumped into William in the second-floor hallway. She nodded briefly and he nodded back. It was odd, she thought to herself, that two people who had been so close could become strangers, just like that. For a moment, she considered turning around and shouting after him that she took it all back, that she had messed up her life, that she needed him, that she actually loved him. But she didn't do it. Because firstly, it would only make things worse and secondly, she no longer thought it was true.

13

Just keep your eyes on the road, Charlie told herself as they headed out of Gullspång town centre. Don't look at the church, or *that* turn-off. Just keep your eyes on the road now.

The potholes made the car rattle.

'What kind of a bloody road is this?' Anders said.

'Just a regular road, I guess.'

'They should repave it. This is worse than a gravel road.'

'You don't seem to get it,' Charlie said.

'Get what?'

'That Gullspång is one of Sweden's poorest municipalities.'

Anders said he did get it, it was just that ... well, wouldn't the cost of the damage done to all the cars far outweigh the cost of repaving?

'The municipality doesn't own the cars,' Charlie retorted.

The church was coming into view in the distance; Charlie wanted to shut her eyes, but kept glancing over at it. It hurts too much, she thought. I should never have come here.

Fredrik and Nora Roos lived in a simple, white wooden house just where the village petered out into fields and meadows. Half the lawn had been mowed; the mower had been left out in the yard. Charlie thought to herself that it would be a while before someone put it away.

The doorbell was broken so Charlie knocked. It was a long time before she heard footsteps approaching. Fredrik Roos opened the door; unshaven and red-eyed, he asked them to come inside. Yes, he had heard detectives were coming down from Stockholm, and it was a good thing, he said, and showed them into the kitchen. He poured coffee with trembling hands. It was a good thing they were calling in outside specialists.

'I'm afraid there's no milk,' he said as he placed two chipped mugs on the table in front of them. They had sat down in the room he referred to as the parlour.

'We don't mind it black,' Charlie assured him. She looked around. The walls were hung with paintings of crying children, the kind that had recently become popular in Stockholm as a kind of ironic gesture. She wondered if they had been inherited from dead parents. White wooden letters spelled out *Carpe Diem* above the fireplace. Charlie had always thought of those words as a taunt, and now they came off as more scornful than ever.

She was just about to ask after Annabelle's mother, when a fair, skinny woman in jeans and a T-shirt appeared in the doorway. The woman said nothing, just stared vacantly at Charlie and Anders.

'I didn't want to wake you,' Fredrik said. 'I thought you could use your rest ... I mean, since you had finally managed to fall asleep.'

'I wasn't sleeping.'

Charlie looked into her haunted eyes and figured she was probably telling the truth.

'These are the detectives from Stockholm,' Fredrik said. 'They've come to ask some more questions.'

'Well, get on with it then.' Nora spread her hands, wobbled and sat down on an ottoman. 'Ask away.'

There was something familiar about Nora. Charlie felt sure she had seen her before, but she didn't think it would have been out at one of the Lyckebo parties. She knew the names of the handful of women who had frequented Betty's house.

'Coffee?' Fredrik said.

'Who gives a damn about coffee?' Nora replied. 'How am I supposed to think about coffee when my daughter is missing?'

'There's no need to raise your voice,' Fredrik said.

'Annabelle is missing. I'll raise my voice as much as I like.' She turned to Charlie. 'Do you have children?'

Charlie shook her head.

'You?' Nora looked at Anders.

Anders nodded.

'I think you can sense …' Nora said and looked out of the window. 'I think as a mother, you can sense when your child is no longer alive.'

'We will do everything we can to find her,' Anders said.

'It's too late. And don't stare at me like that, Fredrik. You were the one who thought we should let her run around as she pleased.' Nora stood up and left the room.

'She's angry because I haven't enforced the rules as strictly,' Fredrik said once Nora was out of earshot. 'We always had different ideas about how to raise her. Nora wants to control Annabelle, while I … I've wanted to give her more freedom.'

'And now look what your freedom's cost her!' Nora shouted. She must have stopped behind the door to listen. 'You must be asking yourself if it was worth it now. Well, was it?'

Fredrik shook his head. He was close to tears now. It was sad to see, Charlie thought to herself, that some men wouldn't allow themselves to cry, that they couldn't let go, even under circumstances like these. But then she thought about the erratic woman behind the door. She supposed someone had to hold things together.

'She's right,' Fredrik said. 'If I had been as strict as her, none of this would have happened. But is it really ... Is it really reasonable to more or less permanently ground a virtually grown woman?' He turned to Anders.

'No,' Anders replied, 'it's not.'

Charlie realised she had to steer the conversation in another direction before Fredrik got bogged down in self-recrimination. She had met parents of missing children before, but none that had seemed as consumed with regret and guilt as Fredrik. Maybe it would have been more understandable if the missing child had been very young, if he had put the child in danger through negligence or lack of attention. But this was a seventeen-year-old, a girl who was one year away from being of age.

'Tell us about that night,' Charlie said. 'Tell us about the night she disappeared.'

Fredrik rubbed his face. 'She was going over to Rebecka's. They were just going to watch a film, but then she didn't come home.'

'And that was when you went out to look for her?'

Fredrik nodded. When Nora started feeling anxious, he had gone straight to the village shop.

'Why not to Rebecka's house?'

'Because neither Rebecka nor Annabelle were answering their phones, so we figured they might have gone somewhere else. Nora was the one who told me to go straight to Vall's.'

'And what time was this?'

'Just before one.'

'Tell us about what happened when you got there.'

'I already have. It was a party that had spun out of control,

74

young people sleeping and talking nonsense, loud music, drunkenness. Svante Linder was sitting in the kitchen with a friend. Well, I'm assuming you know who everyone is already. Either way, everyone seemed completely unperturbed.'

'What do you mean by that?'

'I mean that if they had done something to her, if they had done something to my little girl ... they probably wouldn't have ... they probably wouldn't have looked so unperturbed. And I found Rebecka upstairs with this guy William. It was when she told me Annabelle had gone home that I knew. I just knew something horrible had happened. I could feel it.'

'And then?' Anders said.

'Then I drove around everywhere, looking. I called Nora and she phoned the police straight away, but they didn't really seem to take it all that seriously. They told us to wait and see.'

'Had you or your wife noticed anything different about Annabelle in the days before she went missing?' Charlie said.

'Nothing comes to mind.'

'How was her mood?'

'I don't know, maybe she was a bit ... no, never mind, I don't know.'

'What?' Charlie pressed.

'A bit blue, or maybe tired would be more accurate.'

'Did you ask why?'

'No, I've only really realised it since I've been trying to think back. It's probably more of a feeling.'

'Has Annabelle ever been depressed?'

'Why would you ask that? You don't think she could have ...'

'I just want to know if she's been depressed.'

Fredrik sighed and shook his head. Annabelle had never been depressed, not as far as he was aware anyway, but she was not one of those girls who are always happy ...

'Continue,' Charlie urged when he fell silent.

Fredrik wondered what she meant; Charlie told him to carry on describing his daughter.

He was quiet for a moment, then swallowed hard and started talking. Annabelle was very special, well, yes, he supposed all parents felt that way about their children, but Annabelle ... they had always been told that, that she was special. He had sensed it when she was born. She had screamed before she was even fully out. How many children do that? Fredrik looked from Charlie to Anders and back, as though he thought they might have relevant statistics to hand. 'She loves to read,' he continued, 'goes through several books a week. It's pure curiosity, Annabelle has always been curious and ... a searcher, kind of. It's been everything from Buddhism to ...' He cleared his throat as though he was trying to remember what else it had been. 'But now it's all about church.'

'Are you and Nora active in the church?' Charlie asked.

'Neither one of us; we're both atheists. Nora says this God thing is just Annabelle's way of rebelling.'

'Against what?'

'Against us. She even got confirmed. Maybe it was because almost all her classmates did. Either way, those Bible studies that seem to bore everyone else her age ... Annabelle enjoyed them. She even said they were interesting, and after a while she started attending services and doing ... Christian things like joining a Bible group. I guess we were a bit relieved. Church is better than hanging out up at Vall's. But, then again, she kept going there too.'

Fredrik stood up and walked back over to the window. His back was hunched. Charlie thought he moved like a person who has given up, who has lost all hope.

'If she comes home, I won't yell at her,' he said. 'I would just ... we would just hug her. Just hold her close ...'

He broke off when Anders handed him a tissue. It annoyed Charlie, because she felt Fredrik had been on the verge of saying something important.

Fredrik looked at the tissue in his hand as though he wasn't aware of the tears dripping onto his T-shirt.

'She was our only child,' he said.

Is, Charlie wanted to tell him. *She is your only child.*

Fredrik sat back down. Charlie noticed his hands shaking when he raised his cup to his mouth. What he had told them didn't help to give a more cohesive picture of Annabelle: quite the contrary. A person of extremes, she thought, a complex young woman.

'That day,' Charlie said. 'Did anything out of the ordinary happen on the day Annabelle went missing?'

Fredrik shook his head. 'Like what?'

'Did you have a fight, for example?'

'I didn't see her,' Fredrik said. 'I left around six and didn't come back until just before seven. I work at Bäckhammar. The paper mill,' he added. 'One of the machines was on the blink. I had to stay late. Annabelle had just left when I got back.'

'And Nora?'

'Well, yes, she was home, so they saw each other both before and after school.'

'Do you know what things were like between the two of them?'

'Nora said they argued a little about curfews, but nothing serious. They always argue about that when Annabelle wants to go out.'

'And at other times? Do they fight about other things as well?'

'Usually only about things related to rules and boundaries.'

Charlie swallowed and decided to ask the difficult question.

'Have you or your wife ever used violence against Annabelle?'

'What kind of question is that?' Fredrik turned to her.

'The routine kind,' Charlie replied. 'There's no need to take it personally.'

'No, we haven't. We're not the kind of people who beat children. And of course I take it personally, being treated as a suspect on top of everything.'

'You are not under suspicion,' Anders said. 'As Charlie says, they're just questions we have to ask.'

Charlie gave him a look that said that we can discuss what is and isn't a routine question later.

'Can you tell us about Annabelle's relationship with William Stark?' she said.

Fredrik shook his head. He hadn't even known they were seeing each other. The police had told him as much a few days ago. Well, he obviously knew she had been dating, what seventeen-year-old girl doesn't. But that she was in a relationship ... she hadn't said a word about it, to him or Nora.

'Annabelle has been in frequent contact with someone calling from a pay-as-you-go phone.' Charlie showed Fredrik the number. 'Do you recognise it?'

Fredrik shook his head.

'I just thought it might be a relative or some such, someone we could eliminate from our investigation.'

'I don't think so,' Fredrik said. 'But I can hold onto it and look into it more.' He took the note.

They sat in silence for a while. Eventually, Charlie cleared her throat and asked if they could have a look at Annabelle's room.

Fredrik said Olof had already been there, that he hadn't found anything of value.

'Even so, I'd like to take a look.'

'Nora is probably in bed,' Fredrik said. 'If she's asleep ... I would like her to be left in peace for a while.'

'We can come back another day,' Anders said. 'Thank you for taking the time to talk to us.' He stood up.

'I'll walk you to your car,' Fredrik said. 'You'll have to excuse me, but I'm exhausted too.'

They went back out into the hallway. As they passed the stairs, Charlie thought she caught a glimpse of Nora out of the corner of her eye, standing by the banister upstairs.

'Was there something else on your mind?' Charlie asked Fredrik after they shut the front door behind them.

'I'm concerned about Nora. I want her to get ... help. She's barely slept at all since ... Not sleeping makes her very peculiar.'

'Has she not been given sleeping pills?' Anders asked.

'Yes, but they're not helping.'

'Does she have a history of insomnia?' Charlie said.

'Why do you ask?'

She could feel his guard coming up.

'Because you said sleep deprivation makes her peculiar, as though it were a recurring problem.'

'She's had bad periods before. She's been ill.'

'In what way?' Anders asked.

'Nerves,' Fredrik said and looked down at the ground. Then he turned to look up at the house as though he wanted to make sure all the windows were closed. 'There have been periods of nervous illness.'

'Depressed?' Charlie asked.

'It's more than that. It's almost like she's ... I suppose you could say she goes crazy.'

'Psychotic?'

'Yes.'

'So she's been sectioned?'

Fredrik nodded. It had happened a few times and now, with all this pressure, he was afraid it would happen again.

'I can understand that,' Charlie said. 'I can really understand that.'

'I would like for us to get some help.'

'We will arrange for someone to come over,' Anders said.

'Who?'

'A psychologist, or a counsellor, someone to talk to.'

'Do we even have those around here?'

Anders said he would make sure support was provided as soon as possible.

Charlie hoped that wasn't promising too much.

14

Fredrik cleared away the cups in the sitting room. There was a sound from upstairs. So Nora was awake after all. He thought about Sunnyside, the empty-eyed patients, the untouched board games in the common room. It wouldn't be long before Nora was back there. On a bed in a white room, completely unresponsive.

He thought about the first time she was sectioned. Annabelle had just turned one. He had taken her out of her crib when she cried at night, placed her warm little body next to his and slept that way every single night until Nora came home and demanded that Annabelle sleep in her own bed. On account of the crushing hazard, she claimed. Did he not see that he could unintentionally suffocate her if she slept in their bed? And he had given way to her and put Annabelle back in her crib. The first few nights, she had cried so heart-rendingly, he had felt like he was breaking into a thousand pieces. Why had he not stood up to Nora? Why had he let his daughter cry herself to sleep when he could have just picked her up and held her? And what was the point, he thought to himself as he put the cups in the dishwasher, of thinking about things like that now?

15

Charlie was breathing heavily when they got back into the car. There was something about people in crisis that made her airways constrict. She thought about the mother, Nora: her fluttering hands, the panic in her eyes, the fury.

'Nervous illness?' Anders said after reversing out of Nora and Fredrik's driveway. 'People still use terms like nervous illness?'

'Apparently,' Charlie said. She thought it was fastidious to get hung up on vocabulary in a situation like this. To have sick nerves, wasn't that what it was?

'What do you think?'

'About what?'

'The mother? She seems fairly ... unstable.'

Charlie turned to him. 'Who wouldn't be when their child has gone missing?'

'I was thinking more about her mental health issues; you're well aware of what psychotic people are capable of.'

'Most psychotic people are completely harmless.'

'Yes, and then there are the dangerous ones.'

'Exactly,' Charlie said, 'and then there are people who are considered perfectly healthy but are in fact heinously evil.'

'All right. Why are you getting so upset?'

'I'm not upset, I'm just so sick of people thinking anyone with a mental illness is a danger to society.'

'I don't think that.'

She sighed and thought about how ignorant most people were about the human psyche. She had always been interested in the subject. It had started in middle school when she was trying to figure out why Betty wasn't like other mothers. Why she would end up in bed for days without speaking. Why she never packed gym bags, baked bread or bought presents for birthday parties.

'This business about them being violent,' Anders said. 'Did you really think it was the right time to ask him that?'

'The question needed to be asked,' Charlie said. She took out her phone and googled *psychologist, Gullspång municipality*, but the only thing that came up was a tourist information website with various activities for families with children. She sighed and thought about everything Gullspång didn't have: psychologists, crisis teams, specialists. Then she googled *priest, Gullspång* instead, hoping the insincere old vicar who had presided over Betty's funeral had retired. A name and a number came up. When Charlie called, it went straight to voicemail, where a young man's voice introduced himself as Hannes Palmgren and apologised for not being able to take the call, but if you left a message he would get back to you as soon as possible. She left a message and redid the google search, thinking there might be more than one priest, but the only thing she found was a list of on-call priests in the region.

'So call one of those, then,' Anders said when she cursed.

'But I want it to be someone who can go over there, obviously. What good is a phone call in this situation?' Then she fell silent, thinking that in this situation, what good was anything, other than finding Annabelle, finding her fast and alive.

'He said they're not Christian,' Anders said. 'Maybe it's not such a good idea to send a priest over.'

'There's a crisis; everyone's Christian in a crisis. And what other choice do we have anyway, seeing how there's no one else?'

'That said, the priest seems hard to reach, too,' Anders retorted.

'We're going to have to try again if he doesn't get back to us soon.'

They started talking about what they had found out about Annabelle. The Bible studies, her reading, her exemplary grades.

'It's contradictory,' Anders said.

'What is?'

'You don't think? A girl who likes partying and flirting, but who also reads a lot, is active in the church and does well in school.'

'Why would those things be mutually exclusive?' Charlie said. 'And don't put too much store on the flirting thing. It's just a rumour. It doesn't take a lot to get chins wagging in places like this.'

'It sounds like you're speaking from personal experience,' Anders said.

Charlie didn't reply. She had neither the time nor the inclination to open up about herself or her experience.

'I recognised her,' she said, to change the subject. 'I've met Nora before, but I don't know in what context.'

'I suppose you must have met quite a lot of the people in this place before.'

'Yes, I suppose I must have,' Charlie replied.

'Still, it's odd,' Anders said and turned out onto the bigger road, 'them not having any relatives over.'

'I'm guessing inviting guests isn't their top priority right now.'

'I suppose I meant their near and dear ones.'

'Not everyone has near and dear ones,' Charlie said and looked out of the window.

16

Olof picked up after the first ring when Charlie called. 'How did it go?' he asked without saying hello. 'Didn't get a lot out of them, huh?'

'Did you know Nora has a history of depression? That she has been sectioned several times?'

'No one told us. But I'm not surprised. That woman has always seemed ... anxious, somehow.'

'Fredrik's worried she's going to have a breakdown. Is there a psychologist we could call?'

'No, no psychologist. All we have is Hannes, the vicar. I'll give him a call.'

'I already did. He's not picking up. But we can head over and see if he's in. That'll give us a chance to talk to him about the Bible group Annabelle was a member of as well. Or have you already looked into that?'

'No. We've had our hands full with the partygoers.'

Charlie hung up.

'Are we going to see the vicar now?' Anders asked.

'Yes. We might as well talk to him now if we're planning on contacting him about Nora anyway. What's so wrong about that?' Charlie continued when she noticed Anders's sceptical look. 'No one has interviewed him yet.'

'You think we're going to get anything out of a priest?'

'He can at least answer general questions. Not everything is covered by absolute confidentiality.'

Anders countered that the whole point of absolute confidentiality was that it was ... absolute.

'At the very least, we have to find out who the other members of the Bible group are.'

'Look up his address then,' Anders said.

Charlie said she didn't need to; presumably he lived in the vicarage and she knew where that was.

I might as well just go over there, she thought. After all, there would be no occasion to go to the cemetery, to find the grave, to think about the decomposing body. She was here to solve a missing person case. Nothing else.

She thought about how she had ridden her bike to the church when she was little. She used to walk up and down the aisles between the headstones, reading titles, names and dates. For some strange reason, it made her feel calm to think about all the dead people under her feet. One time, when Betty had turned up to an end-of-the-school-year ceremony for once, she had shown her the most beautiful of the stones. But Betty hadn't been impressed.

I don't want one of those ridiculous pecking doves on my grave. You know I've never liked birds. And besides, you're going to spread me over Lake Skagern anyway. Yes, I know it's not allowed, but who's going to stop you? Just bring the urn one night and row out there.

Betty thought it was madness for Charlie to spend so much time in the cemetery, but she wasn't going to forbid her from hanging out with dead people all day if it made her happy. She wasn't the type of person who prevented people from doing things they liked.

Sometimes, Charlie had wished that Betty would be stricter, that she would have rules like everyone else's parents and demand to know where Charlie was and when she was going to be back. But Betty was not the anxious type and later on, after Mattias moved in, Charlie had fewer restrictions than ever.

He's not my dad, Charlie would object when Betty yelled at her for being rude to Mattias. But how was it Charlie's fault that she hated listening to Mattias's stories about the little boy he had lost? It was as though he couldn't wrap his head around why social services had granted the mother full custody. Betty and Mattias would talk about the boy, about trying to get him back, about being a family of four. When Charlie heard them talking like that, she would go to her room and pray to the God she didn't believe in not to let it happen. She prayed Betty's relationship with Mattias would end and become something they could laugh about, she and Betty. But when it came to Mattias, Betty never laughed. Because he was the exception that proved the rule.

What rule?

The one about all men being pigs. Mattias was forgiving and good, the only person who knew everything about her and still liked her. Maybe that was why Charlie started resenting him in earnest. She didn't want this man who knew everything about Betty around. She didn't want Mattias's son to come and live with them. They would never be a normal family anyway, whatever Betty imagined. Because Mattias drank and wore weird clothes, and Betty ... it was the same thing with Betty. Everything would just be doubly weird.

A pothole yanked her back to the present.

'You've passed it,' she said. 'You were supposed to take a left at the last intersection.'

'Why didn't you say?' Anders asked.

'Because my mind was elsewhere. Shouldn't you have figured it out anyway? The church isn't exactly invisible. Now you're going to have to do a U-turn.'

'The road isn't wide enough.'

'Sure it is. You just don't know how to judge distance.'

'Why don't you just focus on where we're going, okay?'

They parked on the well-raked gravel path in front of the red vicarage and walked up the steps to the front door. When they knocked, a dog started barking inside.

A woman with a little boy on her hip opened the door.

'No, Kafka,' she told the labrador who was jumping at Charlie. 'He still thinks he's a puppy,' she apologised. 'He doesn't realise how big he is. Are you all right?'

'It's okay,' Charlie said. 'I'm a dog person.' She bent down, scratched the dog behind the ears with both hands and explained to the woman why they were there.

Vicar Hannes appeared behind his wife. He was dressed in his full vestments.

'They're here to talk about Annabelle,' the wife said.

'We called,' Charlie offered.

'I'm afraid I don't keep too close an eye on my mobile,' Hannes said. 'But, please, come in. Have some coffee.'

Charlie looked around the large, rustic kitchen. By the window was an old oak table with a matching kitchen bench with a red-and-white checked cushion, and the walls were hung with textiles extolling the safe hearth of home and praising the Lord Almighty.

'Left by the previous vicar,' Hannes said. 'Apparently, his wife loved embroidery.'

A girl of about four entered the room with a toy car in each hand.

'Would you mind taking the children upstairs, Louise?' Hannes said.

His wife nodded, called her daughter and disappeared.

'I was just about to change,' he continued. 'These clothes don't exactly breathe. I've been over in the church with a group of young people, praying for Annabelle. Everyone is very upset.' He wiped sweat from his brow. 'In these situations, we all feel ... we feel powerless.'

'Have you been in touch with the parents?' Charlie said.

'I've called but they don't pick up.'

'It might be good if you went over there. The mother isn't doing well at all.'

He nodded. Of course he would.

'How long have you been with this congregation?' Anders asked while Hannes got out blue and white coffee cups with matching saucers.

'Just three years.'

'You moved here?'

'Yes, from Stockholm. We were tired of the big city. My wife wanted a garden, a safe place for the children to grow up. But I suppose we may as well accept there are no such places.'

'How well do you know Annabelle?' Charlie said.

'I confirmed her and then she joined my Bible group. It's a small group where everyone has got to know everyone else.'

'Why do you think she was drawn to the church?'

'I can only speculate. But it's not unusual for young people with difficult home situations to be drawn to the church.'

'Are you saying Annabelle's home situation was difficult?'

'I was speaking generally. But she certainly enjoyed the conversations we had during her confirmation course. I tried to set up a young people's group afterwards, but everyone except Annabelle dropped out after a few meetings. That was when I suggested she join the adult Bible group. I figured she would only come once, since the other members are so much older. But Annabelle seemed to appreciate that. She is ... different from her peers.'

Charlie asked him to expand on that.

'She just feels more mature and thoughtful. And when she speaks, people listen. I suppose you might say she's ... intelligent, simply put.'

Charlie asked about the other members of the group.

Hannes told them there were six in total, but when Charlie asked for their names, he added that he was sure no one in the group had anything to do with Annabelle's disappearance.

How could he be so sure, Anders wanted to know.

'These are women in their seventies.'

'Even if they aren't suspects,' Charlie said, 'they might know something that could help move the investigation forward.'

She pulled a notebook and pen from her bag and asked Hannes to write down the names of the members of the group.

'Did you ever speak privately, you and Annabelle?' she asked when Hannes pushed the notepad back over to her.

'From time to time.'

'Did anything out of the ordinary come to light during those conversations?'

'I can't discuss that.'

'I think you comprehend how imperative it is that we are told about anything that can lead us to her.'

'And I think you comprehend the meaning of absolute confidentiality. If you'll excuse me' – Hannes glanced at his watch – 'I have a funeral tomorrow that I need to prepare for.'

'Just one more thing,' Charlie said. 'Where were you the night between Friday and Saturday?'

'What do you mean?' Hannes said. 'Are you implying that I ...'

'We ask everyone,' Charlie said, 'so there's no need to be offended.'

'I'm not,' Hannes said. 'Just surprised. But I was home all night.'

'Was your family at home with you?' Charlie asked.

'No, they were in Stockholm, visiting relatives. I had an early Sunday service so I had to stay here.'

'I told you so,' Anders said when they were back in the car. 'Did you really think a priest would tell us anything?'

'I rather think he did,' Charlie retorted.

'He did?'

'Sure, what with the home situation.'

'He said that was generally speaking.'

'Oh come on, of course it wasn't general.'

'Either way, it's hardly news,' Anders said. 'We already knew about the mother, that she's over-protective and ...'

'He drinks,' Charlie said. 'I think the vicar drinks.'

'Based on what?' Anders turned to her.

Charlie didn't know how to respond. It was his breath, of course, the unmistakable smell of alcohol when she shook his hand, but that didn't have to mean he had a drinking problem. Was there something in his eyes? The slightly red nose with its burst blood vessels?

'It was just a hunch,' she said. 'It was just a hunch I had.'

'Does that make him suspicious in any way?'

'No, but you know as well as I do what alcohol does to a person's judgement.'

'Not quite as well as you do,' Anders said with a grin.

'Regardless, I don't like it that we can't verify his alibi.' Charlie pulled out the notepad and read the names Hannes had written down: Inez Gustavsson, Gunlis Andersson, Anna-Britt

Estberger, Marit Höglund and Rita Oksanen. 'Maybe Annabelle told the other people in the group something,' she said. 'Either way, someone has to talk to these women.'

'Is that really a priority? It seems a bit far-fetched. Wouldn't it make more sense to focus on the partygoers?'

'It won't hurt to check in with these people, too.' She called Micke and gave him the names of the women in the group. Could he dig up their phone numbers and have a short conversation with each of them?

'I spoke to one of them just yesterday,' Micke offered. 'Gunlis Andersson. She's my grandmother. And I can tell you this much right now; if she knew anything of significance, she would have told me a long time ago.'

'Contact the other ones,' Charlie said.

There and then

Rosa says that if there is one thing she's always wished for, it's a sister. She's even prayed for God to give her one.

'And what do you know,' she says and strokes Alice's cheek, 'it's almost enough to make you believe he exists after all.'

'He doesn't exist,' Alice says.

'We don't know that,' Rosa retorts with a gentle punch on the arm.

Alice punches back.

Rosa hits her again, a bit harder this time. Before long they are rolling around in the grass.

'Do you yield?' Rosa asks. She is straddling Alice's waist and has locked her arms and hands with her knees.

'I yield,' Alice says and laughs.

'Do you understand that I'm stronger than you?'

'I understand.'

'I'll promise you one thing,' Rosa says, leaning forward so her hair tickles Alice's face, 'if anyone ever hurts you, they'll be punished. I'm serious, Alice, they'll be punished.'

Rosa's not afraid of anything, not even the moped guys who drive up next to them, much too close. She spits after them and gives them the finger. Alice doesn't understand how she dares.

Once, one of them stops, pushes his black visor up and shouts at Rosa that she should be raped with a limp cock.

'Both you and your whore of a mother should be raped with a limp cock,' he shouts.

Alice looks at Rosa, waiting for the explosion.

But instead of lunging at him or kicking his moped, Rosa bursts out laughing.

What kind of threat is that? Is that supposed to scare her, or what?

'So lame,' Rosa says as they walk away, 'like I'd be scared of something like that.'

Alice nods even though she barely understands what was said.

'You can't fuck a person with a limp cock.' Rosa punches her in the side. 'Even toddlers know that.'

17

'I'm driving down to the news-stand,' Charlie said when they reached the motel. 'Need cigarettes.'

'Then why didn't you tell me to go that way?' Anders asked.

'Because I forgot.'

A small group of young people were hanging out by the news-stand. Was it the same ones that had been there before? Charlie stopped. When she climbed out of the car, she noticed one of the boys pushing one of the girls around. She went over.

'Everyone good here?' she said.

The teenagers looked at her in silence.

'I asked if everyone's good here?' she said again and fixed her gaze on the boy who had done the pushing.

'What's it to you?' another, bigger lad said.

Charlie brandished her badge.

'We were just goofing around,' said the one who had done the pushing. 'Don't the police have better things to do right now than worrying about a harmless gag?'

'Did you think it was funny?' Charlie turned to the girl. Only now did she realise it was Sara, one of the girls who had stayed at Vall's until the small hours the night Annabelle went missing.

Sara shrugged. She was drunk, Charlie realised. Thirteen years old and drunk before dinner on a school night.

'Come on, I'll take you home.'

'Leave her alone,' said the one who had pushed her. 'She's better off with us.'

'She's going home,' Charlie said.

Sara shrugged and followed her without protest.

'You're Sara, right?' Charlie said once they were in the car.

'How did you know that?' Sara asked.

'You were there, at the party, the night Annabelle disappeared.'

'Yeah, but I already talked to the police about it. I didn't see anything. I didn't notice anything strange.'

'No one noticed anything strange, but something strange happened.'

Sara's phone rang. She rummaged around her bag for a while, but gave up when she was unable to find it.

'Where do you live?' Charlie asked.

Sara gave her an address Charlie knew.

'Will your parents be angry?'

'*Parent*,' Sara said and hiccuped. 'And no, he won't be angry. I don't even think he's realised I'm not there. Alcoholic,' she explained. 'The only thing he ever tells me is that I can't get into cars with strangers.' She started laughing. 'I hope he meant strange men.'

Sara's house was made of brown brick; an advent candle holder twinkled in the window. Charlie couldn't help remembering the Christmas curtains they'd had in the windows their last year in Lyckebo.

'Do you want me to go in with you?' she said.

'No need,' Sara replied. 'I'll go by myself.'

97

And yet she stayed in her seat, not even unbuckling her seatbelt.

'Good song,' she said with a nod to the radio where Alphaville's 'Forever Young' was playing. 'But the lyrics are proper sad.'

Charlie agreed. They were sad.

Or even horrible, Sara felt. Because who wanted to be young forever? She couldn't imagine anything worse. Grown-ups who claimed to want to relive their youth must have forgotten what it was like or were just fucking stupid. She started laughing again. Charlie laughed too and told her she agreed, that she was one of the people who hadn't forgotten. She couldn't think of anything worse than being forever young.

'In a way, I kind of wish I was her,' Sara said and put a hand on the door handle.

'Who?'

'Annabelle.'

'How come?' Charlie fixed her tensely.

'Because at least she got away from here; wherever she is now, at least it's somewhere else.'

'Do you know her well?'

Sara shook her head. Annabelle wasn't the type to hang out with younger girls.

'Are you sure you don't want me to go in with you?'

'Dead sure,' Sara said.

'Maybe you could take my card?' Charlie searched her bag and pulled out a business card.

'What for?'

'I just figured you might need it. If you think of anything else about that night, anything at all, or ... if there's anything else.'

'Okay.' Sara took the card, turned it over for a minute before climbing out of the car and starting to walk towards the house.

Charlie watched her staggering progress in the rear-view

mirror, her skinny legs in those short shorts. For a few seconds, Charlie felt as though she was her, on her way towards bedlam. She wanted to open the door and shout that everything would be okay, that things would turn out all right in the end, but who was she to make that kind of promise? Social services, she thought, on her way back to the motel. I'm going to call social services about this. But it would probably make very little difference. At least not if their methods were unchanged from when she had needed them. Everything is the same here after all, Charlie thought to herself. Nothing has really changed.

18

Fredrik took a big swig of whisky. He thought about the unpleasant questions the police had asked. Had they ever used violence against their daughter? Had he really answered that question truthfully? At times, the rows between Nora and Annabelle had got out of hand. He had been forced to step in and separate them so they wouldn't hurt each other. Had he been wrong not to tell the detectives? No, he decided. It would only lead them down the wrong path. But the two of them had fought the day she went missing. At least he had told the police that. He went over the previous Friday in his mind, yet again. Nora had had dinner ready when he came home from work. She had seemed upset, he remembered that; upset and distracted. Annabelle had left before dinner. He had asked if they had fought, she and Annabelle. Nora had replied that they had had a disagreement about Annabelle's curfew after she noticed her dress was missing. It was nothing serious.

Fredrik took another swig. What did he really know about his wife?

She had no family, she had told him, when he had finally managed to persuade her to go out for a coffee with him so many years ago now; only a foster family in Mariestad that she wanted nothing to do with.

How come?

Not a subject she wanted to discuss.

And how did she end up in Gullspång?

It was the rents, the cheap rental flats. He had laughed and said it was the same for him. He had tried to learn more about her, but she hadn't wanted to answer any more questions. She said she was the kind of person who looked to the future, not the past.

When Fredrik proposed, just a year later, he still didn't know much more about her background than what he had been told during that first date. Back then, it hadn't bothered him. But later on, he realised that whatever Nora liked to believe, it was in fact impossible to suppress such a large part of one's life. Her nightmares woke him up at night, her flailing fists in his face, her screams. Then, when he asked her about the dreams, she said she couldn't remember. When Fredrik told her about the hitting, the screaming, she just shrugged and told him she had been like that ever since she was a little girl. She had always been a child with very vivid dreams.

Fredrik thought about Nora's elation the day they moved into the house. Everything was crooked and askew, but it was as though she didn't see it.

This place, Fredrik, I think I can be happy in this place.

But had she ever been happy?

19

'Hungry?' Erik asked when Charlie returned to the motel. 'Your colleague is already seated over there.' He pointed to Anders, who was sitting at a window table further in. 'You have a seat and I'll bring the food.'

It was not until Anders commented that she'd been gone a long time that Charlie realised she had forgotten to buy cigarettes.

'I drove a drunk girl home,' she said. 'Sara Larsson, the thirteen-year-old who was at the party.'

'What?' she said when Anders gave her a look.

'A drunk thirteen-year-old,' Anders said. 'She's just a child. It's all so tragic.'

Charlie agreed. It was tragic.

'She tell you anything new?' Anders said.

'As I said, she was in a bad way. We're going to have to interview her again.'

'We're going to have to interview everyone again,' Anders said. He opened his mouth as though he wanted to say more, but fell silent when two people sat down at the next table. He looked towards the kitchen and asked why they hadn't been given a menu, how Erik could possibly know what people wanted to eat.

'I think they only serve one dish at a time,' Charlie said, 'at least that's how it was when I lived here.'

She would actually have preferred to eat in their room so they could go over the facts of the case more thoroughly. What's more, she was struggling with a kind of flight impulse. All the people in the restaurant. She didn't think she recognised anyone, but at the same time, every face she saw seemed familiar.

Anders started talking about the summer, about his time off, which wasn't turning out the way his wife wanted. She wanted to visit her parents in Torekov in July and then go to her sister's; but now that it wasn't going to be one continuous period, it was going to be much harder and ...

What difference did it make, Charlie wondered, which weeks he got off, since she was on maternity leave anyway?

Anders launched into a long explanation of how his holiday didn't line up with his in-laws' holiday and that Maria had been hoping her parents would be able to relieve them and give them time to themselves and ...

They were interrupted by a woman with a notepad squatting down next to their table. She apologised and said she just wanted to ask a few questions about the investigation.

'No comment,' Anders said.

'But I ...'

'I said, no comment. You'll have to come to the press conference like everyone else.'

'I don't know anything about a press conference.'

'I'm sure you'll be told when there's something to tell,' Anders said.

The journalist turned hopefully to Charlie, but when she realised that door was closed, too, she stood up abruptly and walked away.

'One thing's for sure,' Anders said, 'we're going to have a

tough time keeping the vultures at bay if we don't get to the bottom of this.'

'If we don't, I suppose they're within their rights giving us a tough time.'

Anders looked at his watch. 'We've only been here seven hours.'

'I'm just saying we'd better not fuck this up.'

'Why are you talking like a teenager?'

'I'll talk whatever way I please,' Charlie said. 'And hey,' she continued when Erik approached with two big plates heaped with chips, steak and béarnaise sauce, 'good luck with those carbs.'

'Still, it's weird,' Anders said with a glance at his plate, 'that they don't give us options. Shouldn't there at least be a salad or something, as an alternative?'

'Definitely,' Charlie said, because she couldn't be bothered to explain to him that anyone who tried to offer a wide selection of anything in this godforsaken backwater would probably end up going out of business.

'This is going to be a disaster,' he said.

'I hope you mean your diet,' Charlie said.

The local regulars seemed to have congregated over at the bar.

'What's with their arms?' Anders nodded to them. 'Have they all just come from a knife fight?'

Charlie looked at their bare lower arms, which were covered in cuts.

'It's the factory,' she said, 'the plywood factory. Most of the locals work there.'

'Don't they get protective clothing?'

'Sure, but it gets hellishly hot in there in the summer. It's the lumber; they cut themselves handling the wood.'

'I thought they had machines for things like that.'

'I'm sure they do, but maybe people are cheaper.'

Anders looked back over at the bar. 'I would never ... I mean, getting cut up in a factory ...'

'Not everyone gets the same opportunities in life.'

'You always have a choice.'

'That's what people who were born lucky like to say.'

'Sure, but you can always ...'

'No,' Charlie said, 'that's utter fucking bullshit.'

They ate in silence for a while. Charlie stared out of the grimy windows. It was still bright out, even though it was almost nine o'clock. The laburnum was still there on the grassy patch between the motel and the smelter. Its yellow flowers were in full bloom. Once, when she was little, she had torn off a whole cluster and started eating it. Shrieking, Betty had prised open her mouth and demanded that she spit. Spit or die. And then, when the pain in her mouth made Charlie cry: *Fine, but I had to get it all out, or you would have died. But maybe that's what you want? Is it? Do you want to die?*

It didn't matter that Charlie tried to explain later on that she hadn't wanted to die, that the flowers had simply looked like corn on the cob. Betty still turned it into a story about the world's youngest suicide candidate. *Imagine what could have happened if I hadn't been there*, she would say, retelling the story at parties. *Imagine what could have happened if the girl had kept munching down laburnum like it was sweetcorn?*

The din of voices and clutter of cutlery faded into a low background drone. She thought about the house out in Lyckebo, the flowering cherry tree grove, Betty opening the windows and turning on the old record player so they could sing along.

*

Charlie was so deep in thought she jumped when Jonas placed two large shot glasses on the table. Before either one of them had time to object, he had moved on to the next table.

'Did you order these?' Anders said.

Charlie shook her head; Anders called Jonas back over. There had been a mistake.

'They're complimentary,' Jonas explained. 'On the house for all diners. And I made yours extra large, to make up for the booking error.'

Charlie looked after him as he disappeared through the swinging doors behind the bar. He seemed stressed, clumsy, nervous.

'What do you reckon?' she said with a nod to the door.

'I think that's a topic for another time. But this much we know: he was at the party when Annabelle went missing.'

'We don't know exactly when she left the party; there's conflicting information.'

'No, I suppose no one there was really keeping track,' Anders said. 'It seems like most of them were more or less comatose. You're going to drink that?' he continued when Charlie raised her shot glass.

'I don't know about you,' she said and took a big swig of the black, viscous liquid, 'but I've always figured that when in Rome ...'

Anders's phone rang. He checked the screen, stood up and walked off. Charlie knew he was going to be gone for a while. His shot glass was sitting right in front of her, begging to be knocked back. Before she had time to think that she shouldn't, she had downed it. As though he'd been lying in wait, Jonas appeared, offering a top-up.

Charlie shook her head. She was there to work.

'I'm sorry about the mix-up with your reservations,' Jonas said. 'I hope it didn't cause any problems.'

Charlie looked out of the window where Anders was pacing back and forth, looking upset, the phone pressed hard against his ear.

'Don't worry about it,' she said. 'We all make mistakes sometimes.'

Apparently, Anders had no intention of getting off the phone with his wife. Charlie had time to finish her dinner and start browsing the internet on her phone. Both national tabloids were giving the Annabelle story top billing on their websites. One featured a picture of the gravel road it was assumed Annabelle had walked along that night. The photograph had been taken at dawn; the spruces glittered with dew. Charlie mused that a lot of people would not opt to walk down a lonely forest road in the middle of the night, that Annabelle clearly wasn't afraid of the dark. She took a sip of water and, from out of nowhere, the nausea returned. She stood up and started zigzagging her way to the bathroom. There was a line for the ladies so she went into the gents, which was empty. She quickly locked herself in a stall, bent down over a toilet seat that reeked of ammonia and threw up. She didn't normally get this hungover. She was reminded of the sertraline again. Maybe she was already experiencing withdrawal symptoms? In fact, when was the last time she had taken a pill? Predictably, she had missed the call from her GP, and then she had forgotten to call back. Tomorrow, she thought. I'll have to sort it out tomorrow.

When she left the cubicle, she found herself staring into a pair of brown, smiling eyes in the mirror above the urinals.

'I think you might be in the wrong bathroom.'

'Sorry,' she mumbled and walked towards the door.

*

'Where did you go?' Anders asked when she returned to their table.

'The loo.'

'Are you okay?'

'Fine. You?'

'There's a bit of a crisis at home. Stomach pains. Maria thinks he might have colic. He's been given something for it, but apparently it's not helping. He won't stop screaming. Maria's exhausted.'

'I'd lose my mind,' Charlie said.

'She has,' Anders said. 'No, I'm sorry,' he said and wiped his mouth with his napkin, 'all I meant to say is, who wouldn't?'

Charlie looked past Anders. The man from the gents was sitting at a table in the corner by the little stage. He was talking to a man of about the same age, but from time to time he glanced in Charlie's direction. He was good-looking in that unaware way she liked. His hair was slightly curly and his stubble one or two days too old. Had she not been on the job, she would probably have gone over, but she never mixed working and pulling. It was a rule she had set herself (Hugo was going to remain the one exception). But if she hadn't had that kind of rule, he was exactly the type she could have used to calm her jittery nerves. She furtively studied his profile. Was there something familiar about it? Was he from Gullspång? She didn't think so, but she couldn't be sure. How old was he? Thirty-five? Younger?

And then he noticed her looking, looked back and she thought she glimpsed an assurance in his eyes, an assurance that he would not object if she decided to cross that boundary.

'Are you done?' Anders said with a nod to her plate where the chips lay uneaten.

'Yes. I'm trying to cut carbs.'

'I'm going to have to watch what I say around you.' Anders nabbed a few chips from her plate. 'Because it all comes back to bite me.'

Charlie pushed her plate over to his side of the table. Yes, he could have the rest, she was full.

'Do you recognise anyone, by the way?' he said after clearing her plate.

'It's been forever since I lived here.'

'What about your mum, where is she now?'

'She's dead.'

'Dead?'

'Yes, dead.'

'Why didn't you tell me?'

'You didn't ask.'

'Yes, I did. I asked if you see her regularly.'

'And I said I haven't seen her in a long time,' Charlie said, 'which is true.'

'Sometimes you'd almost think you have Asperger's, the way you always take things so literally.'

'I don't always take things literally. Only when it suits me. There's a big difference. If I had Asperger's, I wouldn't be able to do this job.'

'Why not?' Anders asked.

Charlie sighed. 'You studied psychology, didn't you?'

'Just one term.'

'Sometimes I wonder if that's really true.'

'Why?'

'Because ...' Because you don't seem to recall the most basic things, she felt like telling him. 'You seem to have forgotten quite a bit of it.'

'I wasn't particularly ambitious. I had just met Maria then, and I suppose my focus was elsewhere.'

'Love,' Charlie said, 'it really does make people stupid.'

She looked out of the window again; a group of teenagers had gathered around a converted tractor in the car park.

'What happened?' Anders said. 'What happened with your mum?'

'The usual. She got sick and died.'

Anders wanted to know what illness she had suffered from, how she had died, how old Charlie had been at the time, but Charlie pointed out that they weren't there to get lost in childhood memories, they had come to find a missing girl.

'The two aren't mutually exclusive,' Anders retorted.

A folk singer stepped onto the little stage at the back of the bar section of the room. He grabbed the mike and started talking about the day's search efforts. He had participated himself and hoped that many more would join in tomorrow. Because one thing was certain: they were going to keep looking until they found her.

A murmur arose: they bloody well were. A middle-aged man raised his glass, but lowered it again as though he had just realised that his attempted toast might not be appropriate.

The folk singer started playing 'Living Next door to Alice'. Anders rolled his eyes.

'I'm going to bed,' Anders said.

'I'll be right up,' Charlie replied. 'Oh, come off it,' she added when Anders gave her a look that said she should be going with him. 'I just want to hear the rest of the song.'

A gaggle of inebriated women had started dancing in front of the stage and when the folk singer reached the chorus, the audience belted out in unison: *Alice. Alice. Who the fuck is Alice?*

Two young men entered the venue. Heads turned when they walked over to the bar. Charlie recognised their faces from the whiteboard at the police station. The broad-shouldered, blond one was none other than the factory owner's son, Svante Linder, and next to him was Annabelle's ex-boyfriend, William Stark. Jonas, who was behind the bar, quickly finished up an order and gave his friends a beer each on the house.

Charlie studied Jonas. He really did look nervous, tense. Maybe he was concerned about being caught handing out free booze, or did Erik and he have an understanding?

A woman in her forties suddenly appeared in front of Charlie, saying she was moving the tables, that people wanted to dance. They hadn't cleared the tables away after the diners were done, as they normally would have. Maybe they hadn't thought people would be in a dancing mood, things being what they were, but apparently, they had been mistaken.

'Isn't there enough room anyway?' Charlie said.

The woman said it was more for her sake; people were likely to dance into both the table and her if she didn't get out of the way.

'It's those bloody liquorice shots. I've told my husband to stop serving them, but he refuses.'

'So you're Erik's wife?'

The woman nodded. 'Linda,' she said and offered her hand.

'Family business, must be nice,' Charlie said.

'It's not. I would prefer to move back to town. I'm from Skövde originally, but Erik refuses to leave this place. He says it's a safe place for our children to grow up and I guess I used to figure he was right. But now ... with all this about Annabelle, I don't know any more. Have you found anything out yet? Do you have any theories?'

'Nothing I can discuss.'

'Of course.' Linda gave a quick laugh. 'What was I thinking? I just get worried. It's all very unsettling. Because everything points to someone ... having done something to her. No one thinks she left of her own accord any more.' She lowered her voice and leaned in closer. 'It's terrible to think the perpetrator might be one of us, someone I serve beer and chat with at the bar.'

'Did you have anyone particular in mind?' Charlie asked.

'No, or I'd have told the police, wouldn't I? The only thing I was thinking was that there's a lot of commotion around that girl.'

'What do you mean?'

'Exactly that. There's often trouble when she comes in here.' Linda nodded at Svante Linder and William Stark, who had suddenly found free seats at a table that had been occupied just moments before. 'The girl certainly knows how to create drama, put it that way.'

'What do you mean?' Charlie said.

'I mean that she's flirtatious, that boys and men are drawn to her like flies to shit, that they puff themselves up around her, competing for her attention.'

'If you're thinking of something specific, I would really like you to tell me,' Charlie said. Linda shook her head and said she had nothing more to add. 'Would it be okay if we just pushed your table to the side a bit, so you can stay?' she said.

'I was just about to leave,' Charlie said. 'I'll go sit at the bar for a bit.'

She ordered a beer, swivelled around on her bar stool and scanned the room. It was as though they were on a ship in choppy waters. People were swaying and leaning against the walls for support. More young men had joined Svante Linder and William Stark's table. What was the dynamic of that group anyway? Were they friends, rivals, enemies? Had one of them, in a fit of jealousy, insanity or evil, done away with Annabelle?

Charlie looked at the time. It was just before eleven. It was really time to head upstairs. She got up, but only made it a few feet before bumping into the man from the bathroom.

'Leaving already?' he said.

Charlie nodded. She was leaving. It had been a long day.

'Are you with Missing People, too?'

'Yes,' Charlie said.

'Johan, by the way,' he said and held out his hand.

'Lisa.' When she looked into his eyes, it was as though there was a hint of something familiar there after all, but the unmistakable Stockholm accent reassured her. She was just about to tell him she needed to go to bed, when she spotted the pack of Marlboros in his breast pocket; before she had time to consider, she heard herself ask if she could cadge a cigarette off him.

Johan held out his pack and a lighter.

'You're going to smoke inside?' he said when she lit her cigarette.

'I'm hardly the only one.' Charlie gestured at the room, where several cigarettes glowed.

'Fine, but I'm going outside,' Johan said. 'Smoking inside makes me feel sick.'

Charlie followed him out onto the small front door steps. The wind must have turned, because the smell of pulp was gone, replaced by the sweet fragrance of lilacs.

'Are you from here?' she said.

'Stockholm. You?'

'Same.'

'I didn't see you today,' Johan said, 'during the search.'

Charlie pondered whether it had been a bad idea to do the lying thing with this man. This wasn't a night out, not a fling, so there was no reason for her to make things up. What was she doing?

'There's quite a lot of us, I guess,' she said.

Johan nodded. It really was amazing to see, he felt, how many people had come to help out. There was something about this community that moved him: the commitment, the sense of togetherness, the hope of finding the girl alive. 'She doesn't seem to be in the immediate vicinity, at least,' he continued, 'unless she's in the lake.'

'It's bottomless.'

'What did you say?'

'I said it's going to take time,' Charlie said. 'That lake ... it's supposedly very deep.'

'So what do you reckon?' Johan turned to her. 'What do you think we're looking for? I mean, is it a body, or ... ?'

'I don't know, but it doesn't look good, does it?'

'I just saw her dad this morning. He wanted to join the search, but he was in a terrible state. I get that he wanted to go out, though. I would lose my mind, just sitting at home, waiting.'

Johan's phone rang. He apologised and said he had to take the call. He quickly disappeared in the direction of the car park.

Charlie went inside to use the bathroom. It was full of giggling women of all ages.

There was only cold water in the tap. She held her wrists under it and studied herself in the mirror. A ghost, she thought. I look like a fucking ghost.

'Charline!' a familiar voice suddenly exclaimed behind her. 'At first, I figured I had downed one too many shots, but it really is you.'

Charlie turned around.

'Susanne?'

'Fifty pounds later. Oh my God, is it really you, Charlie? I saw you at the bar and I thought you looked familiar somehow, but not in my wildest dreams ... but now that I see your eyes and that scar.' She pointed to Charlie's temple. 'Fuck, Charlie. You finally came back.'

20

'You have no idea how much I've missed you, Charline Lager,' Susanne said. They'd gone back to the pub section and sat down at one of the tables by the wall.

'Me too,' Charlie said and realised it was true. She had missed Susanne, had missed having someone around who knew so much about her history; had missed their conversations, the way they had laughed when things looked truly dark.

'Surely if you missed me so much, you could have called,' Susanne said with a smile. 'Oh, it's okay,' she added when she saw Charlie's face. 'I know you had to get out of here. That you wanted to start over.'

'I should have called,' Charlie said. 'I don't know why I haven't.'

They sat in silence for a while, as though they both needed to stop and ponder all the time that had gone by.

'And now?' Susanne said. 'How come you're back now? Are you with Missing People?'

Charlie told her why she had come.

'Detective?' Susanne smiled. Actually, yes, she could see how that would be. She could really see it. Then she turned serious. It was awful, she said, this thing with Annabelle. She couldn't understand how a person could just disappear without a trace.

'There are always traces.'

'I really hope you find her. I can hardly imagine what her poor parents must be going through.'

'Do you know them?'

Susanne shook her head. She knew who they were, but they were older. 'How would you feel about a shot, by the way?' she said. 'For old times' sake?'

Charlie looked longingly at the bar and said that sounded fun, but that she was on the job and ...

'One won't hurt you,' Susanne said and before Charlie could object again, Susanne had started pushing her way towards the bar; moments later, she was back with two brimming glasses topped with whipped cream.

'I don't get,' she said, 'I really don't get how anyone can make this curdle.' She held her glass up to show that the coffee had infiltrated the Galliano. 'It's because they buy crappy booze from lorry drivers. I'll bet you anything this is just vodka with dye in it, otherwise it wouldn't look like this. But never mind,' she continued and pushed one of the glasses towards Charlie, 'it's all going to the same place in the end anyway.'

'I couldn't tell you the last time I had a shot.'

'Well, it's about time then. Cheers!'

'Cheers!'

They downed their liquor.

'So how are things with you?' Charlie said.

'Well, where to start?' Susanne said and wiped away some cream with the back of her hand. 'A lot of things have happened, put it that way.'

'How are your parents?'

'Dad's dead.'

Charlie offered her condolences, but Susanne said what else can you expect. She was surprised he'd survived as long as he had. And his passing hadn't been all bad, she added, because it had made her mum sober up. It was almost like she had gained a parent rather than lost one.

'I think my mum's the only one left of the old gang.' Then Susanne started listing off all the people who had used to party out in Lyckebo and who were now dead.

When she was done, Charlie thought to herself that Susanne had left out the one who died first. She had left out Mattias.

'I put a flower on Betty's grave sometimes,' Susanne continued. 'When I'm there for Dad anyway.'

'Thank you,' Charlie said. She looked over at the bar and wished she didn't have a job to do.

'Your mum. She was a proper alcoholic, but at least she knew how to make people laugh. People really laughed when Betty was around. Cheers to that. Cheers to Betty.'

'Cheers.' Charlie raised her glass and tried to think of a different topic. 'Are you married?' she asked.

Susanne nodded. She was married.

'Anyone I'd know?'

Susanne shook her head and said he wasn't from around there.

'Children?'

'Four,' Susanne said and held up four fingers. 'All boys.' She shrugged as though she felt their sex was a failure in itself. 'And you, do you have children?'

'No.'

'Smart decision.'

'I'm not married either,' Charlie said to pre-empt the follow-up.

'Even smarter. I don't know a single happily married person. And the kids thing, I know it sounds terrible, but kids are really overrated.'

Charlie laughed and replied she'd always suspected as much, but that she wasn't allowed to say it, being childless and everything.

'You can't say it as a mother either,' Susanne said. 'Definitely not as a mother.' She started talking about her sons, about how they were killing her. They fought, quarrelled and shouted at one another. She said she needed both wine and oxazepam to bear it. Yes, she was aware she wasn't supposed to talk openly about it, especially the pills, but she didn't have the energy to craft euphemisms. That's just the kind of person she was.

'Maybe that's why I was drawn to you,' Charlie said. 'There was no one else like you here.'

'And you.' Susanne smiled. 'And you, Charlie Lager.'

Charlie thought about the time she and Susanne had promised each other never to drink. They had been spider swinging on the swing in the oak tree in Lyckebo and had sworn never to have children, never to drink, never to become like their parents. At the time, they had really thought they could do it, but their genes, or upbringing or whatever it was, seemed to hold strong sway over both of them. It had started with leftovers from glasses at the Lyckebo parties and before long they had moved on to stealing whole bottles of spirits and wine. Getting drunk for the first time had made Charlie understand Betty's love for alcohol. Because that feeling, that amazing feeling when everything went calm and still inside her, that was ... she had loved it from the first.

'Life didn't turn out the way I thought it would,' Susanne said.

'Does it ever?'

'Maybe not.' Susanne took a big sip from her glass. 'But it was nice back when you could still dream.'

Charlie nodded and said she knew what she meant.

'Cut it out,' Susanne suddenly exclaimed to a man who had come over and put his hand on her shoulder. 'Come off it, Svenka.'

'Why are you always in such a bad mood?' said the man called Svenka.

'Maybe because you can't seem to understand I don't want your hands all over me.'

'Can't we just chat for a bit?'

'I was just on my way to the bar.'

'And what were you going to buy?'

'Hot shots,' Susanne said, 'more hot shots for me and my friend here.'

'Arne!' Svenka shouted to a man behind the bar. 'Arne! Bring two hot shots as well.'

Susanne rolled her eyes at Charlie.

'Here we are,' Svenka said proudly when the hot shots arrived. 'Maybe now you'll let me join you?'

'We were actually having a private conversation,' Susanne replied.

'And who is your little friend then?' Svenka asked. His bleary eyes turned to Charlie. 'Are you one of the people searching?'

'I suppose you could say that,' Charlie said.

'She's with the police,' Susanne said, 'so that's putting it mildly.'

Svenka's bloodshot eyes opened wide and he leaned across the table. About fucking time they brought in some back-up, he felt. Had they been up to Skärven? Had they started interviewing the coloured people up there?'

'What do you mean?' Charlie said.

'I'm just saying that if I were the police, that's where I'd look first.'

'Good thing you're not the police then,' Susanne said.

'You do realise, don't you,' Svenka pressed on without paying any attention to Susanne's comment, 'that one of the coloured fellows did it. Just think about all the bikes that have disappeared since they came. This is not a laughing matter, Susanne. Before the nineties, there were no fucking bike thefts, that's for sure!'

'You're full of it,' Susanne said. 'People have always been stealing bikes in these parts.'

'And then there was the thing with the pizza place,' Svenka continued, unfazed.

'We don't know who started the fire.'

'Definitely not a local, I'll tell you that much.'

'He's not just an assaulter of women,' Susanne said and slapped away Svenka's hand, which had landed on her thigh. 'He's a racist too.'

'I'm nothing of the kind. It's just that nothing good has happened here since the Yugoslavs invaded every part of our society, and then, with that pack of Somali people that arrived last year ... it's no wonder things are happening. I'm just saying,' he continued and put his used pinch of snuff in a glass on the table, 'if it had been my daughter ... if she was the one who was missing, I would have blown all of Skärven to hell.'

'And would that bring her back?' Susanne said. 'A bombing?'

'Maybe not,' Svenka said, 'but an eye for an eye. Even the Bible says so.'

Susanne laughed again and said the Bible also said something about turning the other cheek and that it was fucking sick to want to blow up innocent people, but Svenka wasn't listening. He just kept ranting on about the scum up by Skärven; that anyone could see it was one of them who had attacked Annabelle and dumped her body somewhere.

'That's enough now,' Charlie finally told him.

'Enough?' Svenka stared at her. 'That might be easy for you to say. I bet you have a nice flat on some fancy street in Stockholm and haven't had to deal with Yugoslavs, Somalis and all kinds of trash ever since the nineties.'

'She's from here,' Susanne said. 'She's Betty's daughter. Betty Lager's daughter.'

Svenka's belligerent attitude changed. He looked at Charlie in that way she hated. After all her years in Stockholm, she had forgotten how annoying that look was.

'So I see,' Svenka said. 'Now I see you're Betty's girl ... Your mum ... what a woman. People in these parts still talk about her parties.'

'I can imagine,' Charlie said. 'I can certainly imagine.'

'Do you remember me?'

Charlie shook her head. She didn't remember. How was she supposed to remember every nut job who had ever been to one of the Lyckebo parties?

'Is it your first time back since ... I mean, how long since you moved away?'

'Almost twenty years.'

'Twenty years ... Well, bugger me if time doesn't just fly. It feels like yesterday that ...'

'Hey, Svenka,' Susanne said. 'I think your friends want you.' She pointed in the direction of the bar where a group of loud men had gathered.

'All right, all right, I get it,' Svenka said. 'But mark my words.' He raised a finger to Charlie. 'Mark my words when I say you're going to find your man up at Skärven.'

'Right now we're just looking for a girl,' Charlie said.

They watched Svenka stagger over to join his friends.

'I don't remember him ever being in Lyckebo,' Charlie said. 'I have no recollection of him being there.'

'I guess every man from around here went to Lyckebo one time or another,' Susanne said.

'About me being from here,' Charlie said. 'Maybe you could keep that to yourself? I would prefer to just ... I just want to focus on solving this case now. And I don't really want to talk to people about Betty.'

'I get that,' Susanne said. 'But to be honest,' she continued, 'I don't think anyone's going to recognise you. You haven't been here since you were a child.'

'You recognised me.'

'That's different.'

'And Svenka?' Charlie nodded to the bar. 'He doesn't exactly seem the type to keep things to himself.'

'Svenka's an old drunk. When he wakes up tomorrow, he won't even remember he was here.'

'Nice bloke, by the way,' Charlie said, 'really friendly and nuanced.'

They burst out laughing.

'But he sounds worse than he is,' Susanne said. 'He's just a confused little failure of a person.' For a moment, she didn't say anything, just gazed out across the dance floor. 'Like most of us here.'

That day

'*Maman died today.* Or yesterday maybe, I don't know.' Kalle stopped reading when Annabelle slunk into her seat.

'You're late,' he said.

Annabelle nodded.

'You were late yesterday as well, and you didn't even show up to the class before that.'

'I was ill.' She thought to herself that Kalle was insanely strict about absences. Why couldn't he just look at her results and leave well enough alone like most other teachers?

'We'll have to have a talk later. I've just started reading from a novel,' Kalle said. And then, to the whole class: 'Could someone tell Annbelle what book I'm reading from?'

Crickets. Kalle sighed. It was incredible that no one remembered. Bloody hell, he'd told them just a few minutes ago.

'*The Stranger,*' Annabelle said. '*The Stranger* by Albert Camus.'

Kalle nodded, she was right. It was a famous opening and a famous book. To know it was general knowledge. That made it extra sad, he felt, that no one had remembered the title.

Annabelle sat down. Kalle cleared his throat and started over. '*Maman died today.* Or yesterday maybe, I don't know. I got a telegram from the home: "Mother deceased. Funeral tomorrow."'

Annabelle thought of her own mother. If she were to die,

Annabelle might get her times mixed up like that. She had always had a lot of difficulty with time. But would she be sad? Guilt rushed over her when she realised she wasn't sure. What if she was actually relieved? Maybe I'm a psychopath, she thought. I might be as numb to things as that Meursault guy. She tried to tell herself it was expected, given how her mum was out to ruin her life. It had been worse than usual lately because she had refused to tell her where she'd been. The last thing she wanted was for her mother to meet Him, for her to show up and act insane.

Kalle's monotonous voice, talking about the analysis they were supposed to write, turned into a dull background drone. Annabelle looked out of the window and thought about her first time with Him. It had been the first dance of the spring down at the pub. She had had too much to drink and had sat down by the lake to sober up. And that was when he had appeared and offered her a ride home.

At first, she had figured he was just trying to be nice, that she would never be able to seduce him, which is why she was surprised when he didn't remove the hand she put on his thigh. She had asked him to stop the car somewhere and he had obeyed.

Class was over, but Annabelle didn't notice until Rebecka snapped her fingers in front of her face. As they stepped into the hallway, her mum called.

Annabelle's first impulse was to not pick up, but then she figured she might as well because otherwise she would just keep calling. Once or twice, she had even come to school and caused a scene when Annabelle made her wait.

'Yes,' she said.

'I had a message you weren't in Swedish class.'

Annabelle sighed. So Kalle had registered her as absent after all.

'I was a bit late.'

'Why?'

'Because ... I was just a bit late. Look, I can't talk right now. I have class.' She sighed and hung up without saying goodbye.

Rebecka came up to her.

'Mummy?' she said and tilted her head. 'Was that darling Mummy calling again?'

'Funny.'

'I don't get where she finds the energy. How can a person keep calling like that all the time?'

'Don't ask me,' Annabelle said. 'But you know she's ...' She trailed off and thought about what she wanted to say. What was her mum? Nervous? Mentally ill?

'She's not going to let you go out tonight.'

'I don't care. I have to go out.'

'Are you going to tell me now?' Rebecka opened her locker and let out a curse when a book fell out.

'Tell you what?'

'Who it was. Since it's over anyway.'

'Can we not get into it now?' Annabelle said. 'I promise I'll tell you everything tonight.'

'All right. But I have something to tell you too. Promise you won't be angry.'

Annabelle nodded and thought to herself that she was probably going to be angry, that that was always the case when you had promised you wouldn't be.

'It's about William,' Rebecka said. 'William Stark,' she added when Annabelle just stared at her without saying anything.

'I know who he is.'

'Yeah, I know, so why won't you say anything?'

'Why don't you go on?' Annabelle said.

'We have ... he called and was sad back when you ... and we have been meeting up and ... don't leave! Fucking hell, Bella, you can't just walk away!'

21

The folk singer took a break and went to the bar. Things were getting very loud at Svante and William's table.

'You know who they are, don't you?' Susanne said with a nod in their direction.

'Yes,' Charlie replied. 'How did you know?'

'I can tell you've been gone a while.' Susanne smiled. 'You can't possibly think a group of teenagers can be interviewed by the police in the case of a missing girl without everyone finding out? Have you forgotten how quickly word gets around here?'

Charlie shook her head. She hadn't forgotten how quickly rumours or truths travelled around town.

'What do you know about them?' she said.

'None of them is the type you bring home to mother, I suppose,' Susanne said. 'You can see for yourself,' she added as Svante got to his feet and put both hands flat against William's chest.

Erik was there in a flash. For a long while, he and Svante just stood there, staring at each other. Then Erik shook his head and returned to the bar.

'He shouldn't be allowed in here,' Susanne said. 'I don't get why Erik doesn't ban him, but I guess he doesn't have the guts.'

'How come?'

'Svante's dad owns plywood.'

'I see,' Charlie said.

'Erik isn't exactly the sharpest tool, but I'd wager he's smart enough to realise no one would help him if he decided to throw Svante out. No one wants to risk their job at the factory.'

Charlie looked back over at Svante's table. Annabelle's friends, she mused. Wasn't it a bit callous to be drinking in a pub when your friend had gone missing? Or was it exactly what a person needed after spending a day in the field, searching?

Susanne's phone rang. She apologised and picked up.

'Sure, but I'm on my way. Sure, but I ran into an old friend and ... yes, I know I said that and no, just like one drink. No, I'll walk.' She rolled her eyes at Charlie. 'Right, but you do realise you can't just leave the kids home by themselves.'

'Your husband?' Charlie asked after Susanne had ended the call.

Susanne nodded.

'He wanted to come pick me up. I don't think it's a matter of thoughtfulness or convenience. He doesn't want me to stay out too late so he has to look after the kids by himself tomorrow. Damn it, I didn't want to leave so soon.'

Then stay, Charlie felt like urging her.

'Give me a call,' Susanne said and raised her hand.

'I don't have your number.'

'Oh, right.'

Susanne asked for Charlie's number, tapped it in to her phone and rang her up.

Charlie stayed at the table for a while on her own after Susanne left. When she pulled out her phone to save Susanne's number, she noticed she had two missed calls from Hugo. What was his deal? Did he really think she was going to cover for him if his wife decided to call? It was becoming ever clearer, she thought to herself, that he was a fucking idiot.

The folk singer had started a second session after a break. This time it was all about the Louisiana cotton fields. The song brought back more memories of Lyckebo. Betty turning the music up and demanding that everyone dance. Charlie thought about the names Susanne had listed off, the people who had attended the parties. To her, they were nothing but fuzzy, indistinct outlines. The only one who still appeared clearly to her mind's eye was Mattias.

She had never been completely able to forget his face. Mattias had turned up at Lyckebo the summer Charlie turned twelve. He was a friend, Betty said. A friend who was in trouble. And since when had she ever closed the door on a friend who needed a place to stay? At first, Mattias had slept in the shed, but by the time autumn came and with it the cold, he had moved all the way into Betty's bedroom; and just in time for Christmas, Betty had told Charlie that Mattias was going to stay.

At first, Charlie hadn't been able to get her head around why. Why was it no longer true what Betty had always used to say, that her home was her castle and that she would never, ever share it with a man?

And Betty had told her Mattias wasn't like other men, that Charline would see that if she just gave him a chance.

I'm sure you're going to like him as much as I do one day.

Anders was still awake when Charlie got up to their room. He had pulled the two beds apart and placed them as far from one another as possible.

'I was starting to think you were going to close the place,' he said before conveniently turning around so she could take everything but her knickers and T-shirt off and get into bed. Charlie looked at the cross-stitch embroideries with messages of love that hung on the walls. One read: *Greatest of all is love*, and above that: *Love is patient and kind.*

'Did you say something?' Anders asked.

'I said all of bloody Corinthians seems to be plastered on the walls here.'

Anders read the wall-hangings and agreed she was right. Hardly surprising, he thought, the words of love, since this was the honeymoon suite.

'If I ever get married, there'll be no reading from Corinthians,' Charlie said, 'that's for sure.'

And what was so wrong with Corinthians, Anders wanted to know; how could she find beautiful words about love so provocative? Besides, the subject seemed moot anyway, he pointed out, since she was set on never getting married.

'Have I said that?' Charlie said.

'You've said you don't believe in marriage.'

'That's not the same thing. Are there even still people who actually do believe in marriage?'

'You're cynical.'

'You're naive.'

Charlie made herself comfortable. The sheets smelled faintly of cigarette smoke even though they were freshly laundered. The pillow was too flat.

'What are you doing?' Anders said when she got up again.

'Looking for another pillow.'

She couldn't find one, so instead she had to roll up a cardigan and put it on top of her pillow. Then she took out one of her books.

'Would you mind turning the lights out soon?' Anders said and turned over in his bed. 'It's one in the morning.'

'I can't fall asleep without reading.'

'And I can't fall asleep with the lights on.'

'Then you have a problem.'

Anders heaved a sigh, threw his duvet aside and got up.

'What are you doing?' Charlie asked.

'I have to find something to cover my eyes. I haven't slept in three months and ...'

'Fine,' Charlie said. 'I get it.' She put her book down and turned off her light.

It was impossible to fall asleep. The pressure across her chest had been tightening all day and lying down made it worse than ever. And every time she closed her eyes, she was back in the house in Lyckebo. She could see the thin curtains fluttering in the living room, Betty prostrate on the sofa with a wet towel on her forehead.

It's the light, Charline. All this light hurts me.

Anders had fallen asleep and didn't wake up when Charlie turned the light on and picked her book back up. She tried to focus on reading, but it was impossible.

It's this place, she thought. This place is what's making me unable to defend myself against it. I can't keep it at arm's length any more.

The dream transported her to Lyckebo. She was in the garden. The cherry trees were in full bloom, the cats were slinking around her legs. Someone was on the tree swing. Betty? Mummy?

She walked over, reached out to touch Betty's back, but at that moment, the swing spun around and it wasn't Betty. It was Mattias.

Why are you here now, Charline? Why are you here now when it's all too late?

22

The dining room was almost deserted at breakfast. Erik came in and said Missing People had eaten at half past six.

'It's going to be even hotter today.' He looked out of the window. 'People are going to be very thirsty tonight. I hope,' he added as though he was ashamed to be thinking about business in the current situation, 'I hope they find her today so all of this can be over.'

Charlie asked Anders to drive on ahead to the police station. She wanted to walk there by herself, think, buy cigarettes. Even though she had taken it easy the night before, she felt clammy and dizzy. It's symptoms of exhaustion, she thought to herself. I need Zoloft. She had called her GP and been told she had three months left on her prescription, so all she had to do was get to a chemist's at some point during opening hours.

When she got to the station, there was tension in the air. Everyone was clearly feeling the pressure of the stalled investigation. Of all tip-offs and interviews proving to be dead ends.

'A girl can't just disappear like this,' Olof exclaimed. He was pacing around holding a coffee cup he wasn't drinking from. 'Unless she disappeared voluntarily, which by all indications she didn't, so … she has to be somewhere.'

He stopped in front of the big map on the wall and started pointing out all the areas that had been searched so far. The bog at the edge of town, the fields, every abandoned cottage and barn within a four-mile radius. The dragging of the river and lake had not yielded any results either so far.

'The river's too damn deep,' Micke said.

'What's depth got to do with it?' Olof wanted to know.

'It means she could be in it, obviously, that they couldn't possibly have dragged the entire river ...'

Olof cut him off and said that no, of course they hadn't dragged the entire river yet, but if she was in there, the current should have carried her to the inlet gates.

'Not necessarily,' Micke retorted. 'There's chasms down there, chasms, roots and spars. She could have got stuck anywhere.' He turned to Charlie and Anders. 'There's a whole fucking under-water landscape down there. People have disappeared before.'

'People?' Olof raised his eyebrows. 'Who would that be?'

'Like ... yeah, what the fuck was his name, the alcoholic who disappeared?'

Charlie realised she was barely breathing. A strange sense of relief spread through her when no one seemed to be able to remember a name.

'That was ages ago,' Olof said, 'were you even born when that happened?'

Micke looked at Olof as though being reminded of his youth was a violation. Yes, he had been born when that happened. And he hadn't forgotten it, because his brothers had always talked about it when they went swimming as children.

'If she's in the river, we'll find her,' Olof said. 'Then it's just a matter of time, and we'll keep doing our interviews in the meantime.'

They ran through the list of young people they needed to talk to in more depth. The ex-boyfriend William Stark was one of them, Olof said ... yes, he supposed everyone could see why. And Svante Linder as well, because he hadn't been particularly co-operative in his first interview.

'They were at the motel yesterday,' Charlie said. 'William Stark, Svante Linder and a few others.'

'Was there trouble?' Olof asked.

'Not trouble, exactly, but they seemed pretty upset. Svante gave William a good shove.'

'Svante's the type to make trouble,' Olof said.

'Well, clearly, everyone has to be interviewed again,' Charlie said. 'But I'm most interested in the best friend, Rebecka Gahm.'

'We've already asked her about that night; she doesn't know more than anyone else,' Micke put in.

'But if anyone knows anything, it'd be her. Would you mind if we do another interview?'

'Of course not. I was just thinking ...'

'Great,' Charlie said. 'And did you get a chance to talk to your grandmother and her friends in the Bible group?'

'Yes, I actually managed to talk to them all. The last ones just now this morning. Retired people,' he said with a smile, 'when they can finally sleep in, they want to get up at the crack of dawn.'

'And?' Charlie said. 'Anything new?'

'Nothing of note, except that Annabelle seems very well thought of by the members of the group. All the old biddies said practically the same things about her, that she's curious, clever and well read. A very unusual young woman.'

Charlie wanted to ask if clever young women were really all that unusual, but she didn't have the time or the energy to challenge Micke again.

'When was their last meeting?'

'Last Sunday,' Micke replied.

'Did they notice anything different about Annabelle at that time?'

'Nothing they shared with me, anyway.'

Charlie pictured Annabelle, sitting on a chair next to the church altar, surrounded by greying old ladies and the minister. She pictured her in deep discussion, saw the old ladies' smiles and appreciative looks. Who are you, Annabelle? she thought. Who are you and where have you got to?

There and then

Alice is endlessly fascinated by the fact that her own house and Rosa's, which are identically built, can be so different on the inside. At Rosa's house, there are curtains instead of doors. Out the back, there are wind chimes in the trees and there's no table in the kitchen. They order food from the pizza place on the corner.

How can they afford it? Alice wonders. Rosa says they get a special deal. And her mum does actually work as well; she makes money. She reads cards. It's crazy, Rosa says, how much people are willing to spend on finding out about their future.

In Rosa's bathroom, there are brown jars full of pills. Rosa shows Alice her favourites: orange, oblong ones that are hard to swallow. They're magical, she says, because after you take one, you go all calm inside. She hands Alice a pill and shakes out another for herself. And Rosa's right, Alice thinks to herself, because she does feel calm. It's like a soft cotton rug unfolding in her chest and Alice forgets about her mum's aching joints, forgets about her dad who never comes back and everything grows calm, warm and quiet. What kind of pills are they?

Rosa shrugs. She doesn't know. All she knows is that they make her happy; what else is there to know?

They are interrupted by Rosa's mother screaming.

'What's the matter, Mum?' Rosa gets to her feet, runs into the hallway and through the rustling drapery to her mother's bedroom.

'It's this man. Could you please tell him to leave.'

Moments later, Alice hears a few terrible curses and a large, sweaty man with nothing on except a towel around his hips appears in the hallway.

'Get out,' Rosa says. 'Beat it.' She has brought his clothes and dumps the bundle by his feet.

But the man doesn't want to leave. He and Rosa's mother have some unfinished business. And besides, he wants to get dressed at his own pace. Rosa says that if he doesn't leave immediately, she's going to call the police.

'Grab the phone, Alice,' she shouts towards the kitchen. 'Call the police and tell them there's an intruder in the house.'

The man swears, scoops up the pile of clothes and disappears.

Having locked and bolted the door behind him, Rosa walks into the kitchen, opens the window and shouts after the man that he forgot his disgusting pants. Does he want them or should she burn them?

The man doesn't respond and Rosa tosses the yellowy-white pants right out of the window.

'Whatever happens,' Rosa says as they watch the man running away with his clothes in his arms, 'whatever happens, I'm never going to have a husband.'

'What about kids?' Alice wants to know.

Rosa's not sure.

'But how are you going to have children if you don't have a husband?'

'How are you going to have children if you don't have a husband?' Rosa mocks. 'Are you a bit dim or what? You just needed a man for a few minutes to make babies. Just look at their own mothers. Both had children and no husbands. 'And no,' she went on when Alice opened her mouth. 'Don't give me that nonsense about your dad sailing the seven seas again. I'm sick of your stories.'

Then Rosa's mother appears in the kitchen, dressed in a silky red robe. Her cheeks are streaked with black mascara. She reaches for her pack of cigarettes and curses when she discovers there's just one left. Rosa pulls out her lighter and her mum pushes her hair behind her ear, puts the cigarette to the flame and inhales.

'I think,' Rosa's mother says and looks at Rosa. 'I think it's time for your little friend to go home now.'

'Go home, Alice,' Rosa says. 'Come on, go home, will you? Don't just stand there staring.'

When Alice gets home that evening, her mother is sitting on the floor attempting to tie her shoelaces with aching fingers. Why does she insist on wearing shoes with laces she can no longer tie?

Alice asks her where she's going. She bends down to help, but her mother waves her away. She doesn't need her shoes any more. She was only putting them on to go out to look for her.

'I was just at Rosa's,' Alice tells her.

Yes, she had replied, but even so, it was time to come home. She didn't have to spend the evenings at Rosa's as well.

Alice asks why she doesn't like Rosa and her mum replies that she doesn't trust her. That it would be good if Alice could meet some nicer friends.

Alice thinks to herself that her mum has only seen Rosa's bad sides, that she uses swear words and is rowdy and doesn't respect grown-ups. What does her mum know about the times when she and Rosa warm each other's bodies in the night, about their games in the tree house and the jokes only they understand?

What does she know about Rosa's whispered words about how they're more than friends, how they're sisters, how they will always protect each other?

23

Rebecka arrived at the station fifteen minutes after being called in. She was staying home from school. They had offered to come to her, but she had told them she was out and about anyway. But there was still one slight problem, Adnan said as he entered Charlie and Anders's office to tell them Rebecka had arrived.

'What's the problem?' Charlie asked.

'She brought her younger sister.'

'Why?'

'I didn't ask, but I assume their mother's away somewhere.'

'Shouldn't she be in pre-school?'

'Apparently not,' Adnan said.

'How old is she?'

'Three, maybe.'

'You're going to have to look after her,' Charlie said.

'But I was just about to head out to check on Missing People's progress.'

'Someone else will have to do that.'

Adnan turned around, muttering something. They followed him to the reception area where Rebecka was sitting on a sofa with her sister on her lap.

'I didn't know what do with her,' she said when Charlie walked over and introduced herself. 'It's a planning day at her pre-school and Mum's at work and I can't face going to school anyway, so ...'

'Would you like to come and have a look at the police car while your sister talks to the lady for a bit?' Adnan asked the little girl.

'Go with him, Noomi,' Rebecka told her. 'Go see the police car and I'll be right there.'

Her sister reluctantly let go of her hand.

Rebecka Gahm took a seat on the other side of the desk. Without make-up, her face looked younger than seventeen.

'We appreciate you coming in at such short notice,' Charlie said.

'It was no problem. It's not like I have anything more important to do than help you find Annabelle. But I don't know what else I can tell you. I've already told the police about that night.'

'I just wanted to meet with you in person,' Charlie said. 'My colleague and I' – she nodded to Anders – 'we've come in from Stockholm.'

'I know. Or I mean, I can tell from your accent.'

Charlie smiled and told her why they were there; Rebecka listened intently.

'How long have you been friends, you and Annabelle?' Charlie said.

'Forever, or at least since pre-school.'

'So it would be fair to say you know her well?'

'Of course. No one knows Bella like I do.'

'How did she seem that night?'

'She was drunk.'

'But before that?'

'I was pretty tipsy myself when she came over, but she seemed a bit ... upset.'

'Did she say why?'

'No, or maybe she did. I have a few memory lapses.'

'Was it just alcohol,' Charlie asked, 'or did you do other things as well?'

'Just alcohol,' Rebecka said. She met Charlie's eyes without looking away or even blinking. Charlie thought to herself that maybe she had read somewhere that that's what people do when they're telling the truth.

'Do you know what time Annabelle left the party?'

'No, not exactly. But I saw her leave. I was about to have a smoke by the window just then and saw her stagger down the road. I called out to her, but she didn't respond, so I went downstairs, but by the time I got outside, she was already gone. I didn't even see her further down the road, even though I ran after her for a bit.'

'Why did you run after her?'

'Why? Because she was drunk, obviously. She was so drunk she could barely walk and I figured she might fall asleep in some ditch somewhere, that she would never make it home and ... I shouldn't have gone back. If I'd just caught up with her and walked her home, then ...'

'That's no way to think,' Anders said.

'Yes it is,' Rebecka retorted. 'That's exactly how I think.'

'What direction was she walking?'

'She walked down the gravel road behind the village shop, as though she were on her way home.'

'I've been told you had a fight that night,' Charlie said. 'Can you tell me about that?'

Rebecka rolled her eyes. She'd already told Olof and Adnan about the whole William thing.

'Tell me,' Charlie said.

'I took him,' Rebecka said. 'William Stark. I took him, but

only because Bella didn't want him any more. Otherwise I would never have taken him.'

Rebecka talked about William as though he were an object without a will of his own. Charlie pondered whether Annabelle was in the habit of doing that too, if it was the common jargon between the two friends when discussing blokes they met.

'Do you like him?' she said. 'Do you like William Stark?'

'What's that got to do with anything?' Rebecka retorted.

'I'm just asking if you like him.'

'Yeah, I suppose I do, but we're not exactly planning our wedding, or whatever.'

'And were you perhaps interested in him while he was together with Annabelle too?'

'What do you mean? You're not implying that I ...'

'I'm not implying anything,' Charlie said. 'I'm just asking.'

She noted the way Rebecka's face changed colour and reasoned that since she was already making her so upset, she might as well continue.

'Were you jealous of Annabelle and William's relationship?'

Rebecka shook her head. Why would she have been jealous of that? And even if she had been, she would never, ever have hurt Annabelle.

'And besides,' she went on, 'who would kill a person over something like jealousy?'

'Actually,' Charlie put in, 'that's a fairly common reason for murder.'

'I would never hurt Bella over some guy,' Rebecka said. 'I would never hurt her for any reason. Maybe you're not getting that I love her, that she's my best friend.'

She put her forearm on the table and showed them the heart on her wrist. *Becka and Bella forever.*

'It's not what you think,' she continued when she noticed

Anders studying the red scratch marks running across the tattoo, 'it's the factory, everyone who works in the factory looks like this. I suppose I look worse than most, actually,' she said and sighed. 'It's because I can't resist picking at it.'

'I thought you were still in school,' Charlie said.

'I am, but I work extra at the weekends sometimes.' Rebecka let her fingertips tenderly trace the text. 'Bella has the same one. We had them done last summer. This too.' She showed them her other wrist. It was adorned with a small, dark blue semicolon. 'It was Annabelle's idea. She said it was a symbol of the fact that our history wouldn't end here, that there was more to come.'

Rebecka pulled a tissue from her purse and blew her nose loudly. It was as though she was trying to focus on something other than the tears that had started dripping steadily onto the table top.

Charlie felt like crying too. There was something about Rebecka's defiant hope that made it difficult to keep control of her feelings. Don't let this story end here, she thought to herself.

'Why did things end between Annabelle and William?' Anders asked.

'I guess it didn't work out. Annabelle's not really the girl-friend type. I guess neither one of us is.'

'So she ended it?'

'William says it was a mutual decision, but I reckon it was mostly Annabelle.'

'Was she sad?' Charlie said.

'Not particularly, not from what she told me, anyway.'

Charlie looked down at Rebecka's fingers on the desk. Nail biter, she noted when Rebecka's hand went up to touch the necklace with the thin gold cross around her neck.

'Are you Christian?' Charlie nodded to her necklace.

'Not really. It was a gift for confirmation.'

'Annabelle is Christian.'

Rebecka smiled. 'I think that's just a phase.'

Charlie asked her what she meant.

'I mean that she goes all in whenever she gets something in her head; it could be anything. She likes to say that she wants to drill down to the core of things to see if they suit her or not. She might be joining a science club or something next.' Rebecka cleared her throat and continued in a quieter voice: 'If there is a next.'

'Would you say she is easily led?'

'Not easily led,' Rebecka said. 'Absolutely not. Annabelle is ... she's smart. She's not the kind of person you can control. But she's curious. She's probably the most curious person I know.'

'Do you know if Annabelle had any social media accounts?' Charlie said. 'The kind only a select few would know about?'

'Like a second profile on Facebook?' Rebecka said. 'I know she used to have one where she helped people with school stuff. But I don't think she's active on that any more. She felt it took up too much of her time.'

'What do you mean helped?' Charlie said and shot Anders a quick glance.

'That she would write essays and do homework.'

'And what did she get in return?'

'Money,' Rebecka replied, 'money, booze or cigarettes.'

'Do you know what her handle was?'

'A Friend in Need. Fitting, don't you think?' Rebecka swallowed a few times and looked out of the window. Her legs had started twitching under the table.

'I need a smoke,' Charlie said, ignoring Anders's sceptical look. 'Want to come?'

Rebecka nodded and stood up.

They went out to the backyard. Two children who looked too young to be by themselves were digging around in a sand pit some way away. Charlie handed Rebecka a cigarette and took one herself.

'I can't sleep at night any more,' Rebecka said and took a deep drag. 'When I'm not out looking, I still can't sleep, and as soon as I doze off, I just dream of her.' She rubbed her eyes with the back of her hand.

'What kind of dreams?'

'Just a bunch of weird stuff. I dream that we're little again, in pre-school, that we're hiding at the far end of a boat they had in the playroom there. We used to do that, Bella and me, hide in there when the food was gross or when we'd done something we shouldn't. There was like this tiny hole at the far end, too small for the teachers to squeeze through. They bribed us, threatened and yelled to make us come out, but we wouldn't listen. It's gone now. The hole, I mean; I noticed when I picked my sister up once, that it had been boarded up.'

They didn't say anything for a while.

'It's so bloody hot,' Rebecka said. 'If this had been an ordinary day, Bella and I would have gone down to Little Rhodes. A beach,' she clarified, 'not the real Rhodes.'

Charlie smiled.

'Surely, if this had been an ordinary day, you would have been in school?'

'Sure, I guess so.' Rebecka threw her butt on the ground, then she changed her mind, ground it out and picked it back up. 'There's no telling what they'll stick in their mouths,' she said with a nod to the toddlers in the sand pit.

'There's a can here,' Charlie said. 'Do you want another one?'

'Are you for real?' Rebecka said gravely. 'I mean this ... kindness, is it some kind of strategy to make me talk?'

'Don't you want to talk?'

Rebecka nodded and took another cigarette from the pack Charlie held out to her.

'You said she was upset,' Charlie said. 'What do you think that was about? What would normally make Annabelle upset?'

'Bella gets upset a lot,' Rebecka said and smiled. 'She has a pretty fiery temper. But I guess it's worst with her mum.' Rebecka leaned in and let Charlie light her cigarette. 'They fight quite a lot. Bella likes to say Nora makes her feel sick.'

'What do you think she meant by that?'

'I guess it's fairly obvious, that her mum's need for control is suffocating her.'

'What do you think of Nora?'

'What do I think of her?'

'Yes.'

'I think she's not entirely right in the head. There's something seriously wrong with that woman.'

'How is she to you?'

'I don't think she likes me very much. I reckon she thinks I drag her little girl along to all kinds of bad things.'

'Do you?'

'I suppose we drag each other, if anything.' Rebecka sucked on her cigarette. 'You need to know one thing about Annabelle, no one drags her along if she doesn't want to go. Annabelle's tough.'

'Does she have enemies?'

'Maybe not enemies, exactly, but sure, there are people who are bothered by her. I think it's because she's smart, because she takes up a lot of space. That kind of thing can get you pretty fucking hated in this place.'

'Do you have anyone in particular in mind?'

'Just generally. But she's been bickering with Svante Linder quite a bit. Though that seems more like she hates him than the other way around.'

'Did they fight that night?'

'No more than usual, I don't think. But I wasn't with her the whole time, since I was upstairs ... with William.'

The door opened behind them. It was Adnan, bringing Rebecka's sister. The little girl was red in the face from crying.

'She wants to go home,' Adnan said.

Rebecka hiked the girl up on her hip. Noomi nuzzled into her sister's neck. Rebecka stroked her back and told her they were going to go home and make pancakes with jam and whipped cream.

Like a mother, Charlie mused, like a mother soothing her child. Adnan went back inside.

'If there's anything else, just give me a call, okay?' Rebecka said.

'Rebecka,' Charlie said to her back as she started walking away. 'What do you think has happened to Annabelle?'

'What I think?' Rebecka stopped dead, turned around and looked at her. 'I hope she ran away. With her mother, I would have. I'm calling and texting her constantly, hoping she'll pick up, that she'll tell me she left town, that she's alive and okay.'

'But it's been almost a week,' Charlie said.

'I know how long it's been. I just told you what I'm hoping. I have to get her home now.' Rebecka nodded to her sister. 'I'll be in touch if I think of anything else.'

Rebecka lifted her sister up onto her shoulders. Her sister started laughing. Charlie watched them until they rounded the corner before going back in.

'Anything new?' Micke suddenly appeared behind Charlie. He laughed when she shrieked. He hadn't realised she was so jumpy.

'I just didn't hear you coming,' Charlie said. 'I need to have a private conversation with Nora Roos,' she continued.

'So you do think Nora ...'

'I don't think anything, but we need to find out more about what's going on in that family; why is Nora so controlling when it comes to her daughter; why ... well, you get what I mean. Could you check out a Facebook profile as well, "A Friend in Need"? Annabelle used it as a platform to do other students' schoolwork for money.'

'All right,' Micke said.

'And set up a meeting with William Stark as well. I need to talk to him.'

'Now?'

'In an hour. I just need to run an errand first.'

'What about lunch?' Micke asked. 'We were just saying we were going to order from the motel.'

'I'll just grab something later.'

24

The heat hit Charlie like a wall when she left the station. She undid the top button of her shirt and walked down the high street towards the health centre and chemist's. She thought about Anders's negative attitude towards the town, the smelter that spoiled the view and the smell from the paper mill, which today was so faint as to be unnoticeable. He was missing something, she thought to herself, because now, with the birds singing and the river rushing and the smell of grass and flowers, this was a very beautiful place. It was exactly the kind of idyll the papers always wrote about in their stupid articles. But it was hot. She regretted wearing jeans, but the dresses she had thrown in her suitcase were all on the short side. She wondered whether the Outlet Barn with its cheap clothes was still in business on the outskirts of town. If the heatwave persisted, she was going to have to buy some new things.

She walked past the old house that had once housed the café. She and Betty had gone their sometimes when Betty had been paid.

Pick whatever you want, sweetie, whatever you want. No, come on, not the flattest cake, you bore. Pick something bigger. Then Betty would normally deposit a small fortune in the old jukebox sitting in the middle of the room.

Request something, darling. Anything, so long as it's upbeat.

Charlie would feel embarrassed by her, by her loud voice and flappy movements. On happy days like those at the café, Betty occasionally butted into other people's conversation, making them feel uncomfortable. And when it went too far and Charlie asked her not to talk to people she didn't know, to stop eavesdropping, stop interfering, Betty just laughed and said she wasn't eavesdropping. It was hardly her fault she could hear every single conversation in the room. It wasn't her fault she didn't have the ability to filter out unimportant things.

In that, they were different, Betty and she. Because Charlie knew her strength was exactly that, filtering out unimportant things and focusing on what was important, homing in on the right signal amid the white noise. At least she had used to be good at that, before she let a lunatic into her life. She hoped it was still possible to regain that ability. Her therapist, who loved words like 'self-medication' and 'insecure attachment patterns', thought her skill at reading people and moods sprang from a need to survive. Charlie had developed those abilities because she had had no choice; at the mercy, as she had been, of a capricious and unstable mother. Unpredictability in particular was damaging for a child, her therapist said. It put the child in a constant state of readiness.

Charlie cursed when she reached the chemist's and read the opening hours on the door: Mondays and Fridays from eleven to two. How was that possible? Zoloft won't even be enough, she thought. I need something to help me sleep, something to help me stay awake, something to alleviate the damn pressure across my chest. Susanne, she thought and pulled her phone out of her purse.

Susanne picked up after just one ring. Screaming children could be heard in the background.

'Charlie, is that you?'

'Yes.'

'Are you okay?'

'I need help with something.'

'Hold on.'

Charlie heard Susanne put the phone down and yell at a child. *You leave him alone, you hear me? No, of course he doesn't want you sitting on his face, now get up.* I'm sorry, I just had to separate them before they kill each other. What can I do for you?'

'Would it be all right if I popped by?'

'Of course. But I'm warning you. The place is a sty and I have the little ones with me because they had a slight temperature yesterday.'

A barking wire-haired dachshund greeted Charlie at the door. Susanne shoved it aside and gave Charlie a hug.

'Welcome to the chaos. I hope you won't feel obligated to call social services on your way home.'

Susanne had taken over her childhood home, but nothing looked the same inside. The walls and floors had been painted white and there was no wall between the kitchen and living room.

'Open floor plan,' Susanne sighed when Charlie commented on the changes. 'It doesn't exactly help to lower the noise level.'

There were stacks of dishes in the kitchen and the floor was littered with toys. Two boys of about five came running into the room. They rounded the kitchen island, skidded on the rug and disappeared before Charlie had time to say hi.

'Excellent manners, no?' Susanne said and smiled.

'Twins?'

Susanne nodded. Double the joy, double the work.

'What are their names?'

'AD and HD.'

'No they're not, Mummy,' protested one of the boys, who had returned. 'We're Tim and Tom.'

'I know,' Susanne said, noting Charlie's look, 'I let their dad name them. I guess I must have been pretty out of it after the labour. The other two are at school,' she continued. 'once they get home it gets even louder. And it's not long until the damn summer holidays start either. Sometimes I wonder how the fuck I'm going to get through it.'

'I wouldn't stand a chance,' Charlie said and smiled.

'Of course you would.'

'Your paintings?' Charlie pointed to the living room wall. Susanne nodded. Everything on the walls was by her and it wasn't to show off, it was ... well, because they just couldn't afford any other art.

'With paintings like those,' Charlie said, 'you don't need any other art.'

'You don't have to ...'

'I know. But I mean it. Don't you remember how I used to tell you that, right from the start, that you would become an artist one day.'

'I'm far from an artist,' Susanne said. 'I put a lot of time into it, but I don't make any money.'

Charlie stopped in front of a meadow with a girl picking flowers and said that it was probably just a matter of time, that she was bound to be discovered sooner or later.

Susanne laughed. She couldn't imagine a worse place to live if you wanted to be discovered. Who would ever find their way to Gullspång?

'You sound like you live in the nineteenth century,' Charlie said. 'Have you heard of social media? You should have a blog, an Instagram account, where you post your paintings and announce when you have an exhibition and ...'

'I can tell you've been living in Stockholm. It just doesn't work like that down here.'

'How do you know if you haven't tried. I just think it's sad that more people don't get to see your paintings.'

'There are things that are much sadder than that.' Susanne walked off to make coffee. 'No filter coffee, I'm afraid,' she called. 'I hope instant works.'

'No problem,' Charlie said and sat down on the sofa. 'I can only stay for a bit.'

One of the boys – Tim? – had found a wooden sword that he was now waving at his brother.

'Drop your weapon,' Charlie said in a pretend stern way and the boy, who was apparently too young to understand irony, dropped his sword and started shouting for his mother.

'What's the problem, Tim?' Susanne said. She had brought two big cups of coffee and a plate of cinnamon buns.

'The lady yelled at me,' the boy sobbed, 'she said I couldn't have my sword.'

'And she's right,' Susanne said. 'He just fights with it,' she said to Charlie, 'so you were completely right.'

'She can't tell me what to do,' Tim said.

'You know what?' Susanne dropped to her knees in front of her son. 'She can. She can tell people things like you're not allowed hit people. Because she's a police officer.'

The boy opened his eyes wide and turned from his mother to Charlie.

'You don't look like a police officer,' he said after a pause. 'Police officers have blue clothes.'

'Not all police officers,' Charlie said.

But Tim wasn't listening. He just kept asking about where she kept her gun, if she threw children in prison, if she ...

'Only inquisitive little children,' Susanne broke in, 'she

throws inquisitive little children straight in the dungeon.' She started laughing when Tim grabbed his brother by the hand and vanished.

Charlie knew she should give Susanne the whole spiel about not using the police to scare children, but she realised this was her only chance to talk to Susanne in peace.

'How's it going?' Susanne said. 'Are you going to find her?'

'Sooner or later, everyone's always found,' Charlie said. 'Most people, anyway,' she corrected herself.

'Alive?' Susanne said. And then: 'You don't have to answer; I realise you can't talk about the investigation.'

'So far, I don't know much more than you.'

'Annabelle Roos,' Susanne said. 'That girl has spent her fair share of evenings in the pub.'

'I know,' Charlie said. 'Strange that she hangs about there, really. I mean, she's only seventeen.'

Susanne burst out laughing. Seventeen, sixteen, fifteen, in Gullspång, you got into the pub whenever you felt like it; Charlie should be well aware of that. A ginger tabby jumped up on Susanne's lap and started tramping round and round.

'So lie down then, Poki, lie down and I'll stroke you.' The cat settled down on her lap and started purring.

Charlie reached out and scratched the cat behind the ear.

'Remember all the cats out in Lyckebo?' Susanne said. 'How many did you actually have?'

'A lot. Betty couldn't deal with spaying and neutering and that; they were all inbred.'

Susanne laughed, because it was true. That weird albino that always followed them around, for example: there must have been something wrong with that one.

'Wouldn't surprise me,' Charlie said. She checked her watch. She had to get back to the station. 'I wanted to ask you something.'

'What?'

'Well, I've been having some sleeping problems and now I've forgotten to bring my pills and the chemist's is closed so ... I was wondering if you had something to ... help me sleep?'

Susanne got to her feet. Of course she had. She had so many pills she'd never have to wake up if she didn't want to.

'Come with me,' she said.

Charlie followed her upstairs. Susanne pushed a hamper aside and they zigzagged their way between toys and piles of clothes.

'I keep everything locked up,' Susanne said when they reached the bathroom. She climbed onto a step stool and got down a key from on top of a white medicine cabinet. 'You can't be too careful in this house.'

'Quite the selection,' Charlie said when she saw the well-stocked shelves.

'I order them online. Well, maybe I shouldn't be telling a police officer that, but what the hell am I supposed to do when doctors are so stingy with prescriptions and the pharmacy is closed more often than not? I hope you understand.'

Charlie smiled. She understood.

Susanne handed her a box of Imovane. Then she rooted around some more and found a box of oxazepam. 'Take these as well. I have plenty.'

'Is that Zoloft?' Charlie asked, pointing at a box she recognised.

'Yes.' Susanne took it out. 'Is that something you need?'

'I left mine at home, and I get pretty shaky without them.'

'I hear that,' Susanne said. She opened the box and realised there were only four pills left.

'That'll do. The chemist is open tomorrow.'

Susanne warned her not to count on it, because you couldn't

really bank on correct opening hours in Gullspång. All it took was for someone to be off sick and it could stay closed for weeks. No wonder, in other words, that people in the area came up with alternative supply chains.

On her way back from Susanne's, Charlie called Anders and told him she would be a bit late. Anders said that was no problem, because William Stark didn't want to report to the police station.

'Why?'

'My guess would be that he's afraid of the gossip, that people will think he had something to do with Annabelle going missing.'

'Let's go to his house instead,' Charlie said. 'I'll be back in a bit.'

'What are you up to?'

'I just need to check something.'

After they hung up, Charlie continued towards the village shop. It loomed, big and white, on the hill on the other side of the river. Halfway across the bridge, she stopped and leaned over the railing. Looking down into the black depths, she couldn't understand that she had once jumped in from this spot. It had been a late summer's night when she and Susanne were twelve. They had escaped on their bikes from a rowdy party in Lyckebo and halfway across the bridge, they had decided they wanted to go for a swim. When Susanne had started skidding down the steep slope next to the bridge, Charlie had laughed and said they should jump.

Then they had stood there, on the other side of the railing, with the green inlet gates in front of them. That's where they were going to end up, Susanne had said, if they suddenly turned on the current. They'd be crushed in the turbine. It would be a horrible way to go.

Charlie had said that first of all the current started out weak and if they actually jumped in when it was already strong, they'd drown long before they reached the turbine. And besides, drowning was supposed to be the best way to go.

And how did she know that? Susanne had asked. Had she been talking to drowned people, or what?

They had talked about that for a while, until Charlie had moved closer and then, without really realising what she was doing, had grabbed Susanne's arm and jumped straight out.

She could still feel the fluttering in her stomach, the feeling that she was never going to land, and then, when she did, the cold in her feet, the suction that pulled her down, the urge to give in and sink.

The police cordons flapped in the languid breeze when she reached Vall's village shop. The yellowed tabloid placards in the windows were so bleached by the passing of time, they were no longer legible.

Charlie went closer. She thought about the first time she and Susanne had dared to come here. How old had they been back then? Twelve? Thirteen? No one at the party back at home in Lyckebo had even noticed them grabbing a can of beer each and sneaking off. They had drunk the beer before they got here and had laughingly tottered into the shop part before realising the parties were thrown higher up the building. Back then, there had still been ageing merchandise downstairs: bags of flour, tinned foods and rock-hard sweets in glass jars. That all seemed gone now.

The main door was locked. Charlie walked around the house and into the garden, sat down on the old bench by the gazebo and lit a cigarette. She looked up at a window on the top floor and remembered how a girl had tried to jump out of it once, how she had stood swaying on the windowsill, shouting that no one could stop her from jumping. And then, when everyone who had gathered behind her was too afraid to move, she had, at length, stepped down onto the floor, pushed through the small crowd and sobbingly run down the stairs. But Charlie had brighter memories from this place, too. She thought about how they had sat on the veranda: her, Susanne and a few older, tanned boys. They had played guitar, sung songs about the summer of '69 and watched the sun rise over the river. Charlie took a quick drag and let her eyes roam across the overgrown garden, wishing the place could speak to her. What had happened here less than a week ago? She walked over to the back door. There was a temporary bar across it. She called Micke and asked him to bring the key over. Because it was their lock, right?

Micke said it was and asked what she was doing there. He had a way of making every question sound like criticism. Charlie tried to hide her exasperation.

'Can you just bring the key down here?'

'I'll send Adnan. And hey, I'm not your personal assistant.'

Charlie hung up. Ten minutes later, Adnan arrived with the key. He offered to go in with her, but she said there was no need. She just wanted to have a look around.

'Just be careful on the stairs,' Adnan said, 'there's a tread missing halfway up.'

I know, Charlie thought. Would you just leave already?

A familiar smell of stale party greeted her as she entered the hallway. The floor was sticky and every step she took made a smacking sound. So far, everything is as it always was, Charlie thought, looking up at the sweeping staircase. The wallpaper had come loose in a few places and people had doodled in ink and black felt tip pen on the white walls. There was everything from the traditional *Wanna fuck, call*, followed by a number, to slightly more witty scribblings like *Why drink and drive when you can smoke and fly?* And then a few racist lines about how a pig born in a stable is still a pig. As Charlie moved in closer to take pictures of all of it on her phone, she noticed the smaller text. It was written with a thinner pen and partly obscured by a strip of wallpaper.

It was many and many a year ago,
    In a kingdom by the sea,
That a maiden there lived whom you may know
    By the name of Annabel Lee;
And this maiden she lived with no other thought
    Than to love and be loved by me.

Not a coincidence, Charlie thought after reading to the end, not a coincidence and not fate. Why would anyone write a poem by Poe on the wall of a house that was like an unsupervised youth centre? She was so preoccupied with the poem she almost put her foot through the hole in the stairs.

The kitchen looked the same. It smelled of smoke and drunkenness. Charlie went over to the table by the window. It was covered in hundreds of notches and cuts. The knife game, she thought, and remembered the game with the knife's point between widespread fingers. In the middle of the table, the surface was darker. Charlie tried to remember what Olof had said about the technical investigation. Wasn't it on the kitchen table they had found blood? Why had she not thought of the knife game when Olof brought that up?

There was a big aquarium in the next room. It wasn't until she was just a few feet away that she suddenly spotted the turtle. It was sitting on a big rock. The water beneath it was a brown murk full of cigarette butts and debris. Charlie couldn't stop staring at the turtle. Was it even alive? She almost hoped it was dead, but then it suddenly opened its eyes and looked at her. Why hadn't the technicians removed it?

'Again?' Adnan said when she called.

'Who owns the turtle in the village shop?'

'How am I supposed to know? I didn't even know there was a turtle there.'

'Well, there is. It's not having a great time.' Charlie fished out a butt floating on the surface. 'This water is foul.'

'And what do you want me to do about that?'

'Get someone to come and collect it.'

'You feel that's a good use of our resources right now?'

'It doesn't have to be an officer,' Charlie said. 'You know half the town, don't you, just call someone, anyone.'

'Fine,' Adnan replied. 'I'll see what I can do.'

She continued through the rooms. Most of the furniture was the same as it had been back then. In the high windows, the familiar, dusty plastic potted plants that had once been brightly coloured, but had now been bleached by time and sunlight. She continued up another flight of stairs, into the room where Fredrik had found William and Rebecka. The room that was probably still called the fucking room.

She walked over to the window and looked down at the small road outside. What happened to you, Annabelle? she whispered. Where did you go? If I were seventeen and drunk, where would I have gone? She tried to recall her younger self, tried to summon the feeling of drunkenness and upset feelings. It wasn't hard. But where would she have gone? After a while, it dawned on her that she wouldn't have gone anywhere, that she would more likely have stayed, drunk more, made a fool of herself. But, she thought, Annabelle's not me. Annabelle is ... She summed up what she knew about her so far. Annabelle was an intelligent, searching, determined young woman. Maybe not so different from me after all, Charlie mused, particularly if you add her fiery temperament (if that was in fact true) and her love of alcohol. And me ... I would never have left a party unless something really bad had happened. Was that true for Annabelle as well?

25

'There you are,' Anders said when Charlie returned to the station. 'Took you long enough.'

He walked over to the fridge. Micke and Adnan grinned at each other when he took out his soya milk.

'What were you up to in the village shop anyway?' Micke turned to Charlie.

'I just wanted to see the place for myself,' Charlie said. 'Are we heading over to William Stark's now?'

'Won't he still be in school?' Anders looked at his watch. 'Could someone call again to make sure?'

Charlie nodded to Adnan who pulled out his phone, stood up and left the room.

'Did you find her second Facebook profile?' Charlie looked at Micke.

'Yes,' Micke said. 'But "A Friend in Need" has been inactive for eight months. And there was nothing of interest on there, just a bunch of cheating, desperate teenagers who needed help with their schoolwork.'

'No weird comments or threats?'

'Nothing.'

'About that blood in the village shop kitchen, by the way,' Charlie said. 'It could be from a game.'

'What do you mean?' Olof stared at her.

'The knife game,' Charlie said, spreading her fingers on the table top, 'you know when you stab between our fingers. There are a lot of marks on the table in the kitchen.'

'The knife game?' Micke said. 'They still do that?'

Adnan returned and announced that William Stark was at his home; they could head over any time.

'Where does he live?' Anders asked.

'Ribbingsfors.' Micke started explaining how to get here, but Charlie cut him short. They had GPS. She liked the idea of people living at Ribbingsfors again. A place as beautiful as that shouldn't be allowed to fade from memory and fall into disrepair.

'The knife game?' Anders said in the car. 'Am I the only one who's not familiar with it? What else did you get up to at your parties out here? Shoot guns at each other? Russian roulette instead of postman's knock?'

Charlie laughed. She thought about the glue cans they had huddled around, the competitions about who dared to lean the furthest out on the cliff above the inlet gates, the fainting games.

'We fainted each other as well,' she said.

'How?' Anders looked at her.

'Squeezed each other's throats, just squeezing until we fainted, basically.'

'Why?'

'Because it was a rush, just before you blacked out, and when you came to, it was like you had a new perspective on the world for a while.'

'I'm sorry,' Anders said, 'but that sounds really twisted. I think you should count yourself lucky you got out of this place. God knows if you'd have survived if you'd stayed.'

Charlie wanted to tell him she might not have, but that would have been because of more serious things than games.

'Didn't you do anything that wasn't destructive?' Anders said. 'Didn't you do anything except try to hurt one another?'

Charlie thought about the nights with Susanne, their conversations down by the river, Susanne's hands in her hair, the sunsets. No, they hadn't only hurt one another. There had been other things too.

Like what? Anders wanted to know.

'Camaraderie,' Charlie said, 'love, warmth.'

Anders chuckled, but stopped when he realised she was being serious.

'I suppose,' he said, 'that a guy like me from Stockholm can't quite understand.'

'Exactly. I'm glad you're finally getting that, at least.'

They turned onto the highway, and from afar, Charlie could see the Outlet Barn was still there.

'Can you turn off here?' she said.

Anders wondered what she wanted to do in there, and she told him straight, that the heat was killing her, that she had to buy something.

'Make it quick,' Anders said.

Five minutes later, she was back, now wearing a thin, floral skirt that reached her knees and a ribbed white tank top.

'Nice,' Anders said when she climbed in. 'Really nice, actually.'

'Shut up,' Charlie said. 'It was the nicest I could find.'

'Then it's a mystery to me how they're still in business.'

'Maybe everyone doesn't share your sophisticated taste.'

'Clearly.' Anders started the car. 'Ribbingsfors, by the way, what kind of place is that?'

'It's a mansion outside Gullspång where Frans G. Bengtsson used to live.'

Anders looked at her enquiringly.

'Frans G. Bengtsson, the author of *The Long Ships* and ...'

'Yeah, I know who he is,' Anders said.

'Then why are you staring at me blankly?'

'Because I didn't know he used to live here. Why haven't I ever read anything about that?'

'Maybe because you don't read much,' Charlie said and smiled. She thought about Ribbingsfors and wondered what it looked like now. When she was little, the big house with its enormous wings had been abandoned. Cows had wandered about on the veranda and even in and out of the massive drawing room where the wealthiest people in the area had once been entertained. The only building that had been in a reasonable state back then had been the west wing, where Frans G. Bengtsson's old desk still stood. Sometimes, tourists would go there, old men and women with thermoses, ready to walk in the great author's footsteps, see the thousand-year-old oak tree in the backyard. It was said Bengtsson had written large parts of *The Tall Ships* sitting on a bench next to the trunk of that tree. The area around the tree had been one of Charlie's favourite spots. She had used to ride her bike there when things were too chaotic at home. Sometimes she had brought a book, sometimes a notepad, but usually she had just sat on the ground, staring up at the vast foliage. Once, she had scared the living daylights out of two older ladies who had arrived at dusk. They hadn't expected a child in the dark, they said in their own defence, they hadn't been prepared for a little girl to be sitting there all alone, that was why they had thought she was a ghost.

'What are you doing?' they had asked. 'What are you doing here all alone?'

And Charlie had replied that she was sitting there thinking her thoughts.

Couldn't she do that at home, one of the ladies had asked. She could catch cold, a urinary tract infection and ...

But there was no peace to be had at home. Betty played music too loudly and could pop in at any moment to ask if she could have this dance. She never understood Charlie's interest in books.

Why do you read so much, darling?

Charlie would reply that it was because she liked it. She never bothered to describe the feeling of entering different worlds, of allowing her own reality to fade away and being someone else. Being somewhere else.

'Is it true?' Anders said.

'What?'

'What we were just talking about, that Frans G. Bengtsson lived here?'

'Well, yes, why would I lie about something like that?'

'But here, of all places?'

Charlie looked at him and said that this was an amazing place, that anyone who wasn't completely blind or stupid would see that.

'Calm down,' Anders said. 'I was just wondering how he ended up here.'

They had reached the long birch-lined driveway that led up to the mansion.

'Love,' Charlie said. 'Love brought him here.'

That day

It was a double history class. Annabelle felt she might die if she had to stay there. She got up as carefully as she could and mimed 'bathroom' to the teacher.

In the bathroom, she had a text from Rebecka. The delivery had arrived, she wrote. Svante was waiting in the car park behind the gym. Could she go and pick it up? They hadn't spoken since Rebecka told her about William; just sat next to each other in class, in silence, so the message felt like an attempt at making contact more than anything. Rebecka wasn't exactly the type to worry about leaving class to sort out something as important as this.

Annabelle heaved a sigh and wrote *OK* back. The last thing she wanted right now was to deal with Svante, but on the other hand they did need the booze. She needed both the booze and her best friend.

She went out to the parking lot. The orange BMW was waiting there, engine running and music thumping from its speakers. Svante smiled at her through the rolled-down window.

'Long time no see.'

She nodded.

'Nice shirt,' he said with a grin.

Annabelle looked down at the T-shirt she had slept in and told him to stop being an ass.

'But you look good in everything,' Svante continued.

Annabelle thought to herself that he was the only person she knew who could make a compliment sound like an insult.

'Do you have the booze?' she said.

'How about a thank you?'

'Do you have the booze, thanks.'

'I meant for what I said about you looking good.'

'I'm in a bit of a hurry. I have class.'

'I forgot you're such a good girl.'

'Well, I wouldn't mind getting a job in the future.'

Svante said she didn't have to worry about that. He would set her up with something at the factory the day she graduated, before then even, if she wanted.

'Great,' Annabelle replied, because she didn't want to piss Svante off by telling him she would never in a million years agree to have her forearms shredded on the factory floor.

Svante leaned over to the passenger side.

'Here,' he said, handing her a clinking carrier bag. Just as she was about to grab it, he pulled his hand away.

'What?' Annabelle said.

'Rebecka hasn't paid.'

'We'll pay you later.'

'Or I might just accept a kiss instead.' Svante grinned. 'What?' he said when she shook her head. 'Do you know how much this would cost you in the shops?'

'I'd rather pay.'

'Hey, Bella, if I were you, I'd fucking watch myself.' He put the bag back down on the passenger seat.

'Neither one of my parents work for your dad,' Annabelle said, 'so your threats don't work on me. I don't need you.'

'Sure you do. You need me more than you even realise.'

'You're wrong.'

Annabelle turned around and started walking away.

'So you don't want it?' she heard Svante calling after her. 'Rebecka already bloody paid. I was just playing around.'

Annabelle didn't bother answering.

'Did you put it in the usual place?' Rebecka whispered when Annabelle sat back down next to her in the classroom. 'You didn't put it in your locker, did you?'

'I didn't get the booze.'

'What the fuck?'

'He's a moron. I didn't take it.'

'But I already paid!' Rebecka glared at her.

'I'll sort it out some other way.'

'How?'

'I'll just sort it out.'

26

As they turned into the gravel yard in front of the house, Anders gave a low whistle. What a house! Charlie thought about what Micke had told her about the Stark family. They had moved here from Kristinehamn. William was an only child and in his final year of upper secondary school. His mother had died a few years before so now it was just him and his dad. According to Micke, the family had been wealthy for generations, so much so that they had been able to buy Ribbingsfors and renovate both the main building and the two wings.

A woman in her thirties opened the door.

'William?' she said when they asked for him. 'He's gone out. He went down to the lake.'

'Are you ... ?' Charlie didn't know how to finish the question.

'I'm his stepmother,' the woman smiled. 'Kristina. Maybe you'd like to speak to his dad? Stefan!' she called into the house. 'You have visitors. It's the police.'

A well-built man in gym clothes came into the hallway and shook both their hands. He was just on his way out for a jog, he said, as though apologising for how he was dressed.

'We're here to speak with your son,' Charlie said, 'but apparently he's gone out.'

'He was just heading down to the jetty,' Stefan said. 'He

always goes down to the lake when he's feeling bad; and the way things are ... well, I'm sure you understand.'

'Could we speak to you for a minute before we go find him?' Anders said.

Stefan nodded.

'Could I offer you a cup of coffee on the veranda?'

The view from the veranda made Charlie stop dead in her tracks. The scene before her was like a painting. The water glittering between the weeping willows, the buttercups, cow parsley and lupins in the meadow. And then the oak tree. The enormous thousand-year-old oak tree.

'Can't fault the view,' Stefan said. He gestured for them to sit down in the wicker garden furniture.

Within minutes, Kristina joined them, carrying a tray of coffee cups.

'They're lattes,' she explained as she put the tray down on the table and took a seat next to Stefan. 'We had to buy one of those proper coffee makers, because we're twenty-five miles from anything but filter coffee out here.'

'Kristina,' Stefan said wearily, 'I don't think they're here to talk about the different types of coffee.'

'We're here to talk about Annabelle,' Charlie said. 'Did you know that she and William used to be involved?'

Stefan nodded. Of course they had known. Annabelle had been over several times. It certainly was no secret.

'But then it ended,' Kristina said. 'William was inconsolable.'

'That might be overstating it a bit.' Stefan looked at her. 'He was a bit subdued for a few days. But then he felt better.'

'How would you describe Annabelle?' Charlie asked.

Stefan and Kristina exchanged a quick look.

'I suppose we didn't see much of her,' Stefan said. 'The two of them mostly kept to themselves. They were in his room, listening to music and … Well, got up to the things teenagers get up to, I guess.'

'Annabelle's parents didn't know about their relationship,' Charlie said.

'Is that right?' Stefan said. 'That's odd.'

'We don't see them socially,' Kristina said. 'They're the kind of couple who mostly keep to themselves.'

Charlie sipped her coffee and turned her eyes back to the lake. She thought about Annabelle's parents, their house outside of town, how lonely they seemed.

When they had finished their coffee, Charlie and Anders walked down towards the water. A cut path through the tall grass of the meadow beyond the veranda led them to the jetty. William was sitting at the far end of it with his back to them.

'Fuck, you really scared me!' he said when he realised he wasn't alone.

'I thought you'd been told we were coming,' Charlie said, 'so there was no reason for you to leave the house. We need to ask you some more questions about Annabelle.'

'So ask,' William said and turned back to gaze out across the water, 'but make it quick because I'm heading out to join the search when we're done.'

'You and Annabelle,' Charlie said, 'were together for a while, weren't you?'

William looked at her. He had answered that question days ago. Didn't the police take notes so they wouldn't have to ask the same questions over and over?

'I was just trying to make conversation, but sure, let me get straight to the point. Why did your relationship end?'

Anders's phone rang. He looked at it and made a gesture to Charlie to indicate that it was important, that he had to take it. He strode off, away from the jetty.

'So, why did it end?' Charlie repeated.

'Because it all fell apart.' William spat into the water.

'How come?'

'I'm not sure. It just fell apart. I suppose that's how it goes sometimes. And no,' he said, 'I'm not a jealous psychopath, if that's what you're thinking.'

'If you were, I doubt you'd tell me,' Charlie said.

William asked her what she meant by that, and she clarified that psychopaths rarely describe themselves as such, that that's part of their pathology, not having that kind of insight.

'So you think I'm a psychopath?'

'I don't know you.' Charlie took her shoes off and sat down next to him on the jetty. 'Are you?'

William smiled. 'I suppose I wouldn't admit it if I was.'

This boy, Charlie thought, was certainly no dummy.

'Did you love her?' she said. 'Did you love Annabelle?'

William shrugged. He guessed so. For a while, there had even been talk about moving in together somewhere after graduation, maybe in Stockholm or Gothenburg. Annabelle was probably going to study and he was going to find a job. It shouldn't be hard to find a job in one of the bigger cities. He didn't mind where it was, so long as he didn't have to go to school any more. He was really fucking fed up with that. But now everything felt meaningless, graduating, the future, the celebration, because if something horrible had happened to Annabelle, if she wasn't found alive, there was nothing to be happy about.

Charlie said she understood, that she was sure many of Annabelle's friends felt the same way right now. She hoped, she said, without sounding particularly convincing, that he would get to celebrate his graduation.

'I already miss her,' William said. 'I missed her even before she went missing.'

'I understand,' Charlie said. 'Was it rough on you when it ended?'

William nodded and said it had been pretty rough.

'Did you fight the night she disappeared?'

'No, at least not as far as I remember.'

Charlie couldn't stop herself from asking if he had trouble remembering things sometimes.

William's eyes flashed. No, he didn't, no more than other people. But maybe Charlie was aware that alcohol could have an effect on a person's ability to recall things.

All too aware, Charlie thought to herself. She continued asking the usual questions, about how Annabelle had acted, if she had seemed sad that night, when he last saw her, what state she had been in at that point. If he had noticed anything unusual. But she found out nothing new.

With further questioning seeming pointless, Charlie realised her last means of getting him to talk was silence. She focused on the water, on the pond skaters skidding across the surface, the shoals of tiny fish underneath, the reddish, wavy sand bottom.

She was just about to give up when William cleared his throat.

'I felt like the reason she dumped me was because she'd met someone else.'

'Why's that?'

'Isn't that how it usually goes? You find someone new and dump the one you have?'

Charlie nodded and said that happened, but that there could be many other reasons for dumping someone.

'Jonas and Svante were talking about that night, that I'd been replaced or whatever. Jonas had seen Annabelle with someone else.'

'Did you ask who it was?'

William shook his head. He hadn't asked; he didn't want to know.

'You should have told me that right away,' Charlie said.

'It didn't even occur to me. People always talk.'

'You and Svante Linder. How close are you?'

'Pretty close, though Svante gets weird when he drinks. Well, to be honest, we both do.'

'I've been told you had a fight down the pub, that you were fighting about Annabelle.'

William gave her a surprised look and Charlie realised she might have exaggerated a little.

'And last night,' she pressed on, 'last night at the pub, you looked like you were at odds.'

'It was nothing,' William said, 'just a bit of a bust-up. I don't even remember what it was about. And we've never had a fight about Annabelle. If you're talking about what happened on Waterfall Day ...'

'Waterfall Day?'

'Yeah, it's when they open the inlet gates. It's the party that night.'

Charlie knew what Waterfall Day was. The dam opening, the frothing water roaring down the cliffside. She had witnessed it many times herself as a child. But she hadn't heard anything about that night, a few weeks previous.

'So what happened?' she said.

'It wasn't Svante and me fighting. It was the two of us, putting Erik, the guy who owns the motel, in his place.'

'Tell me more.'

'He was groping Annabelle. And it makes no difference that things were over between us at that point, he can't go around fucking groping girls against their will. So incredibly fucking disrespectful.'

Charlie tried to look unperturbed.

'Does Erik grope underage girls a lot?'

'Not that I know. He'd had a lot to drink that night. By the end, he was barely able to serve his customers. Either way, I don't think he's ever going to touch Annabelle again. We scared him. I think we scared him pretty properly that time.'

Charlie couldn't remember reading anything about that incident in the interview records. Why had this not come to light sooner? There must have been a lot of witnesses.

'Why has no one told us about this?'

William shrugged. 'Drunkenness maybe. And besides, it's not like anyone thinks Erik has anything to do with Annabelle's disappearance. He's an upstanding family guy who went a bit wrong one night and couldn't keep his hands to himself.'

'And how can you be so sure he's upstanding?'

William shrugged again. It was just his opinon. Erik wasn't exactly the type to kidnap young girls.

'Do you know anyone who is?' Charlie asked. 'Who is the type to kidnap young girls?'

'I don't know what you're getting at.'

'What I'm getting at is that that type might not be so easily identified.'

'I guess not,' William replied.

'From now on, you're going to leave it to the police to determine what's important and what isn't.'

'Absolutely.'

'And if you remember anything else from that night, or anything else at all, call me.' Charlie handed him her card and got to her feet.

*

She could feel William's eyes on her back as she walked away. Anders was nowhere to be seen, so she assumed he'd gone back up to the car.

Who is William Stark? she pondered on her way back to the house. Is he the dumped boyfriend who consoles himself with his ex-girlfriend's best friend, or is he more profoundly aggrieved than that? Impossible to know. But he had an alibi for the time around Annabelle's disappearance. He'd stayed in the village shop until dawn.

Her phone rang. The *H* on the screen. She was going to decline, but for some inexplicable reason her left middle finger was drawn to the green receiver button instead.

'What do you want?' Charlie said.

But it wasn't Hugo. It was a sobbing woman who introduced herself as Anna, Hugo's wife.

'What were you thinking?' she said.

Charlie stopped dead. 'What do you mean?'

'I'm just curious how a person thinks when they ... You did know he was married, didn't you?'

Charlie considered playing ignorant, but realised it was too late for that, so instead she replied that she had been aware. She had known he was married, but surely that was Hugo's problem, not hers.

'It's true what they say about you,' Anna said. 'It's true that you don't have a fucking semblance of a conscience, that you don't ... I get why Maria didn't want you and Anders working together. I assume you're fucking him too?'

Charlie's first impulse was to ask her to go to hell, but then she calmed herself.

'You don't know me,' she said.

'I know enough. I know your sort. A lonely, bitter person who wants to destroy other people's lives, who ...' Anna sobbed, caught her breath and continued. 'Do you think you're the only woman he's amused himself with when he's been bored?'

'I think this is something you should discuss with your husband,' Charlie said and hung up. She started walking faster. Fuck, fuck, fuck. She tried to erase Anna's words from her memory, *do you think you're the only woman?* Why did she even care? After all, she'd known from the start that she was the other woman. And yet she didn't want to believe that there had been others like her; she wanted what she had had with Hugo to have been something more, more than just lust. She thought about his over-the-top words about how beautiful and amazing she was.

Watch out for men of big words, Betty had told her once. *Men of big words are the worst. They may seem kind and even funny, but most of them are really stupid. Remember that, Charline.*

Charlie thought about Anna. How must a person feel in that kind of relationship? Why would they stay? And calling your husband's mistress? She couldn't understand it. If Charlie was ever to get married and then cheated on, she would never in a million years call and degrade herself like that. She would focus her wrath on the guilty party: the cheater.

And what about your own guilt? A voice in her head insisted. What on earth were you thinking?

Anders was standing by the car when she arrived.

'I'm sorry,' he said, 'but it was Maria. Sam's apparently running a temperature. She took him to A&E, but the doctors didn't think he was in any danger. You see that I had to take it, right?'

Charlie nodded and said she did. Then she felt ashamed for thinking that maybe Maria was overplaying things in order to control her husband.

'I hope he feels better,' she said.

Anders nodded and said something about high fevers not being the same thing for children and adults, but that he had to take every call from Maria at the moment.

Charlie thought to herself that that was no different from usual.

'Did you get anything out of him?' Anders asked when they were back in the car.

'Yes, he said he'd heard Annabelle had somebody new. Jonas Landell told him that night, that he'd seen Annabelle with someone else. We have to talk to him, and then to Rebecka,' she added. 'If it turns out Jonas was telling the truth, that Annabelle was seeing someone, we have to talk to Rebecka about it. We have to ask her why she hasn't mentioned it to us.'

'Maybe she doesn't know.'

'She's her best friend,' Charlie retorted. 'Of course she knows. And then there's Erik, the guy from the motel.'

'What about him?'

'William told me he groped Annabelle during a party a few weeks ago. It turned into a fight; Svante and William roughed him up.'

'I'll grab Adnan or Micke and take care of those interviews,' Anders said.

'Why?'

'Because you look like you need a rest. You're really pale. Are you okay?'

'It's my head,' Charlie said. 'I just feel a bit dizzy.'

Anders said he would drop her off at the motel so she could have a nap. Charlie tried to object. There was no need for him to exaggerate. The last few days had just been a bit intense.

'I get that.' Anders looked at her searchingly. 'It must feel weird, I mean, coming back after such a long time. There must be a lot of memories and whatnot?'

Charlie nodded.

'Do you miss her?'

'Who?' Charlie asked, even though she knew full well whom he meant.

'Your mother?'

'Yes,' she said. 'I miss her very much.'

'It's okay to cry,' Anders said. He put a hand on her arm but quickly removed it again.

'I know,' Charlie said, 'it's just that …'

'What?'

'It doesn't help.'

There and then

Alice and Rosa walk past the old mill house on the hill. Big, red and imposing, it casts its long shadow towards the smaller, boxy cottages further down the street. Rosa doesn't like going close to the manor, as she calls it, but to get to the beach, they have to walk past it. Benjamin is sitting with his brother on a blanket in the grass. Benjamin is in the year above them at school. Rosa calls him stupid-head. Why? She says it's because he's ... stupid. She doesn't like stupid people.

'What are you looking at, stupid-head?' she shouts at Benjamin. And when he doesn't respond, she walks up closer and asks what he's reading.

'Nothing,' Benjamin says and shuts his book.

'And what is that around your neck? Is it a necklace?'

'No, it's a birthstone with a genuine pearl.'

'And here I was thinking it looks just like a necklace.'

'Necklace,' John-John says and touches his neck, where he has the same kind of necklace as his brother.

Rosa shakes her head. Boys with necklaces. And birthstones, she's never heard of birthstones.

'Our dad gave them to us,' Benjamin says. 'They're real pearls.'

'They're real pearls,' Rosa mocks. And then to Alice: 'I don't get why anyone would buy little kids real pearls. Do you, Alice?'

Alice shakes her head, because she doesn't get why anyone would buy real pearls at all.

Benjamin gets up and says he's not a little kid, that he's actually older than them. Rosa retorts that she supposes she must have meant John-John.

Then Benjamin's mother comes out on the porch. She shouts at them to get off her property, right now.

Rosa points to the ground and says they're not even on their property, that they're on public land, but Benjamin's mother doesn't care and for her information, they own the land on the other side of the fence too, all the way down to the lake as a matter of fact. And she wants Rosa to stay as far away from them as is humanly possible.

Rosa just stands there, staring at the stupid-head's mother. Alice thinks she's creepy when she stares like that, without moving. She grabs Rosa's arm and tries to drag her away, but she can't.

'Maybe I should get my mum as well,' Rosa says.

And then Benjamin's mother retorts that Miss Manner is probably busy with other things, that she's probably lying on her back at home, working.

'What are you trying to say?' Rosa says. 'What the fucking is that supposed to mean?'

'You know what I'm talking about. Everyone knows what your mother does for a living. She might as well have a sign on the roof.'

'I'm guessing your husband told you that?' Rosa says.

She has barely finished the sentence before Benjamin's mother is there, slapping her face.

'Are you crying?' Alice says when they reach the water's edge. 'Are you sad?'

Rosa shakes her head. She doesn't seem to notice the tears rolling down her cheeks. Alice sits down next to her.

'Never mind that family,' she says. 'They're full of it.'

Rosa says nothing. She picks so hard at a mosquito bite on her shin, it starts bleeding. Then she turns to Alice and says she's glad they're best friends, that everything is easier now that she has a sister, that you might say they've saved each other.

27

Charlie went up to the motel room. Anders was right. She really did need a rest. She lay down on her bed, pulled out her phone and googled Edgar Allan Poe's poem 'Annabel Lee'.

According to Wikipedia, it was the last one he wrote. The death of a young woman, the source said, was a theme he returned to again and again in his works.

She opened her photos and studied the picture she had taken of the village shop wall. Who had written it? Annabelle herself?

She swiped back one step and found the picture of the number on the same wall, the one you were supposed to call if you wanted to fuck. Without pausing to think it over, she dialled it. After three rings, a girl answered.

Charlie recognised her voice but couldn't place it.

'Who is this?' she said.

'Sara. Who is this?'

'This is Charlie, from the police.'

'What do you want?'

Charlie detected a hint of anxiety in her voice.

'I ... I just wanted to check in on you.'

'I'm okay. Thanks for driving me home yesterday.'

'No worries.' There was a pause. Charlie didn't know what else to say. A man shouted something in the background.

'I have to go,' Sara said. 'Maybe I'll see you around.'

*

When Charlie woke up, it took her several seconds to figure out where she was. How long had she been asleep? The room swayed when she stood up. She found her phone and breathed a sigh of relief when she saw it had only been an hour. She called Anders.

'What's happening?' she asked.

'We've just talked to Jonas. He's confirmed William's information about Annabelle seeing someone.'

'Who?'

'That's what we don't know. Jonas has seen her with someone, but it was from a distance when he was out on the lake. He didn't see who it was. He saw them on an island, Golden Island or some such.'

'Gold Island,' Charlie said.

'Yes, that's the one. He's sure it was Annabelle because of her hair. But the only thing he could tell us about the man was that he was older. At least that was the feeling he had.'

'Didn't he ask Annabelle who it was?'

'Yes, but she just told him he was mistaken, that she hadn't been there.'

'And Erik?'

'He says it was just a drunken mistake, that he must have misinterpreted Annabelle's signals. It wasn't a big deal, according to him.'

'Does he have an alibi for the night she disappeared?'

'Yes, he worked until midnight and his wife says he was home twenty minutes later.'

'Working's one word for it,' Charlie said. 'And the wife? Could she be wrong about the time?'

'She says she's sure, that she's a light sleeper, that she woke up when he got in and that it was twenty past twelve. That doesn't give him much time to get up to any dodgy business.'

'She's his wife though,' Charlie said. 'Don't forget that she's his wife.'

That day

The school day was finally over. How had she managed to get through it? Annabelle took a shortcut across the meadow and thought about a couple of lines she'd read in *Jane Eyre*.

Reason sits firm and holds the reins, and she will not let the feelings burst away and hurry her to wild chasms.

Too late, she thought. Her emotions had already hurried her to ruin. She was on her way towards the wild chasm. But tonight, she was going to try to take her mind off it. She regretted promising to tell Rebecka everything, because all she wanted to do now was forget.

She was almost home when she realised she had to get booze. Rebecka would pitch a fit if she turned up empty-handed tonight. She briefly considered calling Svante and apologising. He would come right over and she wouldn't have to go through the trouble of sorting it out some other way. She stopped, pulled out her phone, found Svante's number, but put her phone away again. Not worth it, she thought.

She turned around and started walking back towards town. She had no money, but she'd find a way. She thought about the fact that this would be her first time at Vall's since she was there with Him. She regretted taking him there, now that place would be associated with their history too. Why hadn't they just stuck with meeting up outdoors? But he felt it was too risky. It was only a matter of time before they were caught. After that time at his house, he had become more cautious. The last few times, he had picked her up in his car. He had driven far from town, down winding forest roads, then he had turned the engine off and pushed his seat back. But then one day, she had taken him to the village shop. It was a weekday afternoon and she was almost sure they wouldn't be interrupted. He had never been there before.

When she opened the door, he had hesitated. It didn't feel right, he said, to just walk into someone's house. Annabelle had had to explain to him again that Vall's didn't have an owner, that no one would press charges if they went inside.

In the hallway by the stairs, he stopped and read the writings on the wall. He wanted to write something beautiful, he said. As a sort of counterweight to all the swastikas and four-letter words.

She handed him a pen from her purse. Write something, she said. Write me a poem.

He took the pen and started writing. When he was done, he let her read it. Did she like it?

Annabelle had said she didn't, because she knew how the poem ended. She didn't like tragic endings.

28

They had gathered for another meeting at the station. It was a slightly crestfallen group sitting in front of Charlie. They went through the new information about the unknown man, the potential lover. Identifying him, Charlie said, was pivotal. She wanted a list of all the men Annabelle might have come into contact with, in any context. They needed to talk to friends of the family, friends' fathers, teachers ... everyone. If only to write them off. Micke interrupted her to say they'd already done all of that. They had talked to almost everyone in Annabelle's life, as she was well aware. Charlie said they had to cast a wider net while also digging deeper in terms of the nearest and dearest at the same time. And all alibis had to be double-checked. She didn't know how to continue without revealing something about herself or offending somebody. It was only a second or two before Micke countered.

'So you're saying the alibis here are less reliable than in other places?'

'I'm saying this is a small place, that a lot of people have strong ties to one another.'

Charlie couldn't keep from rolling her eyes at Anders before carrying on.

'Don't forget to check if anyone has an extra pay-as-you-go

mobile. Have you talked to Rebecka again?'

'We weren't able to reach her earlier, but I'm calling her again now,' Adnan said.

'Great, and tell her it's important, that the usual rules about secrets are not in play here.'

'Charlie,' Micke put in. 'He gets it. We're not completely incompetent down here.'

'And ask her if she recognises this handwriting,' Charlie pressed on, ignoring Micke's comment. She held up her phone and showed them the poem before forwarding the picture to Adnan.

Micke asked what it was and Charlie told them she'd found it on a wall in the village shop.

'I thought that was the technicians' job,' Micke said.

'I guess they let themselves down this time.'

'And what are you going to do now?'

'Anders and I are going to go see the parents.'

'Do you think that's such a good idea?' Olof said. 'I mean, Nora's very upset ... I'm not sure I would go over there given the circumstances.'

'Our visit yesterday was cut short. There's something in that family that feels ... I can't quite put my finger on it. And I also want to have a look at Annabelle's room.'

'We've been over it,' Olof said. 'There was no diary or any other clues to what might have happened.'

'I know, but I would still like to see it for myself,' Charlie said. 'Anders and I will stop by and then we'll head over to the school to talk to her teachers. Micke, call the headteacher and let them know we're coming.'

Fredrik Roos received them dressed in the same clothes he had worn the day before. Charlie quickly informed him they had no news, but that they wanted to take a look at Annabelle's room and have a little chat.

Fredrik didn't offer them coffee this time. He just showed them into the kitchen and asked them what they wanted to know.

'We were wondering about Nora and Annabelle's relationship. About Nora being a little ... over-protective of Annabelle. Why do you think that is?'

Fredrik looked at them and said he didn't know. His wife had just always been like that, he had told them as much, so where were they going with this?

'I guess we just want to know if there was a particular reason, if Nora has reason to think someone is out to hurt Annabelle.'

'No,' Fredrik said. 'She would have told me. I suppose some people are just worrygutses.'

'Then let's drop it,' Charlie said and stood up. 'Would it be okay if we looked around her room briefly?'

Fredrik asked them to keep it down if they really had to go in there, because Nora was resting in the bedroom across the hall.

On their way upstairs, they ran into Hannes. He was dressed in jeans, a shirt and a clerical collar.

'She's asleep,' he said, nodding upstairs. 'I've been sitting with her for a while and was just heading down for a cup of coffee. I want to be there when she wakes up, but it would be better to let her sleep for a while now.'

'We'll be quiet,' Charlie said.

Annabelle's room was pink, as though it belonged to a much younger girl. The bed had a white canopy and dolls and teddy bears lined up on it, nestled between lace cushions. Along the other wall was a desk and above it a noticeboard with photographs. Charlie leaned forward for a closer look. Annabelle on horseback, squinting at the sun, Annabelle smiling with a big gap from a lost tooth, Fredrik with a chubby, ice-cream-eating little Annabelle on a beach. And then the more recent photos, a beautiful, strawberry-blonde girl with her arms around friends who were almost as beautiful.

Charlie moved on to the bookcase and read the backs of the books: *The Hunger Games, The Circle, Alice in Wonderland.* And on the higher shelves: *To Kill a Mockingbird, Crime and Punishment, The Stranger.* This, Charlie thought, really is a girl who likes to read.

'Doesn't it strike you as strange,' she said, 'that a person who reads so much doesn't seem to write?'

The two don't necessarily go hand in hand, Anders replied.

'But usually they do.'

'Maybe she has a good hiding place. Or maybe she just writes notes on her phone.'

Charlie opened the closet door. The necklaces hanging on a hook on the back of it rattled.

'She seems to have a fairly bold fashion sense,' Anders said when he saw dresses in every pattern and colour. Charlie said nothing. She just pulled the dresses aside, one after the other. She wouldn't have called Annabelle's taste bold, more like ... original.

Anders looked through the desk drawers. There was nothing unusual in them, pens, erasers, a notebook full of quadratic equations. Her bedside table held a box of ibuprofen and a pack of gum. Charlie knelt down on the floor, lifted the valance and had a look. Nothing.

Fredrik suddenly appeared in the doorway. He was carrying a number of books.

'How's it going?' he said. 'Finding anything of interest?'

'I suppose we're mostly interested in forming an accurate impression of who Annabelle is,' Charlie said.

'Could you do me a favour?'

'Yes,' Charlie said.

'I was just wondering ... if you could return these?' Fredrik stepped inside and put the books down on the desk. 'Nora and I can't face going into town.'

'I'm sure the librarian won't mind them being returned late,' Anders said.

'We'll return them,' Charlie broke in. 'No problem. We're staying at the motel anyway, so the library's right there.'

'I was thinking about the book club as well,' Fredrik said. 'I believe Annabelle was talking about starting a book club in school, but I don't know if it actually happened. It might not have been easy to get people to sign up.'

'We can ask the people at the school if they know anything about it,' Charlie said. She picked up the books on her way out of the room.

They walked past the door to Nora's room, which was standing ajar. Nora was crying inside.

'My little girl,' she said, sobbing, 'my darling little girl.'

Then Hannes's voice: 'A lot of people are praying for her, Nora. Your daughter is ... she's a very special girl.'

'Get me more water,' Nora said. 'I need more water and something to help me sleep. I don't want to be awake any more.'

Hannes came out onto the landing just as they were about to walk downstairs.

'How is she?' Charlie asked. 'How is she holding up?'

'Poorly,' Hannes replied, 'very, very poorly.' He turned to Fredrik. 'She wants more pills.'

'They're on the kitchen counter, I'll show you.'

'Could I use the loo?' Charlie said. Fredrik nodded and pointed to a door on the other side of the hallway.

'It's that one.'

When the others had disappeared downstairs, Charlie went straight into Nora's room. Nora was slumped in her bed, her face red from crying and her hair dishevelled. She barely reacted when Charlie entered.

'Nora,' Charlie said, 'I need to talk to you.' She went over to the bed. 'I was just wondering if you know something about Annabelle that you're not telling us?'

Nora shook her head.

'I've been told you've been fairly ... concerned about her. Is that for any particular reason?'

No reply. Charlie was just about to reformulate her question when Nora cleared her throat.

'The world is evil.'

'What do you mean?'

'I mean that's the reason. I wanted to protect her.'

'Are you thinking about anyone in particular? Has anyone threatened you?'

Nora shook her head. The world was just evil. The world and the people in it. That was all.

'What did Nora say?' Anders said when they were back in the car. 'I'm assuming you didn't actually need the bathroom.'

'She said the world is evil, and the people in it too, and that was why she wanted to protect her daughter.'

'Did she have any particular evil in mind?'

'Not as far as I could wheedle out of her anyway. She's not the easiest person to talk to.'

'It's good you tried, at least.'

'What do you think of the priest?' Charlie said. 'Could he be the lover?'

'The priest?' Anders turned to her.

'Well, he's not just a priest,' Charlie said. 'He's a person as well.'

'Wouldn't he have a lot to lose?' Anders said.

'That's what I mean. I get the feeling he knows more than he's told us. We need to talk to him again.'

29

Gullspång Central School was a large orange brick building with strange annexes and portable classrooms. The upper secondary school was at the far end of the parking lot. Charlie never made it that far. She hadn't even had time to graduate from the secondary school housed in the larger building. School. She had been the kind of unusual child who loved it. It had started with a teacher with a warm lap and a gentle voice, continued with another who encouraged her to read and let her use a maths book for the higher classes. It didn't matter that Betty forgot to go to the parent-teacher conferences and parent meetings, that she never bothered to help Charlie with her homework, because Charlie did well regardless. *High achiever*, that's what a teacher had called her in year eight. *The only one who can stop you is you*, she had added. That wasn't true, Charlie reflected now; plenty of factors were categorically beyond her control. She thought about Betty and Mattias, who would routinely keep her up on school nights. If it wasn't Betty clinking on the piano, it was Mattias with his guitar. *Play something for me, darling. You're the first person I've ever met with perfect pitch.*

The smell of fossils, stones and books washed over her when she opened the heavy double doors to the upper secondary school. Classes were over for the day and the corridors were silent and deserted.

The headteacher received them in her office. She told them how shocked all the pupils in the school were. In tiny Gullspång they just weren't used to things like this happening. Children who disappeared were always found and everyone … well, everyone knew everyone else and …

'Do you have anything to tell us about Annabelle?' Anders said.

'I've already told the police,' the headteacher said, 'that Annabelle is our most promising student. True, she has skipped some classes and been late several times recently, but other than that, there's not a lot to say.'

'The lateness and absences,' Charlie said, 'is that new?'

'I think so, but I could check the records further back if you want.'

'We could do with a list of her teachers as well,' Charlie said.

'Sure,' the headteacher turned on her computer and sighed about the slowness of the school's intranet. 'All the teachers are listed as abbreviations, so I'll write them out for you.'

She turned around and pulled a paper from the printer. Then she picked up a pen and started to write. Charlie asked her to note down their ages as well. The headteacher looked up and said she would have to check their contracts to make sure she got it right.

'Then please do,' Charlie said. 'Annabelle's father talked about a book club she wanted to start. Do you know anything about that?'

'No,' the headteacher said. 'But check with the librarian. He might know. The library is at the end of the corridor. I think he's still there. Unless the printer gives me trouble I'll be by with the list shortly.'

As they walked towards the library, Anders had a text message and Charlie realised she'd forgotten that his son was ill.

'Was that Maria?' she said. 'Is the baby okay?'

Anders nodded.

There was no sign of the librarian in the library. Charlie walked over to the counter and rang the little bell. A man came out of an adjoining room with a stack of papers under his arm.

'Can I help you?' he asked.

Charlie looked at his tight, light blue shirt. He looked nothing like what she had expected. To her, a school librarian was a middle-aged woman in colourful clothes with big pockets; if it was a man, it was supposed to be a slender little thing with glasses and tiny hands. But this librarian was a good-sized man of about thirty-five. His handshake was firm and self-assured when he introduced himself as Isak Sander.

'Could we speak to you for a minute?' Charlie said.

'Sure,' Isak said. 'Why don't we use the back office. There are several chairs in there.'

He showed them into a room behind the lending counter. On his desk was a framed photograph of four blond, happily smiling boys. So this is him, Charlie thought to herself. This is Susanne's absent husband. She'd had the feeling he worked in some kind of office, but he was apparently in fact a librarian.

'I'm not sure what I can do for you,' Isak said. 'But I certainly hope you find her soon. This ... disappearance has stirred up the whole area.'

'How well do you know Annabelle?' Charlie asked.

'Know? She's a student at the school, one of my most frequent borrowers, but I wouldn't say I know her. We've talked a bit about books for the book club she started.'

'So she did start a book club?' Charlie said.

'Yes,' Isak replied.

'Do you know who was in it?'

'Rebecka Gahm,' Isak said. 'Rebecka, William Stark and a few girls from the senior class, and sometimes he came to, the one who works at the motel, Jonas.'

'Jonas Landell.'

'Yes, isn't that his name?'

'So the book club wasn't just for students at the school?'

'No,' Isak said. 'I can see no reason to exclude somebody who wants to join in and read books simply because he's a few years older than his friends.'

'That's not what I meant,' Charlie said. 'It just strikes me as a bit unusual that a young man who has finished school joins a book club there.'

'Young men with an interest in literature do exist,' Isak said and smiled.

Sure, Charlie thought. But they would more likely be interested in the girls in the book club.

The bell on the lending counter dinged. It was the headteacher. Isak asked her to join them.

'Here's a list with names and personal identity numbers,' she said. 'Not just teachers, but all the school staff. Yes, you're on it too, Isak.' She smiled. 'You and the janitors, cleaners, well, everyone. The ones I circled are the ones who taught Annabelle,' she clarified as she handed the papers to Charlie. 'And about her absences. There was a slight uptick during the past five weeks, but it's not unusual for a lot of our students to feel a certain amount of school fatigue in the spring term.'

Charlie thanked her and stood up. 'We'll let you know if we need to speak with you again,' she said. 'And if either of you think of anything else concerning Annabelle, anything at all, call us straight away.'

On her way to the car park, Charlie went over the names of the school staff. Annabelle had three male teachers. Two of them were close to retirement, and one was in his forties. Her eyes continued down to the janitors and miscellaneous staff.

'Maybe you could wait to read that until we get to the car,' Anders said when she stumbled.

Back in the car, Charlie took a pen from her bag and marked the people who would be their first priorities.

'Kalle, the Swedish teacher, might be the most interesting prospect,' Charlie said. 'He's the youngest of her male teachers and he teaches a subject she's very interested in.' She pulled out her phone and called Adnan, asking him to contact Kalle immediately to set up an interview.

'And what do you think of the librarian?' Anders said and turned out from the school. 'He seems to have the same interests as Annabelle too.'

'I know his wife,' Charlie said. 'She's a childhood friend of mine.'

'Okay, but what do you think of him?'

'I don't think anything,' Charlie said. 'I'm just underlining his name. And then there's Jonas Landell,' she went on. 'What is he after, going to a school book club?'

'You heard what the librarian said. Young men with an interest in literature do exist.'

'So you don't think he was there for Annabelle, that he is in love with her too?'

'I don't know,' Anders replied, 'but when they talked to him it seemed like he spent quite a lot of time with her, that he was almost like her private chauffeur. He used to drive her around.'

'Drive her where?'

'Wherever she wanted to go, to friends' houses, from school sometimes, to the parties in the village shop.'

'But how did he describe their relationship, how he felt about her?'

'He said they were just good friends. After all, she'd been going out with William.'

'We still need to ask him about the book club.'

A few hours later, when they had all gathered at the station again, Adnan told them Rebecka had confirmed Jonas's information. Annabelle had been seeing someone. Rebecka had kept it to herself because she'd promised not to tell anybody and because she didn't want to drive Nora batty for no reason. At first, she'd thought Annabelle would come back and then she'd been scared they'd think she was lying if she told them after the fact. Besides, she didn't even know who it was. And either way, it was over. Annabelle had promised to tell her everything the night she disappeared, but it hadn't turned out that way. The only thing Rebecka knew was that he was older. Nor could she recall the nickname Annabelle had used for him once or twice. The best she could manage was that it started with an R and sounded English.

Micke had interviewed Kalle, the Swedish teacher. He had no substantial relationship with Annabelle. She was the most gifted student he had ever had, but they were not particularly close and had never interacted outside of school. Furthermore, he had a watertight alibi for the night in question since he had taken his mother, who had suffered a stroke, to A&E.

'Convincing enough for you?' Micke turned to Charlie and Anders.

'And the poem?' Charlie said and looked at Adnan.

'She didn't know who had written it on the wall,' Adnan said.

'She didn't recognise the handwriting but it's not Annabelle's. Why are you so hung up on this poem?'

'I'm not hung up,' Charlie said. 'But whoever wrote it ... I'm thinking that person might have deep feelings for Annabelle.'

'Why?' Adnan asked.

'Didn't you read it?' Charlie said.

'Yes.'

Charlie sighed and recited the second stanza:

I was a child and she was a child,
    In this kingdom by the sea,
But we loved with a love that was more than love –
    I and my Annabel Lee –
With a love that the wingèd seraphs of Heaven
    Coveted her and me.

Olof, Micke and Adnan stared at her in silence.

'Why did you learn it by heart?' Adnan said after a long pause.

'Words just tend to stick in my head, that's all. In any case, I think it's important to find out who wrote that on the wall.'

'I thought our current priority was finding an older lover,' Micke said, 'so surely we shouldn't be focusing on the people who hang out at the village shop parties?'

'It might not be one of the young people,' Charlie said. 'It might be someone Annabelle had secret rendezvous with there.'

'I'm having a hard time keeping up now,' Micke said.

'What's the problem?' Charlie said. 'Seriously, what's your problem?'

'What?' Micke feigned surprise. 'I'm just saying I'm having trouble keeping up.'

Not my problem, Charlie thought to herself.

'Besides, it doesn't sound like something an older person

would write,' Micke pressed on. 'What with both of them being children in the first lines.'

'Maybe we'd do better not to take it so literally,' Charlie suggested.

'And maybe we'd do better not to get bogged down brooding over some random words on a wall.' Micke glared at Charlie.

'How did it go at the school?' Olof said. 'Anything new?'

'Annabelle's been skipping lessons lately and they gave us a list of all the teachers and other staff at the school.' Charlie put the document on the table. 'I've marked the ones we need to speak to. The Swedish teacher is done already, but there are several others who will need to be interviewed as well. We're also going to try to find out if any of them use a pay-as-you-go phone. And we discovered that Annabelle ran a book club at the school, which both William Stark and Jonas Landell attended. I think we need to go one more round with Jonas about his relationship with Annabelle. Would you mind doing that?' She turned to Adnan.

'Sure, I'll talk to him right now.'

'By the way, did you find anyone to rescue the turtle?'

'Yes. It'll be in safe hands soon. But there's a risk it's been permanently damaged by the filthy water it was in,' Adnan said with a smile.

There and then

'One day,' Rosa says and points up at the house on the hill, 'one day, I'm going to burn that one down.'

'Why?'

'Because it ruins the view of the lake. It ruins the view of the lake and also I'm sick of seeing that stupid grin every time I want to go for a swim.'

And Benjamin ... what had he ever done to her?

He was a sissy, a teacher's pet, a nerd. Rosa almost wishes he was dead. And that whiny kid ... John-John, what kind of stupid name was that anyway? Wasn't one John enough?

'Want to go for a swim?'

'You're supposed to be careful,' Alice says, pointing at Rosa's head. She has a bandage around it from falling out of the tree house the day before. She's really supposed to be resting, the doctor said, because she probably has concussion too. But Rosa doesn't want to stay home. She says it's because of her mum, her mum wants to be alone.

'Maybe we should just dip our feet in,' Alice says.

But Rosa says dipping their feet isn't enough, because it's as warm as hell out. She gets up, runs out onto the jetty and dives in. When Alice get there, Rosa is nowhere to be seen. The ripples on the water subside, but no Rosa breaks the surface.

Alice's heart starts to beat faster. Then she spots Rosa's hair further out. She's floating face down, arms out; her bandage has come off her head. Alice jumps in. When she is just a few feet away, Rosa suddenly turns over.

'Did I scare you?' she says and laughs. 'Didn't you get it was a joke?'

But Alice doesn't laugh. Instead, she points to Rosa's head where blood is trickling from the taped-up wound and says she's bleeding again. Back on the beach, Alice wraps her towel around Rosa's head.

'I didn't actually scare you, did I?' Rosa says.

'Yes, you did. You scared me, staying under for so long.'

And Rosa says that's one of her talents, holding her breath for a long time. She's the kind of person who can get by on less air than most.

'Does that feel all right?' Alice says when she's done with the temporary bandage.

'It feels like nothing,' Rosa says. 'Feels like nothing at all.'

30

They left the car outside the station and walked the short distance through the town centre to the motel. They were going to have a late dinner and then catch a few hours of sleep.

'What are you doing?' Anders said when Charlie stopped and took her shoes off.

'I want to walk barefoot,' she replied. 'I never wore shoes as a child, not even in school. You might say I was a barefoot child, like in the poem.'

'I'm starting to understand you better,' Anders said. 'You're a dog person, a barefoot child ...'

'Who has lost my paper slip,' Charlie added, paraphrasing Nils Ferlin.

When they entered the pub part of the motel, Erik came to meet them. He was waving a key that he gave to Charlie.

'Good news,' he said. 'We have a free room, so you don't have to share.' Charlie noted the relief that spread across Anders's face.

They decided to head upstairs and sort out their rooms and then meet back in the restaurant afterwards.

'I'm glad that worked out so I don't have to get divorced,' Anders said as they walked up the stairs. 'I actually do think Maria was suspecting something.'

'Don't jealous people always suspect something.'

'She's not jealous. She's just a bit of a ... worryguts.'

Charlie laughed and said that was a delightful euphemism. She tossed her suitcase on the bed in her new room. It was upstairs from the wedding suite and had no Bible quotes about the power of love on its walls. She went over to the window and looked out across the meadows, forests, water, all the way to the church in the distance. Where are you? she thought. Where have you gone, Annabelle? Did anyone out there know?

The phone rang, cutting short her reverie.

'Is this the police?' The voice on the other end was thick with tears.

'It's me,' Charlie said.

'It's me, Sara, I need to talk to you.'

'Where are you?'

'Little Rhodes, I mean ... the beach at ...'

'I know where it is,' Charlie said. 'I'm on my way.'

She called Anders and told him there was something she had to take care of, could they meet in the restaurant in an hour instead?

'I'm going to die of starvation before then,' Anders said. 'What's this you're taking care of?'

'I'm going to see the girl I drove home yesterday. Sara Larsson.'

'How come?'

'Because she wants to talk to me.'

'I'll go with you.'

'No need.'

'You're not supposed to respond to calls on your own.'

'I'm going to see a sad teenage girl,' Charlie said, 'and I don't want to be mean, but I think it'll be easier if I go on my own.'

*

Little Rhodes was a public beach a mile or two outside town. It had few similarities with the beaches of the real Rhodes. Maybe the name had been intended as a joke once upon a time. Charlie took in the changing rooms, the jetty, the swings, the firepit. Sara was nowhere to be seen. It was only when she looked up at the diving tower further down the beach that she spotted her. The girl was perched on the edge of the highest platform. Charlie hurried over and climbed the ladders. Sara must have heard her but didn't turn around when she got there.

'Sara?' Charlie said behind her. 'Are you okay?'

Sara shook her head.

'Is it all right if I sit down?'

Sara nodded and moved aside to make room for Charlie.

'I remember it being a lot higher,' Charlie said.

'What do you mean, remember?' Sara looked at her.

'I used to live here. But then I moved away. I left when I was fourteen.'

'I'm going to leave too,' Sara said. 'This entire place can just … it can go to hell.'

'Did something happen?'

'Yes, it did, but my life's going to be hell if I tell you about it.'

'And yet you want to tell me,' Charlie said.

'Yeah. I figure it could hardly get much worse. My life is hell already.'

Charlie looked down at the water. The little eddies below them indicated that the current had been switched on. She wanted to say something encouraging to Sara. Something about how life can serve up all kinds of surprises, not just bad ones. She wanted to tell her there was help to be had, that things would get better, but she couldn't bring herself to do it.

'Can I smoke?' Sara asked.

'Why wouldn't you be able to?'

'I'm thirteen,' Sara reminded her. 'I'm not allowed to buy cigarettes.'

'True,' Charlie said, 'but smoking one isn't against the law, is it?'

Sara smiled.

'You're not like the others. You're ... all right.'

She pulled a packet of cigarettes from her purse.

'They're hand rolled,' she said when she noticed the look Charlie gave her. 'They're not the other kind of cigarette, if that's what you're thinking.' She held one out to Charlie.

They smoked in silence for a while.

'The inlet gates are open,' Sara said. She looked down at the water. 'If you were to jump in now, you'd be pulled under. There's really deep parts further out as well. You could disappear down one of those and never come up.'

'What's on your mind,' Charlie said. 'What did you want to tell me?'

Sara took a deep breath.

'That night,' she said, 'that night when Annabelle disappeared, we hadn't just been drinking. Svante had brought some other things as well. I think that's why we're having such a hard time remembering stuff; most of us were completely out of it. Svante told me I couldn't tell the police. He said we'd all get into trouble if I did, that my dad would get fired. My dad works in the factory, the plywood one, and he'd be absolutely broken if he lost another job. The last time he did ...' Sara pulled out a new cigarette and lit it. 'I thought he was going to drink himself to death for real.'

'The last time?' Charlie said. 'It's happened more than once?'

Sara told her it happened all the time. She handed Charlie another cigarette while she talked about all the other times her dad had been let go. He had worked in that damn factory since she was born and they still wouldn't give him a permanent position. It was something about machines that were supposed to be coming, which made the owners not want to hire the people on the floor.

'The machines,' Charlie said. 'They were talking about those machines back when I was your age. My mum worked there. Regardless, Svante can't just fire your dad for no reason. You know that, right?'

Sara said she did know, but that even so, she was still scared.

'Something horrible happened that night,' she said and flicked her glowing butt into the water. 'I ... I even filmed it.'

'What?' Charlie turned to her.

'You can see for yourself.' Sara pulled out her phone and pressed play. 'It's not the best quality, I mean, you can see the image fading in and out. I even forgot I'd done it. It was only today, when I was looking through my pictures, that I realised what I'd filmed. Luckily, I don't think anyone noticed.' She handed the phone to Charlie. 'You'll have to watch on your own. I can't bear to see it again.'

31

Nora had fallen asleep again. She was breathing so quietly Fredrik had to lean over her to make sure she was still alive. The floorboards creaked under him when he sneaked out into the hallway and down the stairs.

The past two nights, he had tortured himself watching video recordings of Annabelle. He had started with the shaky footage from her birth, the black-eyed, wrinkly bundle on Nora's chest. By now, he had reached her first birthday. Annabelle in a red dress with a clip in her hair. A few friends they were no longer in touch with around the table, the laughs when Annabelle shoved her chubby hands in the cake. Then there was a gap of a few years. Annabelle was on her bed with her hair spread out across her pillow, smiling.

What did you do today, sweetheart?

And the little girl's face that lit up.

Sweets!

Yes, you had some sweets. Were they tasty?

Deep nods.

But we're not going to tell Mummy.

No, no telling Mummy.

That was the end of the tape. Fredrik went to pour himself a large whisky before putting the next tape in the video camera, which was connected to the television. The case said Summer 2004. A close-up of a child's hand appeared on the screen.

It looks like a bird's eye, Daddy. Can you see it, that my hand looks like a bird?

Yes, sweetie, I see it. But weren't you going to go swimming? Wasn't I supposed to film you jumping off the jetty?

I'm cold. Can you warm me up.

Come here then.

The camera films the sand.

I love you, Daddy.

Fredrik hit stop, reversed and pressed play again. He did it over and over.

I love you, Daddy.

'Come home,' he whispered with tears streaming down his face. 'Just come home, sweetheart.'

That day

Nora was at the shops so Annabelle had had no trouble getting the blue dress from her closet. She had worn it that time when she went to Gold Island with Him. She had sat at the prow with her hand in the water, telling him the lake was bottomless. And he had laughed and told her that wasn't true, that everything had a bottom somewhere.

And then he had pulled the boat up and spread a blanket on the dry grass underneath the pine trees. He had brought crackers and wine. After drinking a glass, he'd wanted to go swimming.

She'd said she hadn't brought a swimming costume.

And he'd replied it didn't matter; he'd already seen her. Felt her.

As she undressed, she thought about how it was the first time she was naked in front of a man in broad daylight. All the fumbling in dark bathrooms, under duvets ... nothing was like this. He took his clothes off as well. For a long time, they just stood there, naked, looking at each other.

'Last one in,' she yelled and ran towards the lake. He caught up with her and they disappeared into the freezing water at the same time.

'Stop staring at me,' she told him when they got out.

'You stop. You're no better. How are you doing?' he added. 'Are you okay?'

'I'm so cold, I think I'm going to die.'

'I'll warm you up,' he'd said and taken her hand. 'Come with me.'

'What are you doing to me?' Annabelle had whispered. Lying on the blanket, she had no longer felt the cold. 'What are you doing?' she'd said again and looked up at the swaying pines above her.

'Do you want me to stop?' he'd asked.

She had shaken her head, grabbed his hair and asked for more.

'More.'

Annabelle studied herself in the full-length mirror. She picked up her phone. Nothing from him, of course. Just as well, she thought. It was over. Even so, she sent him the picture, the digital stick with the text *ten weeks pregnant*.

32

Olof had called an urgent meeting. Micke was dressed in a dated, oversized suit. He had been interrupted in the middle of a birthday dinner, he explained when Adnan ribbed him about his sartorial choices.

'Charlie has something we need to see,' Olof said, 'but I can't get the damn projector to work, so you're going to have to make do with the computer.'

They crowded around the screen.

'What is this?' Adnan said.

'A video clip,' Charlie said. 'From the village shop that night.'

'Where did you get this? Who filmed it?'

'Shut up and watch,' Charlie said. A picture appeared on the screen. The world was swaying in an unsteady hand. A punk song, 'Staten och Kapitalet' by Ebba Grön, was blasting in the background.

Three teenagers on a green plush sofa: William Stark, Svante Linder and Jonas Landell. They were passing around a pipe.

'Fuck, that's a good hit,' Svante shouted after a deep toke. 'This shit's outstanding!'

Then it cut to a turtle in a murky aquarium.

'Who's filming?' Adnan asked.

'Sara Larsson,' Olof replied, 'Svenka's daughter. What are you doing?' he added when Charlie pressed pause.

'Sara's Svenka's daughter?'

'Yes,' Olof replied. 'Why?'

'I just met him briefly yesterday,' Charlie said. She pressed play again.

Annabelle's face appeared in close-up, partly obscured by curly strands of hair. Her make-up was smeared and the straps of her blue dress had slipped off her shoulders. She was dancing, eyes closed, arms above her head. Charlie had always felt provoked when victims of crime were described as beautiful, but this girl's obvious beauty was difficult to disregard. Then, the kitchen, Annabelle with her hand on the table and the knife between her fingers. Neither she nor anyone else seemed to notice that she missed, that blood was dripping from her hand onto the table.

'Why wasn't this handed over to us before?' Micke exclaimed. 'How the fuck can that brat wait to show us something like this?'

'She didn't know she had it,' Charlie said. 'She still doesn't remember filming it. She discovered it today when she was deleting pictures on her phone.'

'And why didn't she come to us?' Micke demanded.

Charlie looked at him and said she didn't understand. Wasn't that exactly what she had done?

'We can talk about that later,' Olof said. 'At least now we know Annabelle was still at Vall's at eleven o'clock.' He pointed to the time-stamp at the top right corner of the mobile phone screen, 11.06 p.m., and then pressed pause.

'Didn't we already know that?' Micke said. 'The question is, what happened next?'

'That's what I'm about to show you,' Olof said. 'I just want to say a few words first. What happens next has to stay between us. Yes, it may seem a bit over the top, but it's important this doesn't get out. Does everyone understand me?'

When he pressed play again, the camera panned across an overgrown garden. A thick blanket of fog covered the tall grass.

'The land behind the village shop,' Olof said.

The hand holding the camera was even shakier now and laughter and shouting could be heard over the music.

Charlie steeled herself for the final scene. She had watched the film about ten times before showing it to Anders and Olof, but there was no getting used to images like these.

Sara took a tumble. A close-up of the grass followed. *Hi there, tiny fiddler guy.*

'Who is she talking to?' Adnan asked.

'The grasshopper,' Charlie said, pointing at the screen.

'How did you see that?' Adnan said, squinting.

The screen turned black for a few minutes and then curses were heard from Sara.

'She dropped her phone,' Charlie said. 'We'll see things again shortly.'

The world was upside down for a few seconds before a flowering apple tree appeared on the screen. And there, on the ground next to the trunk, was Annabelle. Her dress was pulled up over her protruding hip bones, someone was kneeling next to her, half turned away from the camera. Despite the distance, his face was clearly discernible when he looked up.

'Svante Linder,' Micke said. 'What the fuck!'

Adnan shushed him.

Svante leaned down over Annabelle. They watched her writhe under his hands, saw his swaying erection when he pulled his trousers and underwear off in one motion, saw him spit in his hand and rub saliva between her legs and then penetrate her. They could see Annabelle trying to turn over, and Svante pinning her wrists above her head and carrying on.

That day

Annabelle's hands shook when she put the phone down on the bed, screen down. She didn't want to know if he replied. What was he supposed to say? And what was the point of telling him about the child when it would all soon be over? Or maybe it wouldn't be?

She had never been particularly interested in children, but now she suddenly pictured herself with a warm, wriggly bundle in her arms. It didn't matter that her realistic side told her it was impossible, that a child would wreck everything she'd ever dreamt of. She knew how things had turned out for the people who'd had children at her age in Gullspång, the ones who had ended up single and were forced to work in the factory. Children could really make life a lot harder and life ... it was hard enough as it was. Besides, the foetus was probably damaged. The way she had been acting lately, it was a wonder anything could live inside her. But she was going to tell Rebecka tonight. And I'm going to say it like it is, she thought to herself. I'm going to tell her who the father is. I have no reason to protect him any more.

33

'This had better be important,' Svante Linder said as he took a seat across from Charlie in the interview room.

'A girl is missing,' Charlie said, 'it's important.' She could hardly look at Svante without seeing the image of him leaning over Annabelle, his coldness.

'So, what can I do for you?' he said self-importantly. He looked from Charlie to Anders and back.

'We've seen a video from the night Annabelle disappeared,' Anders said. Charlie concluded that what Sara had said must be true, that Svante hadn't noticed her filming, because now he looked genuinely uncomprehending.

'From the garden behind the village shop,' Charlie said. 'Someone filmed the whole thing.' She had a pleasant feeling of satisfaction when she detected a slight shift in Svante's face.

'Okay? And what does that have to do with me? Am I under suspicion of something?'

'What do you think?' Charlie said.

'To be honest, I've no idea what you're talking about right now.'

Charlie noted a popping vein on his forehead. 'Well, so say something, then,' Svante went on. He stood up suddenly.

'Sit down,' Anders said. 'Take a seat.'

Svante shook his head and sat back down.

Charlie shot Anders a look telling him not to ask any questions.

'I haven't kidnapped her,' Svante said at length. 'No one can have filmed that, because it didn't happen. Why are you looking at me so weirdly?'

'I'm just waiting,' Charlie said.

'For what?'

'The rest of the story.'

'I don't know what you mean.'

'So there's a video of you and Annabelle from the garden behind the village shop,' Charlie said. 'Does that clear things up for you?'

'Who the fuck was filming?' Svante said. He turned pale.

'That's neither here nor there. What matters is what you did to Annabelle.'

Svante leaned across the table.

'Just because I had sex with her, doesn't mean I ... Well, because I assume that's what you're talking about.'

'Had sex?' Charlie said. 'You call this having sex?' Her laptop was on and the clip cued up at the exact point where Svante grabbed Annabelle's wrists and held them over her head. She turned the screen so Svante could see.

'What's that got to do with anything?'

'Oh my God. Are you as dumb as you seem or is it an act?'

'I'm not dumb,' Svante said. 'Dumb's the last thing you could call me.'

'One of the problems with stupid people,' Charlie said, 'is that they rarely get just how stupid they are.'

'Is that what we're here to talk about. My IQ?'

'No. Definitely not. We're going to talk about how you raped a girl, a girl who disappeared that same night.'

'Rape?' Svante looked genuinely surprised. 'That wasn't rape. It's not like she said no.'

'She was in a helpless state; that counts as rape.'

'I don't think that's how she saw it. The parties in the village shop ... they're always pretty wild. People drink, fight and fuck. It looks worse than it is.'

Charlie pressed play again, zoomed in and played the part of the clip where Annabelle tried to resist.

'How does this look to you?'

'I'm not a rapist,' Svante said.

'If you have sex with a person in a helpless state, that's exactly what you are. And now I want you to tell me what you were doing on the night Annabelle disappeared. Aside from raping her, I mean.'

'You know I was still at the party when she left,' Svante said.

'You could have got rid of her quickly and then returned to the party.'

'But people saw her leave, and I was back by then! Why don't you go have a word with Jonte and the others?'

'Are they reliable?'

'What do you mean?'

'Maybe they want to protect you. Maybe you've already threatened them?'

'Why would I threaten them?'

'I've been told you're in the habit of doing that when things don't go your way, that you threaten your friends with making their parents unemployed.'

'Don't believe everything you hear,' Svante said.

'That's why I'm asking,' Charlie said. 'But,' she went on, 'I still believe what I can see with my own eyes.'

'Stop it,' Svante said when she hit play again. 'I get it.'

'Does it make you feel uncomfortable? I thought it was the

kind of thing that happened at these parties. The question is what you did with her afterwards.'

'Nothing. You have to believe me.'

'You lied about this,' Charlie said. 'Why wouldn't you be lying about the rest of the night as well?'

'I'm telling the truth now.'

'How generous of you.'

They were interrupted by someone shouting outside. Someone who was there to pick up his son.

'My dad,' Svante said. 'He's probably pretty pissed off at you right now.'

'That's nothing compared to what he's going to be with you later,' Charlie said and left the room.

There and then

And one day, Rosa tells her about the child, about the sister she would have had if that bastard of a man hadn't come to their house and punched her mum in the stomach, punched and kicked until the baby died and came out.

Alice doesn't say anything. She's waiting for Rosa to tell her it was a joke, that she's the most gullible person ever. But Rosa says nothing of the kind. She just pulls out the little box where she keeps her cigarettes, lights two and hands one to Alice. Then she starts talking about the blood.

'I've never seen so much blood in my life,' she says. 'I didn't think people had that much blood inside them.'

'How do you know it was a sister?' Alice says after a while.

Rosa said it was obvious. How else would she know? All her parts had been ready, nails, hair, eyebrows, everything. It had all been ready, even her lungs. But what difference did it make when she couldn't breathe with them? What difference did it make that she was perfect when she was dead? And then Rosa tells her about all the nines you had to dial to get an ambulance. It was like they never ended.

'When was this?' Alice asks.

'When I was seven,' Rosa replies. 'I had just turned seven.'

'And who was he?'

'Who?'
'The violent man?'
Rosa pulls hard on her cigarette.
'He was just some guy.'

34

It was just coming up to eleven when Charlie left the police station and started walking towards the motel. Anders was going to stay behind for a while to write the interview report. Svante, despite his father's vociferous protests, had been sent to the detention facility in Mariestad for further questioning in the morning. They had also decided to interview all the young people who had been at the village shop again. There was a risk they were withholding information, that Svante had manipulated or threatened them.

Her phone rang. That familiar *H* on the screen. Was it Hugo, or his wife? Charlie declined the call. A text popped up instantly. 'I have to talk to you. It's important.' It rang again. She figured she might as well accept it. To end things once and for all.

'Yes?' she said.

'Can you talk?' Hugo asked.

'I suppose the real question is, can you?'

'I really need to talk to you, Charlie.'

'Make it quick,' she said, 'we have a lot going on here.'

'How's it going?'

'Not great, but I'm sure you didn't call to talk about work.'

'No, I suppose not. Are you alone?'

'Yes.'

'Maybe you didn't get my message. It's Anna, she's ... been through my phone and she found our texts.'

'I know,' Charlie said. 'She called.'

'She called you?'

'Yes, she gave me a ring and called me all kinds of lovely names.'

'She's fucking insane,' Hugo said. 'She's saying she's going to leave me and ...'

Charlie felt like telling him that sounded more like good sense than insanity to her. She couldn't quite figure out why he was calling. What was he after? Did he want her to console him?

'I've told her it was just a fling,' Hugo went on, 'but she doesn't believe me.'

'Big shock,' Charlie failed to stop herself from replying. She thought about the contents of their texts. They were impossible to misinterpret. 'Hugo,' she said. 'Why are you calling me about this?'

'I don't know, I guess I figured you could talk to her, but now it turns out you already have.'

Neither of them spoke for a while.

'I thought you were tired of her?' Charlie said at length. 'Seems you get your wish if she does decide to leave you.'

'I'm not tired of her. I love my wife. I thought you'd figured that out by now.'

Charlie was surprised by how calm she sounded when she replied that that had not been her impression, but that she was sure she had just misunderstood the whole thing.

Hugo was apparently too upset to catch the sarcasm, because he just confirmed that she most certainly had. What they had ... it was just ... fleeting passion. He didn't want anyone but his wife.

'Well, that's lovely then,' Charlie said. 'I hope it works out for you.' Then she came pretty close to hurling her phone away, but instead she contented herself with just hanging up on him.

It felt like her brain was overheating with too much stimulus. Svante Linder's smug grin, the video of him and Annabelle running on a loop in her head, and on top of everything else, she was going to have to play the part of the other woman. Enough, she thought. She'd rather die than be in his wife's position; anything she'd ever felt for Hugo was gone. But if that was true, what was this thing throbbing inside her, if not jealousy? I don't want him to be happy, she thought. I'm a spiteful person, a bad person, but then she thought of the things people had done to seek revenge, all the things she had seen on the job, women's faces destroyed by acid, battered bodies in pits. There were always people who had it worse. The world was full of them.

That day

I have to stop thinking of it as a child, Annabelle thought. She stroked her still-flat stomach. She hadn't been able to keep herself from going on her phone to see what was happening with the foetus this week. Mostly to reassure herself that it was just a small clump of cells. But instead, she had read that the foetus was one to two inches long from head to bottom in week ten. When she measured it out between her thumb and forefinger, she felt that was worryingly big. And she didn't like the phrase *from head to bottom*. That meant there was something inside her that had a head and a bottom and looked nothing like the billowing water creature she had imagined. But it didn't have feelings, she told herself. The brain in that tiny head could hardly feel pain, or could it? She was too afraid to do a search on it, scared that would make her waver. She already felt more emotional than usual. No, she had to focus on tonight, had to try to feel like herself again.

She put her hair up and when she looked in the mirror it occurred to her that her mother's mourning gift, the small sparkling diamond earrings, would go really well with the dress. But where were they? She had only used them twice before, then her mum had caught her and hidden them someplace. Where could she have put them? Annabelle went into her parents' bedroom and rummaged through the shelves in the closet. Nothing. She pulled out a drawer in the bedside table, but found nothing but tissues and empty medicine packets. She sighed. Where to look next? Then it occurred to her she hadn't set foot in the attic since she ran into a mouse up there several years earlier. If her mum wanted to hide something from her, she would obviously put it in the attic. Like looking for a needle in a haystack, Annabelle thought when she opened the creaky attic door. The memory of the mouse made her shudder. Were the earrings really worth putting herself through this unpleasantness?

They were, she decided. Now that she'd made it up, she might as well look around. There was a thin layer of sawdust on the floor. It had fallen from the ceiling, her dad had explained once, some kind of animal had probably chewed its way into the roof ridge, he'd reckoned. Annabelle had been scared. She thought the house might be about to cave in on them, but her dad had reassured her, saying there was no danger at all. He would never allow a house to collapse on top of his family, would he? Now, the sawdust was helpful, she realised, because it showed the footprints leading in a straight line across the floor, in under the slanted roof on the south side, where boxes were lined up.

Annabelle pulled out the outermost one and opened it. Nothing but moth-eaten knitted jumpers. She sighed and pulled out the next box. It contained her old baby clothes. Floral dresses with frills. She was just about to push the box back into place when she noticed the small wooden chest. Annabelle was sure she'd never seen it before. She grabbed the wooden handle and pulled it out, only to discover it was locked. Was her mum so concerned about her earrings that she'd locked them up? She looked around the attic for something to break the lock with and soon found a rusty hammer. She took careful aim and then struck the lock as hard as she could. Mum's going to lose her rag, she thought to herself when the lock gave way after the second blow, but her curiosity was stronger than her fear of the consequences.

Annabelle opened the lid. She quickly pulled out a number of soft black notebooks, old newspaper clippings and letters. But the tiny box with the earrings was nowhere to be found. She read the headline on the topmost yellowed newspaper article. Then she read the whole article and then the next one, the hairs on her arms standing straight up. She had just opened one of the notebooks when she heard the familiar creaking of the front door.

35

'Is the kitchen still open?' Charlie asked when she entered the pub.

'No reason why not,' Erik replied, 'since I'm still here.'

She sat down at the only free table. The famous Gullspång salmon was on the menu tonight. Anders called and said he'd brought back pizza. He was going to eat it in his room and then go to sleep. It bothered Charlie that she replied she was going to finish her meal and then hit the hay; that she felt a need to explain this to him.

The folk singer was already on stage. He looked tired. Like almost everyone else in the pub, he had probably helped with the search all day. Now he was singing the county anthem, a beautiful tune known to everyone in the room.

Charlie was drinking a glass of wine when Johan from Missing People appeared.

'Long day?' he said and sat down without asking.

She nodded. A bloody long day.

'Did you hear the police arrested someone? A local hooligan, from what I hear.' Johan took a sip of his beer. 'I hope they solve it soon; it feels like this whole community is about to explode.'

Charlie said nothing.

'Want another one?' He pointed to her half-empty glass.

'I'd love a glass of white.'

Johan went to the bar. Charlie thought about the pills she'd taken. She really shouldn't drink more now. Just one more glass, she thought when Johan returned, one more glass, then I'm done.

Things were rowdy over at the bar. Charlie saw Svenka swaying against a younger woman. Given what had happened, he should be with his daughter. Where was Sara now? Was she alone? Charlie pulled out her phone and typed out a text saying she could call her anytime, for any reason.

No one else from the village shop posse was in the pub tonight. Charlie thought about Svante Linder. How uncomprehending he had been about what he had done to Annabelle. Clearly, he didn't think of himself as a rapist. What else was he capable of?

'Do you want to be left alone?' Johan asked.

'No,' Charlie said and realised it was true. She didn't want to be left alone.

The folk singer struck the familiar opening chord of 'The River'.

'He's good,' Johan said, nodding at the folk singer.

'Sure,' Charlie said. 'Maybe just a little bit too ... predictable. His song choices aren't exactly original.'

'Maybe that's what I like. The predictability.'

'If that's the case, we're pretty different; I prefer to be surprised.'

'Oh yeah?' Johan's eyes flashed.

Charlie looked at the stage again. The folk singer had reached the chorus and was now singing with his eyes closed.

Johan looked out across the room and said Gullspång really was a special place. He had never seen anything like it.

'Look around. Everyone's so ... I don't know what, but they're different, pretty direct and ...'

'I suppose it's the booze. Don't all people get like that when they drink too much?'

Yes, Johan agreed with that, but he'd never seen so many people drinking so much before.

'As you say, it's a high-pressure time too,' Charlie said. 'People are probably tired, scared, stressed.'

Johan said she was probably right. And wasn't that the essence of small-town charm, that people cared about each other.

One glass of wine turned into two and three. The tightness in Charlie's chest had subsided and Charlie knew if she had one more glass, air would start reaching the bottom of her lungs instead of getting stuck halfway like now. *Which is easier for you to say no to*, a lady from social services had asked Betty once, *the first or the second glass?*

Betty had laughed and said her problem was more likely that she had a hard time saying no at all.

Linda called out last orders. Johan looked at Charlie and asked if she wanted to stay a bit longer.

'If you like unpredictability,' he said with a smile, 'maybe you might want to ...'

To Charlie's mind, that seemed fairly predictable. But maybe it was just what she need right now. She thought: just one more time. It's for the thrill. I need the closeness, the blowout.

They left the dining room to the lines of the final song of the night, 'Hotel California', that place you can check out of any time but never leave.

Maybe it's no wonder, Charlie thought, that so many people confuse chance with destiny.

36

In her dream, Charlie was back in the house. Summer in Lyckebo, Betty in her floral-print reclining sunlounger in the untended garden. Charlie herself on her knees in the overgrown driveway, the thistles that refused to relinquish their hold on the ground. The cats around her feet.

You have to pull them up by the roots, honey, otherwise they just grow back.

And Charlie digs at the soil with her bare hands; the roots turn into fingers. They slither around her wrists like snakes and try to pull her down into the dark.

Loud knocking woke her.

She got up slowly and clasped her head as she staggered towards the door.

'Come on, open up properly so I can get in,' Anders said.

'What time is it?' was the first thing she could think of to say. She realised she must look terrible, but that it was too late now.

'Half eight. You were supposed to be at the station half an hour ago.'

'Did anything new happen?'

'Yeah, you might say,' Anders took out his phone and showed her a tabloid headline: *The video of missing Annabelle.*

'What the fuck,' Charlie said. 'Who the fuck leaked?'

'I have no idea, but the guy you brought back to your room last night wrote the article. He's a freelance journalist.'

A tornado was growing inside Charlie. Had Anders seen them? She turned hot and cold by turns. I'm going to die now, she thought. It's over.

'Anders,' she said and sat down on the bed. 'I didn't ...'

'Olof has been on the phone with Fredrik Roos since the news hit the internet. As you can imagine, her parents are wondering what the fuck this is about.'

'What have you told them?'

'That they shouldn't believe everything they read in the paper. At the moment, that's all we can do. That's why it was important that the video thing was kept under wraps.'

'I haven't said anything,' Charlie said. 'I swear. You have to know that I wouldn't ...'

'This one, Lager,' Anders said. 'I don't know how you're going to get out of this one.' He turned around and left.

Charlie wanted to run after him, to try to explain ... but what was there for her to explain. What had she told that arsehole of a journalist? They had talked, afterwards, but *what* had they talked about? No matter how hard she tried, she couldn't recall a single word. When she stood up, she felt light-headed. She had to lean against the wall to keep from falling over. She didn't make it to the bathroom before throwing up. And it was just too fucking typical, she thought, that the motel still had the same old carpets.

She had just finished gagging when her phone rang. It was Challe.

He asked how the case was going and Charlie could tell instantly that he knew everything.

'Anders told me,' Challe said. 'Now, there's no reason to be pissed off at him. There are limits, Charlie.'

'I didn't know. I ...'

'You've assured me you never drink on the job.'

'This was an exception,' Charlie whispered. 'It was ...'

'It was once too many.'

There was a long silence. Charlie saw her entire career washed away, all those years, all the extra hours to become the best; and all because of a drunken night, an idiotic journalist and ... because of her own poor judgement. I'm an idiot, she thought.

And then what she had expected: the news that she was suspended from the investigation and an offer to see a psychologist. It was for her own good, Challe said. She clearly couldn't work when she was on the brink of a breakdown.

Charlie sighed and thought to herself that Challe was clueless.

'I love my job.'

'I know that,' Challe said, 'but you need a rest. Rest and professional help and ...'

'I think I'm the best judge of what I need.'

'I don't. If you were, you wouldn't be making such terrible decisions.'

Challe went on to talk about how many people had been worried about her well-being recently, that he should never have assigned her to this case in the first place.

'Then why did you?'

'Because you're one of my best.'

Charlie hung up on him, lay down on the bed and cried.

That day

Annabelle quickly shoved a few newspaper clippings and one of the notebooks under her dress and tried, as quietly as possible, to get down the attic stairs.

Her mum had already started calling her from downstairs.

Annabelle just managed to slip into her room and put on a long cardigan that hid the dress before there was a knock on the door. As usual, her mum opened the door a millisecond later, without waiting for a *come in*.

'Is everything okay?' her mum's X-ray eyes scanned her.

'Yes.'

'You look ... upset.'

'I'm not.'

'All right.' Her mum stepped into her room. 'Do you have plans tonight?'

'I'm going over to Becka's. Or maybe watching a film with your best friend is forbidden now too?'

He mum said it wasn't, but that she didn't like being lied to.

Annabelle wanted to scream that she felt the same way about being controlled, but she didn't want to start a fight and get grounded, so she said she wouldn't be out late, that they really were just watching a film. And yes, it was just her and Becka.

'Twelve,' her mum said. 'You're going to be home by twelve

at the latest, and I don't mean ten past or half twelve, I mean twelve. Can you promise me that?'

'I promise,' Annabelle said, and couldn't help adding: 'And I won't stray from the path or talk to wolves, I'll go straight to Grandma's house.'

'Twelve o'clock,' her mum said and left.

Ten months, Annabelle thought. I have to stay here for another ten months, but then, I'll be free.

She pulled out the notebook and clippings. From the parts she had read, she sensed she was onto something important, something important and terrible. Why else would the articles, books and letters be hidden in a locked trunk? I'll read more when I get home tonight, she thought. But where to hide them until then? She didn't dare leave them in her room. The way her mum went through her things, she couldn't even keep a diary any more.

That was when she thought of the secret stash. Her mum would never find that. When the things were safely stowed away, she packed what she needed for the night in a small bag. She had hidden the booze on the way.

Her mum wasn't in the kitchen when she got down, nor in the living room or the study. Had she gone up to the bedroom? Annabelle walked over to the stairs.

'I'm leaving now,' she called.

'Why is the attic door open?' her mum shouted. 'Have you been in the attic, Annabelle?'

37

Charlie lay in bed for an hour, staring at the ceiling, incapable of getting up. Shower, she thought, I have to at least shower.

The hot water ran out after only a few minutes. She stayed under the jet, letting her body grow numb with the cold.

It's all Hugo's fault, she thought. If he hadn't called and stirred everything up, she wouldn't have drunk too much, wouldn't have brought the fucking journalist back to her room, wouldn't have … But then she realised she was acting like the least insightful category of perp, the weak kind that always blamed their crimes on others. Anders liked to tell them we all make our own decisions. She had never fully believed him.

'I just cleared away the breakfast buffet,' Erik said when Charlie entered the dining room. 'But if you want, I could fry you up some eggs and bacon.'

'I'm good, thanks.'

'Everything all right?'

Charlie nodded. She poured herself a coffee, walked over to a table and started flipping through the local paper. Naturally, it was full of the latest news about Annabelle, pictures of people searching through ditches, the unanswered questions. But it said nothing about the video. Charlie hoped they wouldn't publish a full spread on it the next day. Maybe the local journalists had stronger ethical backbones.

Anders came over and sat down across from her.

'I want to be alone,' Charlie said.

'And I would like to talk to you.'

'Shouldn't you be at the station?'

'As I just said, I would like to talk to you.'

Charlie wanted to ask: What exactly did you tell Challe? But then she realised she didn't want to know. She couldn't bear hearing about it, so she just said she was going to take some time off, rest up.

'Good,' Anders said. 'You need it.'

'I'm so glad everyone seems to know what I need,' Charlie said.

'Maybe you should be, since you don't seem to be getting it yourself.'

'As I said,' Charlie said without looking up from the paper, 'I want to be alone.'

'It's not to mess with you, if that's what you're thinking,' Anders said. 'What was I supposed to tell Challe when he called and asked how you were and I knew you had dragged a journalist back to your room in what was probably a drunken state? All right, there's no reason to look so reproachful. It's not my fault you woke me up, coming up the stairs and ... when I heard your voice, I obviously had to get up to see what was going on.'

'Great,' Charlie said, 'that's enough. How did you know he was a journalist anyway?'

'He tried to ask me some questions yesterday. You didn't know?'

'The bastard said he was with Missing People,' Charlie said. Why didn't you stop me, she wanted to ask. Why didn't you say something?

'You might have got away with it if it hadn't ended up in the paper.'

'And how can you be so sure I was the one who leaked it?'

'It does look that way, doesn't it?' Anders said. 'Either way, it might be a good thing it came out. Don't look at me like that,' he went on. 'You know I'm only looking out for ...'

'The investigation?' Charlie sipped her coffee; it burnt her tongue.

'You,' Anders said. 'I'm looking out for you, Charlie.'

'Thanks for your concern,' she said and stood up.

'Are you going back to Stockholm?'

'I don't know. I don't know anything any more.'

'Where are you going now, then?'

'Upstairs to pack my stuff.'

Charlie tossed the clothes strewn all about her room into her suitcase. Under a rumpled cardigan, she found the bag with Annabelle's library books. She put it in her suitcase, thinking she could stop by the town library before she ... Yes, what was she going to do now? She thought about her messy flat in Stockholm, the thirsty plants in the windows, the heat. What on earth was she going to do in Stockholm if they wouldn't let her work?

I can't go back there, she thought. Not today.

When she got down to reception, Anders was waiting on one of the sofas.

'I thought you had to work?' Charlie said.

'I figured I could give you a ride to the train station?'

'I'm not going to the train station,' Charlie said.

'Then where are you going?'

'To an old friend's house.'

'I'll drive you,' Anders offered.

Charlie was just about to say there was no need, but then she realised she couldn't possibly walk the three miles to Lyckebo with her suitcase in all that heat, so she accepted.

They said nothing in the car. Charlie wanted to talk about the case, about Svante who was detained, about the video, about whether new information had surfaced since last night, but she didn't dare risk having Anders remind her that she had been taken off the case, having him make it clear yet again that they were colleagues first and friends second.

She showed him where to turn off. The forest grew denser. The spruce branches reached far into the poorly paved road.

'Where are we going?' Anders asked.

'Home,' Charlie replied.

'Home?'

'In here.'

'Is that even a road?'

'Just drive.'

'I don't see a house,' Anders said when they reached the end of the narrow gravel road.

'It's further on,' Charlie said.

'Lyckebo,' Anders read on a white wooden sign that was sinking into the ground. 'Who's waiting for you at Lyckebo?'

'I don't know. That's what I don't know.'

'Is this where you lived?'

Charlie nodded. She opened the door and climbed out of the car.

'Oh, but surely you're not going to ...' Anders called after her. 'I don't know if it's such a good idea to ... I mean, for me to leave you here, alone in the middle of nowhere, when you ...'

She turned around, squinting at him in the sunshine.

'I don't care what you think.'

She'd just got through the first thicket of undergrowth when she heard him calling again.

'And how am I supposed to turn around?'

'I guess you'll have to reverse,' she shouted. 'Good thing you're such a fucking outstanding driver.'

Charlie was almost surprised the house was still standing. The garden was completely overgrown. It was as if the forest had rushed back in to reclaim the land.

Lyckebo. Betty had picked this house for three reasons. First, she loved the name. Second, it was in an ideal location, at a perfect distance from the town. Betty had never understood why people wanted to cram houses together and live cheek by jowl with neighbours they hadn't chosen. And then, there was the water. It was a dream, Betty felt, to live so close to water.

If you didn't know, it would have been hard to tell the house had once been red. The paint had started peeling pretty badly during their last years there, and Betty used to joke about how it would have been better if it were wood-coloured so you didn't have to worry about it.

Now, the facade was grey; green damp had spread along the edge of the foundation and thistles and nettles had completely overrun Betty's spot in the sun. The climbing roses, the ones Betty had loved, had spread and now covered the windows on the south side. The swing in the old oak tree was moving gently in the breeze.

There was a stabbing pain in the left side of her chest. Is this for real now? Charlie thought. Am I having a heart attack? Am I going to die when I'm this close? She had to sit down on a rock. She put her head between her knees and tried to just focus on breathing. Breathe in and out, she thought. In and out. It's just a regular panic attack. I'm not going to die. I'll survive.

When her breathing returned to normal again, she looked over at the cherry tree forest and could almost hear the music Betty had used to play.

There and then

They're in the tree house. During the day, the sun seeps in between the planks, but now only the faint light of the moon reaches them

'These are the rules,' Rosa says. She's sitting cross-legged on the floor of the tree house, warming the glass over the candle. 'You can't ask about death and if you come into contact with the devil, you have to smash the glass and burn the board. Got it?'

Alice looks down at the piece of brown cardboard with circles, numbers and letters and asks how you know if you've made contact with the devil.

'You can tell,' Rosa says. She points to the number six and says that if the glass ends up there three times, you can be sure he's got involved.

'How do you know it's a he?' Alice says.

And Rosa retorts that everyone knows the devil's a he. What else would he be.

'Are you scared?' she asks.

Alice shakes her head.

'Let's get cracking then.' Rosa puts the glass down on the board. It's all sooty and too hot to touch. 'You're supposed to only just touch it. The spirit will do the rest.' She picks up the glass and whispers something, then they both put their index finger on the sooty surface.

Alice's stomach flips when the glass slowly starts moving from letter to letter. They read each letter out loud: 'B-e-n-j-a-m-i-n.'

'What did you ask?' Alice wants to know.

'I asked who the stupidest person on our street is,' Rosa laughs. 'Your turn.'

Alice thinks to herself that she's going to ask about her mum, about her fingers. She wants to know if they're ever going to straighten out, if the pain will ever go away. But then she thinks about something she heard somewhere, something about how you shouldn't ask questions you already know the answer to. Rosa shoots her an impatient look so in the end she just whispers some nonsense words and puts the glass down.

'What did you ask about?' Rosa says when the spirit spells out s-o-o-n.

'I asked when we were going to become famous.'

Rosa finds the question ridiculous. She snatches the glass from Alice and whispers something short.

'Fuck,' she says when the glass flies through the letters, forming her name. 'Fucking shit.'

'What?'

'I asked which one of us is going to die first.'

'But we weren't supposed to ask about death!' Alice gets to her feet.

'What's the point if you can't ask about death?' Rosa says. She starts laughing.

Before they part, she looks Alice straight in the eye.

'There's no reason for you to be afraid,' she says. 'You're not the one dying first.'

38

The fence around what had once been a garden had given up and toppled over. Charlie looked at the moss-covered gateposts and it was as though she could see herself as a child. How she would sit on top of one of them, shouting out rules to the grown-ups at the party, all the things she knew you weren't supposed to do: not make fires when there was a draught, not let go of the handlebars, not give kids beer. She just wanted everyone to obey the rules. Betty liked to remind her who the adult was in their relationship. She, Betty, made the rules. *And if there's something I hate, honey, it's rules. It's like they're begging to be broken.*

And it didn't matter that Charlie told her that some things really weren't allowed. Betty just laughed and said she had the world's most precocious daughter. She didn't know any other little girls who were as old as her.

The curtains in the living room were still there and for a moment Charlie thought she could see Betty standing there behind the sheer white fabric, looking down on her.

An overzealous therapist had once asked Charlie to return to the house in her mind. *Let me come with you to Lyckebo, Charline. Close your eyes, take my hand and let's go inside.* And Charlie had brought her into the hallway and on towards the kitchen and parlour. She had even gone upstairs, but there, on the upstairs landing, her courage had failed her.

Describe what you see. Tell me what you see. But then Charlie had opened her eyes and said it was a sight she had no desire to relive. She didn't think putting words to her feelings would make them more manageable.

So how was she going to solve it, the therapist had wanted to know; how was she planning to confine it to the past and move on?

You have to accept, Charline, accept and forgive.

And Charlie had thought to herself that she would never be able. She would never forgive Betty.

Challe and Anders were probably right. She was a person who didn't know her own worth, who made bad decisions. It's just going to drive me insane if I go inside, she thought, yet even so, she picked up her suitcase and walked towards the door.

The pallets were stacked like steps in front of the side door. The notch from Betty's clog gaped at her like an open mouth in the wooden door. Hand on the handle. Locked, of course. What had she expected? Was there a key? She couldn't remember if she'd been given one. But it's my house, she thought as she walked around the corner and picked up a rock. It's my house so if I want to enter through a window, I will.

And then she was inside. In her dreams, her visits to the house were invariably like scenes from a horror film, but now, with the sunlight streaming in through the dirty windows and the familiar smell of wood greeting her, it didn't feel as ominous. Yet even so, she felt dizzy again, her head crackled. Charlie braced herself against both walls in the corridor leading in from the hallway.

Flies were buzzing around the kitchen. The table was set with cups and saucers, as though someone were expecting company. It made her think of the story of Goldilocks that Betty had used to tell her. It had always seemed unfair to Charlie that it was only the little bear's things that were eaten and broken. And Betty told her that's exactly what the world is like. Unfair.

She walked into the living room: the parlour as Betty had jokingly called it. *Come now, friends, let's enjoy a drink in the parlour.* She ran a finger through the dust on the black piano. Betty had played at every party.

Make a request, anything.

Climbing roses covered the window by the piano. They turned the light in the room a beautiful shade of green. Charlie thought that it was true what Betty used to say, that trees and plants didn't need pruning and trimming, that people should let things grow in peace. She looked over at the steep stairs leading up to the first floor. No, she wasn't ready to go up there yet.

The only family photograph in the house was sitting on top of the piano. Betty as a little girl and next to her, a beautiful young woman who was her mother. Charlie thought about all the fruitless attempts she had made to make Betty talk about her family, relatives, everything that had been before they ended up in Lyckebo. The only thing Charlie knew was that her grandmother's name had been Cecilia and that she, according to Betty, had been a wonderful person. Cecilia had been brave enough to go her own way, Betty would say, and if there was one thing she loved, it was people who went their own way. It was a family trait, something they should be proud of.

Charlie figured it might not be much to be proud of since going their own way seemed to have led them all to an early grave, seeing how everyone was dead. But death had nothing to do with making wrong decisions, Betty would tell her. They had simply been unlucky. That's just how life was. Unfair.

But we have each other, Charline. You and I don't need anyone else. We're strong together.

What about her dad then, was she never going to tell her who he was?

Betty had sighed and told her there had never been one. As she was well aware.

In the end, Charlie had contented herself with that. She had contented herself until Betty had let Mattias move in. Because if they were so fine on their own, just the two of them, then what did they need Mattias for?

Charlie went into the room behind the kitchen. The white wallpaper with roses had come loose in several places and thick layer of dust covered her old desk and bookcase. Outside, the rope from the first floor was still there, the one she and her brother were supposed to use to send letters to each other. Betty had said that's what she had always wished for, a sibling to share her secrets with.

Betty had thought she was a stick-in-the-mud when she tried to explain that people didn't become siblings just because their parents were together. Charlie realised she really needed a drink. What was the point of staying sober when you weren't allowed to work anyway? She opened the basement door and sent up a prayer that Betty's treasure trove would still be there.

A smell of soil and damp hit her when she walked down the stairs. The grimy little windows barely let any light in, so she had to feel her way until her eyes adjusted to the dark. It didn't take her long to find the door to the wine storage. Was it still drinkable? She was about to find out. Quickly, she snatched up two bottles and turned back up towards the light.

It took her a while to find a corkscrew. Everything was jumbled in the kitchen drawers. Betty had never seen the point of having a system for things. That was one of the issues the stubborn woman from social services would bring up with her, the importance of tidiness and order, regular hours and a clear structure. *If you want to keep the girl, Betty, you have to prove you're a grown-up and that you can be responsible.* That would induce Betty to shoot her an exaggerated smile and say that greatest of all is love, and then the social worker would sigh and say that the one did not preclude the other, that it all went hand in hand.

Is she going to take me? Charlie would always ask after she came by. *Is the mean lady taking me away?*

Over my dead body, Betty would say. *You're safe with me, Charline.*

But it was hard to feel safe with Betty. It wasn't because every drawer and shelf was untidy, that there was no structure and that Charlie was allowed to roam about freely. It was because of Betty's capricious mood, because of the unpredictability of what kind of day it was. Granted, there were days with singing and dancing in the cherry tree forest, days when they swam all the way out to the platform and played piano four-hands in the parlour. But there were also days when Betty couldn't get out of bed. When life revolved around shutting out all sounds and light. Days she just lay on the sofa, staring. And then, once she got back up again, the parties started. All the drunk people with guitars and confused German shepherds. Betty standing there on the front steps welcoming everybody. Why did every last weirdo in the world have to come to their house?

Because Betty wanted an open home, a home filled with song, laughter and music. Yes, life was too short to be bored. Surely Charline didn't begrudge her mother a bit of a fun now that she was finally happy again?

And it made no difference that Charlie said she didn't like it, that the drunk people scared her. Betty didn't understand what she was on about. She would never invite bad people to her home. *And if anyone so much as lays a finger on you ... if anyone even looks at you, then ... I'll protect you, my darling.*

But those nights when the parties went off the rails, when Betty fell asleep in the bathroom and couldn't protect her from anything at all, Charlie had wished the mean social services lady would come and take her away, take her away to a better place.

That evening

'There you are!' Rebecka exclaimed when Annabelle entered the living room. The TV was on and the sound was turned up so high she had to shout. 'What the fuck's wrong with you?'

Rebecka reached for the remote and turned the sound off.

'What?' Annabelle said.

'You look like you've seen a ghost.'

Maybe I have, Annabelle thought to herself. She looked into Rebecka's bleary eyes and realised there was no point talking to her about anything serious right now. That it would have to wait until the next day.

'I started early.' Rebecka raised her glass to her.

'I can see,' Annabelle replied. She looked at the coffee table, the overflowing ashtray, the alcohol, the Fanta. 'Where did you get the booze?'

'The drinks cabinet,' Rebecka said. 'You're going to owe me a life when my mum notices. I just don't get how you could mess it up with Svante. You do know I already paid, right? Three hundred kronor.'

'He's just going to give you the stuff later. Besides, I sorted it out anyway.' She held up her clinking bag so Rebecka could see it.

256

'Who did you buy it from?'

'Since when do I reveal my sources?'

Rebecka heaved a sigh and said all the secrecy was really getting on her nerves, really fucking getting on her nerves. They'd gone from telling each other everything to suddenly keeping everything secret. She didn't see the point of having a best friend if she was always fucking clamming up.

Annabelle started pulling the bottles out of the bag. Rebecka whistled when she saw the bottle of liquorice shots.

'Your source has been revealed,' she said and smiled.

'What are you watching anyway?' Annabelle sat down next to Rebecka on the sofa. Gruesome scenes were taking place on the muted screen in front of them, pictures of a big, bloated corpse.

'It's *Seven*. Mum recommended it. I asked her what the scariest film she ever saw was and she said this one. I've just watched the whole thing, but I just started over from the beginning. It's about the seven deadly sins. This fat guy, for instance, he's guilty of ...'

'Gluttony?' Annabelle interjected.

'Right. I forgot I was talking to the Bible expert. It's still really messed up that you've started hanging out in church. It's for him you're actually going, though, right? It's not for God, the old ladies or the Bible talk. Just tell me straight, Bella. You're hot for the priest, right?'

'Give it a rest,' Annabelle said, 'you already asked me that. Hannes would never ... don't forget he's a priest.'

'Priests are the worst,' Rebecka said. 'Priests, police officers and social workers. You can't trust people who do those things for a living. Do you swear it's not him?'

'I swear.'

'On the Bible?'

'On the Bible.'

'Then who is it? I've guessed, like, every single man in this whole bloody town.'

Annabelle kept her mouth shut and waited her out. Rebecka had trouble focusing on anything for long, particularly when she was drunk. She had planned to tell her tonight, about Him, the baby, everything, but now ... It would be catastrophic to say anything about it now.

'And it's going to be greed in a minute,' Rebecka said, nodding at the TV. 'Fuck, I'm going to have to go Christian too soon, because I'm guilty of every one of the deadly goddamn sins.'

'Who isn't?' Annabelle said. 'By the way, do you have cigarettes?'

'I'm out. Check Mum's stash in the cupboard above the fan. And grab a whole pack from the carton. That way, she won't notice.'

Annabelle went to get a packet of Prince and sat back down. She took a sip of the drink Rebecka had mixed for her from the booze she had brought. It tasted horrifically strong. After the second drink, she started feeling that familiar sensation of her arms growing heavier. She leaned back in the sofa.

'Just don't pass out now,' Rebecka said. 'It's going to be a hell of a party tonight. The whole gang's already there.'

'Who?'

'The usual crowd. William's coming too.'

'Well, isn't that swell,' Annabelle said.

'You're not upset, are you?'

Annabelle shook her head. No, she wasn't upset. She just didn't feel like seeing him. Not him and not Svante.

39

The corkscrew was in a spice box above the hob.

Charlie took a few deep swigs straight from the bottle. She had never been a connoisseur, and at least it didn't taste like vinegar. She went over to the counter by the kitchen window and looked out at the shed, remembering that Betty and Mattias had painted in there and started building a wall so the boy could have his own room when he arrived. But then Mattias had moved into the house instead, so the project had been left unfinished.

Why couldn't he have stayed in the shed?

Because, she had to understand, Betty loved him, they loved each other, and when people love each other, they want to live together. What was so strange about that?

What's strange about it, Charlie wanted to say, what's strange about it is that I'm not enough.

What's so wrong about Mattias? Betty wanted to know. She couldn't see what Charlie's objection to him was. He had never done anything to her, had he?

Charlie hadn't known what to say to that. He had never done anything to her, and yet she wished he had never come, that he would go away. Because everything got worse after he moved in with them: the parties, the drinking, the chaos. Was it so strange then that she hated him?

After a glass of wine, Charlie had made her mind up. She was going to stay here. She was going to do what that stubborn therapist had advocated: face her demons. Nothing else had worked, so what did she have to lose? She pulled out her phone, called Susanne and told her where she was.

'What are you doing there?'

'I couldn't keep staying at the motel. I've been put on sick leave.'

'How come?'

'I suppose it's because I'm ... sick.'

'Would you like me to come over?'

'Yes.'

'Do you need anything?'

'Yes, I need ...' Charlie looked around. 'I need cleaning supplies, sheets, water, a camping stove if you have one. I need, like, everything.'

Susanne arrived within the hour with two big Ikea bags.

'My God, it's overgrown,' she said. 'You'd have to cut it all back and get rid of the undergrowth and ...'

'It's not like I'm moving in permanently,' Charlie said. 'I was just thinking ... I mean, since I'm here anyway, I might as well check in on the house.'

'Sure. It really looks like it needs to be checked on, to put it mildly.'

They went inside and unpacked the things Susanne had brought. She started wiping down the cupboards and sighed when she realised the fridge wasn't working. How had Charlie planned to get by without a fridge?

Charlie told her they could put things in the basement, that it was pretty cold down there.

'Have you been upstairs?' Susanne asked.

'No.'

'Because we could go up there together and ...'

'Sorting out the downstairs will do for now.'

When they were done, they sat down at the kitchen table and Charlie poured Susanne a glass of wine.

'So, what's up?' Susanne said. 'What's really going on?'

'I've been having a tough time lately. It's been ... I've been drinking quite a bit.'

'Who hasn't?' Susanne lit a cigarette. 'Things never turn out the way you thought they would. Look at us, thinking we wouldn't ... that we wouldn't turn out like them, but the genetic inheritance or whatever it is. It's bloody hard to resist.'

'We're not like them,' Charlie said. 'We are not our parents.'

'I'm not far from, myself. I feel like I could very easily take that final step, if you know what I mean, and just let it all go.'

'But you haven't been suspended from work.'

'Probably only because I don't have a job,' Susanne said. 'If I had one, I would definitely have been suspended.'

Charlie had to laugh.

'Tell me,' Susanne said. 'What happened?'

So Charlie told her about her night with the journalist, that she must have leaked privileged information. She had no memory of doing it, but either way, her boss had had enough and suspended her.

'Is it about the video?' Susanne asked. 'I read about it online.'

Charlie nodded.

'So there is a video?'

'I can't comment on that. I've fucked up enough as it is.'

'It wasn't necessarily you who leaked though,' Susanne said. 'You know how people are, how they sniff out every last thing.'

Charlie nodded. She did know.

'But sometimes they sniff out the wrong thing,' she said. 'They may even muddy up the track.'

'And sometimes they sniff out the right thing,' Susanne said.

Charlie looked out of the window and said she wanted to go outside.

They brought their glasses and chairs and went out to sit in Betty's sun nook. They started talking about the parties. How many parties had actually been thrown at Lyckebo? A hundred? A thousand?

They laughed about the old man who had fallen down climbing on the gutter outside Betty's room, laughed about when they caught Susanne's dad with another woman in the shed. They talked about all the nights they had spent together in Charlie's single bed, how they had told each other whispered horror stories, about nails in coffin lids and ghosts in the woods, when all the time, the ghost were actually there, all around them, alive in the house.

'Should you really take the car?' Charlie said when a few hours later, Susanne cursed about how late it was.

'It's all back roads,' Susanne said. 'And the police are busy with other things, obviously.' But fuck, time had got away from her. Isak was going to kill her. She had promised to make dinner, clean the house and ... yeah, fuck, she'd promised a lot of things. On the other hand, she continued as she stood up, Isak had promised a thing or two as well, like being faithful to her.

'Is he ...?'

'Yes,' Susanne said. 'My husband's an adulterous shit. I have no idea why I ever got married in the first place.'

'I suppose maybe you don't know those things before they happen,' Charlie said.

Susanne laughed and said she could hardly blame ignorance. She knew what most men were like, after all, so she should have figured out that the likelihood of her, of all people, finding a normal person among the swine was marginal.

'Why don't you leave him?' Charlie said.

'The usual reasons,' Susanne said. 'The kids, too tired, no sense it would improve things. Money.'

'What is this, the nineteenth century?'

'For some of us, yeah. Some of us have no choice.'

For a split second, Charlie was about to parrot Anders's stupid line about how everyone has a choice. Had his view of things affected her after all? Maybe sometimes there was a choice, she thought, but usually chance, fate or whatever it was stood in the way.

There and then

Rosa says you have to do what the spirit tells you to.

Or else?

Or else one of them will die, and she doesn't want that, does she?

Alice says she doesn't want to die. Her mum and dad would be sad if she died.

'What dad?' Rosa says. 'You've never had a dad, have you, Allie?'

And Alice says she does have a dad, one who's sailing the high seas, and Rosa laughs and says Alice should give up her Pippi Longstocking fantasies and face the truth: Her dad left. He doesn't love her. *No one loves you like I do, Allie.*

40

Charlie stayed outside after Susanne left. She leaned back and closed her eyes in the warm afternoon sun. She must have dozed off but was woken up by something touching her bare legs. Her first thought was that it was a badger, an animal she was inexplicably mortally afraid of; but before she could scream or kick she realised it was a cat. It looked just like a skinnier version of the albino they'd had once, the same snow-white fur and light blue eyes. How long did cats live for?

No, she thought to herself as she sat down and called to the animal. That cat had been old back then. Betty had even used to joke about it, that she had the world's oldest cat – the world's oldest cat and the world's oldest daughter. But it might be one of the albino cat's offspring. Charlie stroked its back, which was lumpy with wounds and scars. One of its ears was jagged and floppy. At first, it seemed suspicious of her touch, but it soon gave in, lay down, rolled over and started to purr.

'Have you been in a fight?' Charlie whispered. 'Who hurt you so badly? Are you hungry?' She went down to the basement, fetched one of the milk cartons Susanne had brought and poured some into a newly washed saucer. The cat was still there when she came back. It greedily started lapping up the milk. Its ribs were clearly visible under its fur. This was a cat that had probably never been dewormed. Betty had never bothered with deworming, spaying or euthanising. She felt life should run its course.

It was past seven, but the heat was still oppressive. Charlie hadn't been down to the lake since the summer she turned thirteen, but now she realised she wanted to go there. Physical memory was a peculiar thing, she mused as she walked the path towards the water; her feet remembered every root and stone. How many times must she have walked this way with Betty, all those evening swims from early June to the end of August?

The lake was like a mirror. Charlie stopped. She had forgotten how beautiful it was. Steam was rising from the water. A gull shrieked, everything was sparkling. She continued onto the jetty. Some of the boards were rotten. She carefully made her way to the end before sitting down and gazing into the dark water.

If you dive down too far, Betty had told her once when Charlie had wanted to show her how long she could stay under, *if you dive down too far, the cold can warp your thoughts so you think down is up and up is down, and you don't realise you're on your way to the bottom until it's too late.*

Charlie dangled her feet in the water, closed her eyes and let the memories wash over her.

It was midsummer. Betty had started drinking early. She had put together a small maypole and insisted that everyone had to dance around it. *Is it Midsummer's Eve or isn't it? What is this group of bores I've invited to my home?*

Susanne and Charlie had tired of staggering around with the grown-ups. They were sitting in Betty's room, smoking and looking down at the idiots wandering about on the lawn.

I feel like we're the only adults around here, Charlie.

There was a fight. Betty was crying over something, pushing

away anyone who came near her to try to console her. It was her party and she'd cry if she wanted to. After midnight, all the guests had left, but Betty carried on shouting and making a racket. She yelled at Mattias that he was a coward, a wimp, and Mattias roared back that he was no knight in shining armour come to save her on his steed, if that's what she was thinking.

Because the truth is, Betty Lager, that no one can save you.

Betty had lunged at him and started punching him in the chest. She wanted to know why he was staying with her if that was the case, if she was beyond salvation. What the fuck was he doing in her house? Why didn't he just fuck right off?

Charlie had escaped to the lake. She had sat down on the jetty and waited for the sun to come up, for a new day to arrive. But then Mattias had appeared. He didn't see her, just staggered straight down to the beach further on, pushed the old rowing boat into the water and waded out a bit before crawling into the boat and starting to pull on the oars. It looked precarious and Charlie thought she should call out for him to turn around, to sit still, that the lake got deep quickly, but she didn't. And then everything happened so quickly. She saw him stand up, stand there for a while before falling overboard and disappearing into the blackness.

And what had she done? Had she swum out to him with the lifebuoy? No.

Had she run up to the house, fetched Betty and called emergency services? No, not that either.

She had just sat there on the jetty, watching the surface of the water grow still again while a strange serenity spread through her.

'What was he even going out on the lake for?' Charlie said to Betty when the police started dragging the lake for Mattias.

But Betty had just screamed she didn't know. How was she supposed to know? He must have ... wanted to row to somewhere. What did it matter why he'd done it? How could she be so calm when Mattias was missing? Mattias was missing!

'He'd just been told his son was going to be allowed to come,' Betty said after she found out the police had stopped searching. They can't stop looking, what's going to happen to the boy?

Maybe he hadn't gone out on the lake after all, she ventured. And Charlie pointed out the obvious, his cardigan in the boat, how everything pointed to ...

Then why hadn't they bloody well found him?

Charlie had had to remind her about the chasm in Lake Skagern again and again. And Betty had cried and said it was all so unfair. They'd had it so good together. And Mattias had been so happy about his little boy.

Charlie had retorted that if he'd really been so happy, maybe he shouldn't have gone out on the lake when he was drunk as a skunk.

'Who the fuck said anything about him being happy?' Betty had snapped. 'I said he was happy about his boy, but in other ways ...' And either way, the drunkenness had had nothing to do with it, it was the swimming. Mattias didn't know how to swim.

Then, afterwards ... it was as if Betty had forgotten that she had a job, or a daughter. All she did was lie in bed, staring at the ceiling.

It's as if everything's coming back.

What, Mummy? What's coming back?

Everything. Everything comes back.

Betty went over and over how it had happened, maybe he'd been afraid, in pain. And it didn't matter that Charlie had tried to comfort her with her own words, that drowning was the best way to go, because Betty had said that actually, they had no way of knowing that, and either way, she didn't give a toss, because she wanted Mattias here with her. Without him, she was like a flapping piece of tissue in the wind; without him, there was no telling where she'd flutter off to. She no longer had anything tying her down.

Charlie thought about the sofa on which Betty had spent most of her time during her last year. How she would lie there shivering even though it was warm and complain about the light seeping in through the gaps between the blankets she'd hung across the windows. *It's the light, honey. We have to shut out all this light.*

Betty kept a bottle of whisky on the coffee table and all her pills. At night, she'd wander about the house like a restless spirit. Sometimes, Charlie woke up with her pale face hovering over her. And yet when social services were standing on the pallets outside the door, asking to come in, Charlie said there was no need, that her mum needed to rest. Everything would be okay if she just had a chance to rest.

But it made no difference how much Betty slept, how much Charlie talked in whispers and covered light sources; weeks went by, the holidays were over, but Betty stayed on the sofa. Her hair got so knotted Charlie thought they would never be able to comb it out again. School started, the leaves turned brown, but Betty stayed where she was. Charlie started going home with Susanne after school; they went to the village shop together, any day of the week. It was as if the partying was the one thing that gave Charlie the strength to look at Betty at all, to force some food down her, to keep hoping she'd come home one day and find her in the kitchen. She'd be standing by the hob, smoking with the phone pressed to her ear, inviting people over for a party. But there never was another party at Lyckebo.

*

Now, Charlie thought. This is when I go upstairs, to Betty's room. She downed another half-glass of wine and told herself it wasn't going to kill her, and if it did, maybe that was fate or whatever. The circle would be complete.

She walked up the steep steps, crossed the landing, opened the creaky white door to Betty's bedroom and crossed the high threshold. Then she paused for a moment. Her knees were shaking, then she got a grip on herself and went straight over to the window and drew back the curtains. The evening light streamed into the room.

She looked over at the bed. It was made. Who had got rid of the vomit-stained sheets and put on clean ones?

Charlie looked at the clothes rail with Betty's clothes. Her favourite red dress was there, dusty and tired next to old fur coats. She walked over and buried her face in one of the coats to catch Betty's unique smell, but it just smelled old. Then she turned to the dressing table. Memories rushed past like a slide show. Betty slumped across the table with her arms dangling at her sides. The buzzing of flies. Charlie had known instantly. Yet even so, she had rushed in, knocked Betty off her chair and tried to arrange her limp body in the recovery position. Betty was already cold, but Charlie had still slapped her face and tried to breathe life into her. She didn't know how long she had kept it up. A minute? An hour? In her next memory, she was in the forest, undergrowth was tearing at her face, but she didn't feel any pain. She didn't feel anything at all.

An accident, they told her later. Betty must have made a mistake with her dosage. The sleeping pills in combination with the alcohol – it had been too much for her body.

Charlie pulled out the white chair and sat down at the dressing table. It had been Betty's most cherished possession because it had belonged to her mother, grandmother and ... Charlie didn't know how far back it went. How many times had she stood next to Betty when she prepared for a party, admiring the way she brushed out her thick, dark hair, put on perfume and red lipstick. Sometimes, Charlie would lean forward with her lips puckered and Betty had painted them a light shade of pink and then she had tilted her head and said it was just nuts how dashing she looked. In the top drawer was a powder brush, an old mascara and a dried-up bottle of nail polish. In the other was a small jewellery box. Charlie couldn't recall ever seeing it before. When she opened the lid, a dancing ballerina with a tattered tulle skirt popped up. She pulled out the tiny drawers inside the box. They contained plastic rings, a few brooches, something that looked like a swimming badge and furthest down, under all of that, was ... Charlie held up the small necklace with the red stone. She certainly was no jewellery expert, but something about it made it look expensive. The chain was too short to be worn around the neck. She wrapped it twice around her wrist and studied the red stone. It wasn't until she was putting the rest of the jewellery back that she noticed the photograph at the bottom of the box. A girl of about thirteen with a pale, serious face. It wasn't Betty, that much Charlie knew. But who was it and why did she look so familiar?

That evening

They staggered down the road with arms linked. Rebecka started to sing: 'I've been a wild rower for many a year.'

'Rower!' Annabelle laughed so hard she had to stop. 'Did you say rower?'

'Yeah, isn't that how it goes?'

'I've been a wild *rover*,' Annabelle said.

Rebecka thought her version was better. It gave her a fun mental image of it, of a drunk crazy person rowing about in a boat.

I've been a wild rower for many a year, and I've spent all my money on whiskey and beer.

Annabelle told her to be quiet. She wanted to sing something more serious.

'Like what?' Rebecka said.

Maybe that song they'd sung at the end of year ceremony in school.

'What fucking ceremony?'

Annabelle reminding her that they'd only ever sung together at one end-of-year ceremony, in year ten, had done nothing to help. Rebecka laughed and said she had no memory of that. It felt like so long ago. But she remembered the song: 'That's What Friends Are For'.

The lyrics were banal, but even so, they made Annabelle feel mournful. Before they knew it, it wouldn't be her and Rebecka any more. A few years ago, they'd made a promise, that they would never, ever part. How many girls had promised each other that? Annabelle thought now. And how many had kept their promise?

When they got to the chorus, they started belting it out.

Rebecka suddenly stopped dead.

'What?' Annabelle said. 'What are you doing?'

'I heard something.' Rebecka peered into the woods. 'Didn't you hear that?'

Annabelle shook her head. How could she have heard anything when they were singing at the top of their lungs? But Rebecka was sure; she'd heard a sound in the forest. What the fuck could it be?

Annabelle told her the forest was full of animals. And Rebecka retorted that they'd better hope so, they'd better hope it had been an animal.

'What else would it be?' Annabelle nudged her. 'You always get so damn paranoid when you drink.'

'And you get too damn relaxed. Never mind then, but don't blame me if some fucking lunatic comes at us from behind.'

'You really shouldn't watch so many horror films, Becka.'

41

Charlie was lying on the bed in her old room, studying the wood grain in the ceiling. She remembered having seen shapes there as a little girl, but now all she could see was ... wood. She heard the faint patter of mouse feet from the floor above. Her thoughts wandered up to the attic. As a child, she had used to imagine the sounds in the house came from the ghost of the man who had lived at Lyckebo before them. He had hanged himself in the attic. Betty had told her that as a lovely little bedtime story one night. Yes, and of course it was sad and all those things, but one person's loss is another's gain, because if that man had gone and killed himself somewhere else, she would never have been able to afford the house, because, well, of course, the price had to go down when everyone in town knew what had happened there. Charlie thought about all the subsequent tragedies that had taken place at Lyckebo. The house would be incredibly hard to sell, she realised now. Her only hope was probably finding a buyer from Germany or Norway. With the house's proximity to the lake, garden and forest, maybe that wouldn't prove impossible.

She didn't feel like reading any of the books she'd brought from Stockholm and was just about to start looking for a young adult book on her shelves when she remembered Annabelle's library books. She still hadn't returned them. She got up and fetched the bag from her suitcase. The top book was *Jane Eyre*. Charlie had read it, but it was a lifetime ago. Maybe she needed a contrast to all the dark violence she'd been ploughing through lately. But this one wasn't from the library, she realised, because there was no barcode on the back and someone had written a message on the flyleaf.

I hope you'll like it as much as I do.
Rochester

Charlie fetched her phone and called Anders.

'Rochester,' she said when he picked up.

'Come again?'

'Annabelle calls him Rochester. That's the nickname that starts with an R and sounds English. Rochester is the married man who has a relationship with the governess in *Jane Eyre*. The one who has a crazy wife in the attic. Has Annabelle been babysitting for anyone? Have we missed her having a baby-sitting gig?'

'I reckon we would have heard about that by now,' Anders said. 'Besides, we're not focusing as much on this potential lover any more. I mean, I'm sure you understand why.'

'Has Svante confessed to anything?'

'You know I'm not supposed to talk to you about this.'

'But since you already are, has he confessed to anything?'

'Nothing, he won't even confess to the rape. Which actually only proves that he's capable of lying. But he's a hard nut to crack. And according to his friends he stayed at Vall's all night, until dawn.'

'Friends who wouldn't dare say otherwise,' Charlie said.

'Exactly. We're trying to find a contradiction in his story, but without further evidence, without a body or even an explicit motive, it's not easy.'

'Do look into whether she babysat for anyone, though,' Charlie said. 'Do it anyway. Ask the priest, all the men around here who have children.'

'Charlie,' Anders said. 'I'm grateful for all your help, but the idea is for you to not participate in the investigation, for you to rest and …'

'I can't just switch off from one day to the next, can I?' Charlie coughed. She was close to tears again, but she didn't want Anders to know how devastated she was. 'You need me,' she said more quietly. 'I can rest when we've found her.'

'No. You need to listen to Challe now.'

Charlie took a deep breath and said she was. She let her silent tears drip down onto her T-shirt.

'Maybe you're too personally involved in this?' Anders said. 'Maybe it's hard for you to keep it at arm's length because … well, because you grew up here.'

Maybe that's an advantage, Charlie wanted to counter, but she knew her voice would break if she did.

'I think,' Anders went on. But Charlie never found out what he thought, because before he could say another word, she had hung up.

42

Charlie was woken up at five by birdsong and sunshine. She was sweating even though she had kicked her cover off. She had had a dream about Annabelle. The two of them had been walking along the gravel road behind the village shop. They'd walked in silence, hand in hand. And then someone had called them. When they turned around, Charlie had seen a small barefoot girl in a white nightgown. The girl moved quickly towards them. She had appeared to age as she approached; first, she turned into a young woman, then a middle-aged one, and when she reached them, she was a skeletal, white-haired old lady. And yet, there was no doubt that she was Betty.

You'll never be a dancer, Charline, she said and smiled. *Anything but a dancer, sweetheart.*

Then Betty had grabbed Annabelle's wrist and started walking.

I have a garden full of cherries, Charlie heard her say. *It's almost like paradise out there. I got it cheap. One person's loss is another's gain, as they say.*

Charlie had been unable to scream or run after them. All she could do was stand there, watching as Betty and Annabelle disappeared over the horizon.

*

She had been so close to something in her dream. She tried to go back to sleep, but it was impossible. At seven, she got up and poured a large glass of water from the jug Susanne had brought. The sun was already warm. Another day of sizzling heat.

She would stay away from the investigation; she had promised herself that after speaking to Anders yesterday. Challe was already angry with her; she should dedicate herself to showing that she knew how to obey orders and wasn't mentally unstable. But it was going to be impossible, she realised now, impossible to quit the investigation just like that. Annabelle was still missing and Charlie was one of the people who had come to find her, and this mishap with the journalist ... it didn't render her incapable of finding the girl. She was feeling increasingly sure she hadn't said anything about the video. Why would she have? Granted, she had a way of making a fool of herself when she'd been drinking, but leaking privileged information about a case? She would never do that; that much she knew about herself. After drinking her coffee, she went inside to fetch *Jane Eyre*. Surely no one could object to her giving Annabelle's book back to her parents?

Betty's red Monark bicycle was where it had been left under the eaves of the woodshed. The pump was attached to the frame. Charlie pumped the tyres and checked the brakes.

It was downhill all the way to Nora and Fredrik's, but even so, sweat was streaming down her back by the time she arrived. She leaned the bike against the fence and started walking up towards the house. The lawnmower hadn't moved.

Fredrik opened the door.

'Has something happened?' he said.

Charlie said nothing had.

'What do you want?' said Nora, who suddenly materialised behind her husband. 'What now?'

'I just have a few questions about a book. Nothing major has happened.'

'And we're supposed to believe that?' Nora gave her a look full of scepticism. 'Given what the newspapers have been writing. But I assume you have nothing to tell us about that video either?'

'Don't believe everything you read in the paper.'

'Who am I supposed to believe then? Why won't you tell us anything?'

'I'm on sick leave,' Charlie said. 'I'm no longer working on the case.'

'Then why are you here?' Nora gave her a vacant look. 'Why have you come here, talking nonsense about some book.'

'I just wanted to return it.' Charlie gave Nora *Jane Eyre*. 'You asked us to return the books to the library,' she said, addressing Fredrik, 'but this must be Annabelle's own. I thought you might know who gave it to her. There's a message in it.'

Nora stared at her without speaking.

'Is everything okay?' Charlie asked.

'Where did you find that?' Nora pointed to the red stone on the bracelet around Charlie's wrist.

'This? It was my mother's.'

'And who is your mother?'

What's it to you? Charlie wanted to say. She had no desire to tell Nora anything about herself. Even so, she told them straight, that she was Betty Lager's daughter.

Nora was still staring at her.

'Is there something ...'

'Leave,' Nora said. 'Leave now.'

'I think it would be best if you left now,' Fredrik said.

'But ...' was all Charlie managed, because Nora took a step forward and shoved her in the chest.

'What are you doing, Nora?' Fredrik grabbed his wife's shoulders.

'I want her out of here,' Nora said, pointing at Charlie.

'What's the matter with you?' Fredrik tried to pin down Nora's wildly flailing arms.

'Get out of here!' Nora screamed. 'I don't want you here, Charline.'

There and then

It starts with the loudly meowing cat. The spirit says: Silence it for good.

'There's only one way to take that,' Rosa says gravely. And then they head outside to look for it. The shouty ginger tabby is never hard to find. Rosa squats down and calls to it. The cat runs over and rubs herself against her legs. Rosa picks her up and they walk over to the brimming water barrel under the gutter in the back garden.

'Now you just grab her and hold her tight,' Rosa says and holds the meowing animal out to Alice. 'Just push her down.'

Alice shakes her head. She can't do it, not to an innocent animal.

But Rosa says it's not about the cat, it's about an order from the spirit; that if she doesn't do it, something horrible will happen to them, and she doesn't want that, does she?

Alice wants to tell Rosa that she doesn't believe in spirits, that she's not going to drown a cat, no matter what Rosa says. But instead, she pushes the clawing, hissing animal down into the water, looks into the yellow, petrified eyes staring up at her.

It's impossible. She can't do it. The cat gasps for air when she lifts it back out. It looks so tiny and sad with its fur clinging to its body. But it's not trying to scratch any more, it's not struggling. It's just breathing fitfully with its eyes closed.

'I can't,' Alice whispers.

'Then I guess I have to do it myself,' Rosa says and snatches the cat from her hands. It's still not resisting, just hangs there like a wet rag. A faint meow is heard before Rosa pushes it back down into the water.

Alice turns around and claps her hands to her ears. She feels like she can't breathe. It's as if she's the one who's drowning.

Afterwards, they bury the cat in Larsson's field. The cows watch them wide-eyed when they come carrying the wet bundle.

'Don't be upset, Alice,' Rosa says. 'Don't you know drowning's the best way to go? Just ask your dad. All sailors know it's the best way to die. But next time,' Rosa says as they walk away from the cat grave, 'next time, you won't let me down. Because you know I'd do anything for you, right?'

And Alice nods. She knows.

'Because if you do, we can't be friends,' Rosa goes on, wiping her dirty hands on the dry grass. 'You have to be prepared to do anything for your friends. Never forget who saved you.'

A few weeks later, Alice's mum tells her their neighbour found four abandoned kittens with the same coat as that ginger tabby who always meowed so loudly. They were brand new, she says, their eyes were still closed. The ginger tabby must have been run over because no mother would ever leave her babies like that.

Alice can't sleep that night. She thinks about the abandoned kittens whose eyes will never open, thinks about the sticky little bodies, hears them whimper with hunger, sees their mouths trying to find something to suckle.

Alice doesn't want to contact the spirits any more. She tells Rosa.

Why?

Because of that thing with the devil. How can they know it's not the devil moving the glass?

Rosa says you just know. And if she were Alice, she would obey the spirit. Because she thinks it might be because Alice is disobedient that her mum never gets better.

Later on, a young police officer will give Alice a very level stare and ask her if she believes in spirits. *Do you believe in spirits, Alice?*

And Alice will look down at the table and say she doesn't believe in anything any more.

43

Charlie's hands were shaking when she got back on her bike. What had got into Nora? Why had she reacted so strongly to the necklace, to her being Betty's daughter. Charline, she had called her. No one other than Betty and her elementary school teacher had ever called her that. She must have known me as a child, Charlie thought. She's someone who was there that I've forgotten. But what was her problem with Betty? Considering her reaction, it was not trivial. That much was clear.

Charlie had to talk to someone who knew this community. She stopped and pulled up Susanne's number on her phone. Ten minutes later, she rode into her driveway. All the boys were home, Susanne had warned her, and Isak was out jogging, so they wouldn't get a moment's peace. Charlie could hear their loud voices long before she got to the front door.

No one came to the door when she knocked, so she entered. The dachshund greeted her in the hallway. She petted it for a while, waiting for someone to come, but when no one did, she took her shoes off and went into the kitchen. Susanne was standing by the counter, leaning her head against the cabinet above it. She didn't turn around until Charlie had almost reached her.

'I didn't hear you,' she said. 'Yeah, I'm not exactly in the running for the mum-of-the-year award,' she went on and pulled two yellow plugs out of her ears. 'It's a survival thing. I mean, you can hear for yourself. It's the opposite of when we were kids. Back then, we needed these things to block out the sound of the adults. Have you had breakfast?'

'No.'

'Then why don't you eat with us? We haven't got there yet.'

Charlie nodded.

'Let's get a bit of a head start before we call the gaggle upstairs,' Susanne said.

'I was just at Nora and Fredrik's,' Charlie said after they had sat down at the table.

'What for? I thought you had been put on sick leave.'

'I just wanted to give something back to them. But Nora threw me out.'

'What? Why?'

'It was when I told her who I was, who my mum was. She went completely crazy.'

'Rumour has it that woman is in fact crazy.'

'But why would finding out I'm Betty's daughter make her so furious? She and Betty didn't know each other, as far as I recall.'

'I suppose Nora's lived here for as long as we've been alive, but she didn't go to the Lyckebo parties, we would have remembered that. But maybe her husband used to go. You know how the men always swarmed around your mother.'

'And that would make her act like that now? And towards me?'

'Maybe she's not in the best mental shape.'

The boys came downstairs. Milk glasses were knocked over and slices of toast ended up butter-side down on the floor. The second oldest boy, Nils, yelled at his younger brothers.

'Where's their big brother?' Charlie asked.

'I assume Melker's upstairs,' Susanne said. 'He already ate. He's a bit of a loner.'

'Hey, police lady?' Nils said suddenly. 'Can I show you my new room?' Charlie looked at Susanne.

'Is that okay?'

Susanne nodded. She might as well go with him now, otherwise he would nag holes in their heads.

Charlie followed Nils upstairs.

They reached the spacious landing. Charlie noted that the piles of laundry had grown since the last time she was there. Nils first showed her his little brothers' room, then his parents', and then his dad's study. Charlie couldn't help taking a quick peek. The walls were covered in bookshelves from floor to ceiling.

'Dad really loves books.'

Charlie turned to face the boy who was the oldest of the four. She hadn't heard him coming.

'He likes books more than films,' the boy went on and pointed to the shelves.

'You must be Melker,' Charlie said and held her hand out.

Melker looked at her, ignoring her hand. Yes, he was Melker and he was just like his dad. He loved books more than films too.

'Me too,' Charlie said.

Melker studied her as though he didn't believe her, that there could be another person like that in the world.

'My mum doesn't like reading,' Nils said. 'She says Dad doesn't need this room, that one of the twins is going to get it before they kill each other.'

'We're keeping this,' Melker said, glaring at his brother.

'Come on!' Nils said. 'I was supposed to show you my room.'

Nils had Susanne's old room. Back then, the wallpaper had been shredded by cat claws and the floor covered by beige vinyl;

now the hardwood floor had been uncovered and the wallpaper was new and pristine.

Charlie sat down on the bed. The bedspread was the same fabric as the curtains, a lot of strange birds of different colours. Children were not minimalists when it came to things and colours, that much she had come to understand.

'Nice, right?' Nils said.

'Really nice. Cool birds.'

'They're not birds. They're angry birds.'

'I see,' Charlie said.

'Angry birds are birds, idiot,' put in Melker, who had stepped into the room.

'Get out of my room,' Nils said.

'I'm not in it.' Melker had stepped back across the threshold and was now ostentatiously leaning into the room.

Nils decided to ignore him and turned back to Charlie.

'You're here because of the girl, right?' he said. 'To find Annabelle.'

Charlie nodded.

'If you don't find her, Dad'll be sad.'

'Yes, because she went to Dad's school,' Melker said from over by the door. 'Of course he'd be sad.'

'But she was Dad's friend as well. She was friends with Dad.'

'No, she wasn't,' Melker said.

Charlie stood up, went over to the door and shut it in Melker's face without a word.

'What do you mean?' she said. 'Do you mean Annabelle and your dad are friends?'

Nils nodded.

'Yes, but we promised not to tell anyone. She was here once when Mum was with a friend in Gothenburg with the twins. It was in the middle of the night, but I had a dream and woke up.'

'Did you tell your mum?'

'No, because Melker says that if I do, we won't get a new dog. Daddy promised us a puppy.'

'It's good you're telling me this.'

'You won't tell Mum, will you?' the boy eyed her anxiously.

'I might have to tell your mum,' Charlie said, 'but no one's going to be cross with you, Nils. You did exactly the right thing.'

When she walked back downstairs, she had to pause for a moment and catch her breath, to avoid coming down looking shaken. Isak Sander, she thought. The lover.

44

Fredrik was leaning over the kitchen counter, looking out at the driveway. How many hours had he stood like this, staring down at the road? Occasionally, especially after taking one of Nora's many pills, he'd thought he'd seen Annabelle unlatch the gate and run up towards the house. The day before, he'd seen her in her white graduation outfit, the one they'd picked out together before she finished year ten. At first, it had scared him, that his brain could turn the figments of his desires into something so real. Maybe he was losing his mind, like Nora?

He couldn't shake what he'd read about that alleged video. 'The filmed sexual assault on Annabelle.' He'd called Olof the second he saw it, wondering what the hell was going on, why they would keep something like that from him. But Olof had just calmly replied that they we're doing everything they could, that they had to keep some things to themselves, that it was for the good of the investigation. It had made no difference that Fredrik had screamed that he wanted to know what it showed, who had assaulted his daughter, was it Svante Linder? Olof just kept apologising and referring to the good of the investigation. And about Svante Linder ... Olof couldn't comment on that either, except to say that he was in detention. Then Olof advised him not to read the papers, that all they were after was selling copies and chasing clicks, that they had a way of twisting and distorting things. Olof had asked him to try to focus on something else, as though that were an option.

Fredrik thought back yet again to his encounter with Svante Linder that night. Was it possible for a person to be so cold that he let a father search a house for a daughter he had … well, what was it he had done, then? That boy with his terrible reputation, was he really capable of …? Fredrik couldn't bear to finish the thought. Nora had lost her mind when she heard about the video and Svante Linder being arrested. She had struck and scratched Fredrik when he prevented her from driving down to the police station. If she was going to carry on like this, he thought and rubbed a scratch on his arm, if she was going to carry on like this, she would have to go back to that facility soon. In a way, that would be good, because as it was, a lot of his energy was spent caring for Nora, making sure she ate and slept and didn't … kill herself. The priest had told him not to leave her unattended.

Fredrik thought about her outburst at that poor detective that morning. Why had her dead mother aroused such fury in Nora? Betty Lager … Fredrik remembered the poor alcoholic woman. He'd never gone to any of her infamous parties, but from what he'd heard, things had been wild out in Lyckebo. He had no memory of Nora ever saying anything negative about Betty Lager before, or had she?

At least Nora had finally fallen asleep on the living room sofa: short, jagged breaths. Fredrik tiptoed past her and went upstairs. He fetched the video camera and the box of tapes and went to Annabelle's room. It was the part of the house where her presence was strongest, where he could still imagine her coming back soon. He sat down on her white bedspread and turned the video on.

Annabelle's big, toothless smile, her tongue poking out the gap. She had lost four teeth, both in her upper and lower jaw and could no longer say *s*.

She laughs, tries. The camera shakes with his own laughter.

'And where's the tooth you lost yesterday?'

'In my secret hiding place,' Annabelle whispers and points to the door in the wall beneath the slanted ceiling. 'I put it in my secret hiding place. Do you think the tooth fairy will be able to find it?'

Fredrik paused the recording and looked over at Annabelle's larger closet. It wasn't really a closet; it was a passage leading to his and Nora's bedroom. Now he remembered the hiding place they'd found when Annabelle was little. They had discovered the loose board in the wall through sheer chance when they were building a fort. Behind the board was a deep hollow in the wall. Annabelle had called it her secret hiding place. When the police had asked for her diaries, letters or notes, he hadn't thought of the hiding place. How could it have slipped his mind?

He went into the closet, hunched down under the slanted ceiling and searched around for the loose board. If she did keep a diary, maybe this is where it was hidden. He felt around. There was indeed something in there. He pulled out a notebook with some newspaper clippings stuck between its pages. He unfolded the yellowed paper and read: 'Thirteen-year-olds behind the murder of a two-year-old.' He skimmed the text. He remembered the case. It had happened when he was a teenager himself and everyone around him had talked about how horrific it was. But what was an almost forty-year-old newspaper article doing in Annabelle's closet? It hadn't been there when he put the money from the tooth fairy in, he was sure of it.

'What are you doing?'

LINA BENGTSDOTTER

Fredrik jumped when Nora's face suddenly appeared in the doorway. He quickly put the article and notebook back.

'I don't know,' he said. 'I thought … I just feel so bad.'

'And being in her closet helps?'

45

On her way from Susanne's house, she called Anders.

'Check out Isak Sander,' she said.

Anders couldn't hear her over the wind, so she had to stop the bike and repeat it.

'We've checked him,' Anders said. 'He has an alibi for that night and ...'

'Isak Sander's the one who had a relationship with Annabelle,' Charlie said. 'He's our Rochester.'

'And how do you know that?'

'His son just told me.'

'His son.'

'Yes, I was over at Susanne Sander's and one of her sons told me that Annabelle and his dad were friends.'

'I thought you were supposed to stay out of the investigation?'

'That doesn't mean I have to stay away from friends, though, right?' Charlie said.

'I'm sorry,' Anders said. 'I didn't mean ... We'll check it out.'

'See if he has a pay-as-you-go phone as well.'

'Of course,' Anders said. 'Hey, Charlie,' he added.

'Yes?'

'Thanks.'

*

Charlie thought about how surprised Susanne had been that she suddenly had to go. Had something happened, she had asked. Charlie had told her it was nothing. Susanne had clearly not believed her, but there was no way Charlie could have told her the truth with all the children at home. How was Susanne really doing? Charlie thought. How much did she know about her husband?

That evening

They could hear the music long before they saw the big village shop loom up on the hill above the bridge.

'Wicked bassline,' Rebecka said. 'I almost feel like dancing.'

'How do I look?' Annabelle said.

'Perfect, as usual. What about me?'

Annabelle studied Rebecka's face, asked her to look up, spat on her finger and wiped off a mascara smudge on her cheek.

'There you go, now you look pretty for your lover.'

'Don't call him that,' Rebecka said. 'He's just ... He's just William.'

'How long have you had the hots for him anyway?'

Rebecka shook her head. She wasn't really hotter for him than anyone else.

'But did you want to fuck him when I was with him?'

'Lay off, will you? Why are you being like this?'

Annabelle didn't know how to answer that. She didn't actually care, but now it suddenly felt important.

'You should know, Bella,' Rebecka said, 'that William would never choose me over you. But I'm guessing you already know that. So I don't understand what you're getting at with that stuff. Sometimes you seem to forget that we're best friends.'

She started walking.

'I don't think best friends are supposed to fuck each other's boyfriends!' Annabelle shouted after her.

Rebecka stopped, turned around.

'He's not your boyfriend any more. You can't take him back just because you've been dumped by that other guy.'

'You should never have gone with William in the first place,' Annabelle countered. 'You just don't do things like that. What are you doing?' she went on when Rebecka bent down and started digging her hands into the gravel by the side of the road.

'Let the person without blame throw the first stone,' Rebecka said and threw a handful of gravel down in front of her.

Annabelle had to laugh. That made Rebecka even more upset.

'Why do you always have to fucking laugh when someone's pissed off at you? When you're always so bloody serious otherwise. What's wrong with you, Annabelle Roos?'

46

Back at Lyckebo, the cat was sitting on the front steps as though it were waiting for her. It followed her in when she opened the door. Charlie poured it a saucer of milk and reminded herself she had to buy cat food. She should try to eat something too, but it was as if her entire body was on strike. She wasn't hungry, just filled with a nagging worry about what she had found out that morning. Susanne's husband had had a relationship with Annabelle. Did Susanne know? Would she have been able to keep it to herself if she did? Charlie thought about Hugo's wife's irate phone call. Jealousy and betrayal could unbalance even the most stable person. She sat with the cat on her lap for a while. It had a big, bloated tick behind its tattered ear and gave her a miserable look when she pulled it out. It was as though its eyes were saying, I thought I could trust you. Are you going to hurt me too? Charlie put the tic on the table and felt the familiar satisfaction at seeing all its parts still attached, its head and all the black legs. She started meticulously searching the cat's fur. There were tics of various sizes everywhere. She pulled them out and stroked the cat's chin and belly by turns. It seemed like it was starting to understand that her intentions were good. She thought about how Betty had used to burn the ticks. It had changed nothing when Charlie had said it was horrible, that it was cruel to the animals. Betty couldn't help it that she loved the feeling when the little creatures burst and turned into a puddle of blood.

When all the ticks were gone, the thoughts of Isak Sander returned. She took out her phone and googled his name. He looked even better in pictures than in real life, she realised when a picture of him appeared on her screen. Other than that, she didn't find much, just basic information about his address, profession and name day. And a short article from the local paper in which he was interviewed about good young adult fiction. Isak Sander, librarian, father of four, Susanne's husband, but also an adulterous, unreliable bastard.

In an attempt to distract herself, she tied two old kitchen towels around her knees and went over to the shed to fetch the bucket containing Betty's gardening tools. The cat followed her. The trowel and cultivator were so rusty the handles turned her hands red. She spent a long time crawling around on her knees, toiling, digging and hacking at clumps of grass, thistles and dandelions. After working for over an hour, she had only uncovered seven tiny tiles. Charlie sighed and tossed the trowel aside. It was no good.

When she went to rinse off, her phone rang. It was Susanne, who between sobs and curses managed to relay that the police had come to pick up Isak. No, they hadn't forced him to go with them, they had just turned up saying they wanted to talk to him in private and then they'd left.

'Where are the children?' was the only thing Charlie could think of to say.

'My mum picked them up. I can't even take care of myself right now.'

'I'm coming over,' Charlie said. 'I'm leaving right now.'

*

'Isak's a fucking arsehole,' Susanne said. She was sitting on the sofa, drinking some weird greenish concoction. The dachshund was lying next to her, shooting its owner anxious glances whenever her voice turned shrill. 'But you should know, Charlie, that even though right now I'm hoping he'll rot in some dungeon, he's not the type to kidnap a young girl. I hope you know that.'

Charlie nodded, even though she didn't really know. How was she supposed to know that? She didn't know Isak; and when people were in a bind, when they felt threatened, the most unpleasant personality changes could occur.

'Did you know?' she said. 'Did you know they were seeing each other?'

Susanne nodded. She had known.

And why hadn't she told the police?

Yeah, right, why hadn't she? Maybe because she hadn't wanted the boys' father, their whole family, dragged through the mud in front of the whole bloody town.

'But Annabelle's missing,' Charlie said. She wanted to add something about how the Susanne she'd known once would never have kept that kind of information to herself, but Susanne was upset enough as it was.

'I suppose I believed him when he said he had nothing to do with her disappearance.'

'Was Isak home that night?' Charlie asked.

'Yes, I think so.'

'Think?'

'I'd taken two Imovane,' Susanne said. 'Two Imovane and painkillers. How the fuck am I supposed to know if he was home?'

'So he could have gone out?'

'Theoretically, yes.'

'And practically?'

'Yes, theoretically and practically, but he didn't do anything to her.'

'Have you told the police everything you know now?'

Susanne nodded. She had told them everything she knew. But she was sure, dead certain, that Isak hadn't done anything to Annabelle.

'Sometimes,' Charlie said, 'you think you know a person, but then ... people aren't always what you think they are.'

'Like I don't know that,' Susanne said and downed the last of what was in her glass. 'But Isak ... Isak wouldn't ... My God, if he were the violent type, he'd have smacked one of the boys a long time ago. You don't understand how their screaming and fighting have messed with our heads. Isak can't keep it in his trousers; he's a liar and deep in some kind of life crisis, but you have to believe me when I tell you he's not capable of hurting anyone, at least not physically.'

For a while, neither one of them spoke. Susanne handed her the bottle. When Charlie shook her head, she heaved a sigh, topped herself up and took three deep gulps.

Charlie steeled herself and asked the unpleasant question.

'Did you see Annabelle?'

'Like I've told you, she comes to the motel sometimes.'

'But that night? Did you see Annabelle that night?'

'What night?'

'The night she disappeared, obviously.'

'No,' Susanne said. 'I didn't see her that night. But I saw her earlier. I saw her earlier that evening.'

That evening

Rebecka disappeared down the road in front of her. Annabelle pondered going home. What was the point of going to a party where almost everyone was pissed off at her, even Jonas? He'd told her he'd seen her with someone out on Gold Island, asked her who it was. She had obviously denied being there. Jonas had been annoyed and said that the next time she wanted a ride anywhere, she should ask someone else. He was fed up.

Annabelle's thoughts moved on to William. He was at least as disappointed in her as Jonas. And Becka, she was probably just going to disappear off somewhere with William all night. She'd probably get stuck with Svante Linder and if anyone could put her in a foul mood, it was him. So why even go?

But what was she going to do at home?

The only thing she really wanted to do was see Him. What would happen if she went over to his house and knocked on the door? But no, she didn't have to make things worse than they already were. Besides, she didn't know what his wife might be capable of. What she had said earlier, by the meadow ... it didn't feel like empty threats.

A girl from the secondary school was smoking a joint on the front steps of the village shop.

'You should go home,' Annabelle said. 'You shouldn't be here.'

The girl laughed and said it was none of her fucking business. If this was such a bad place, what was she doing here herself?

'I'm older,' Annabelle said.

'A couple of years doesn't make a lot of difference, Bella.'

'How do you know my name?'

'Why wouldn't I know your name? Doesn't everyone know everyone's name around here?'

'Not everyone,' Annabelle replied, because she couldn't remember this girl's name, even though she'd seen her before.

'I'm Sara. I'm just here because ... I want to see Svante.'

'He doesn't sell to little kids.'

'He usually gives it to me for free.' Sara glared at her defiantly.

Annabelle opened her mouth to say that Svante never gave anything away for free, but then she reckoned there was no point.

'Go home,' she said, 'and don't get mixed up with Svante.'

The hallway was full of shoes. It was funny, Annabelle mused, that the people who graffitied on the walls, carved notches in the furniture and threw up all over the house still respectfully took their shoes off before entering. She felt she needed more to drink. She would need a lot more to make this a good party.

As she walked up the stairs, she realised Svante Linder had already arrived, because the weird music pumping through the house had to be his choice.

47

Coming back from Susanne's, Charlie went straight down to the lake. She didn't have a swimming costume, but what did it matter, she thought to herself as she took off her clothes and got in.

She hadn't swum in Lake Skagen since Mattias disappeared, because she had always had a feeling his bloated corpse would surface right next to her, but now ... now she knew better. She reckoned a swim might help her gather her thoughts together and calm down.

The water was just the right temperature. She waded out a bit and then started swimming. Maybe she should have stayed with Susanne for longer, but it was hard for her. She had sat there for hours, listening to the story about the message from Annabelle on Isak's phone, the panic Susanne had felt seeing the positive pregnancy test. She had been so fucking pissed off, she'd stamped on the phone and broken it. And then, how she'd got in her car to drive over to Annabelle's house to talk to her. She'd almost run her over on the gravel road by her house, had stopped and shouted atrocious things. She'd regretted it afterwards. It wasn't that poor girl she was angry with, after all, it was Isak. She'd confronted him that evening and then all hell had broken loose. She'd asked Isak to go to hell, bellowed at him that they were over, that he had to get out of their house. But then the boys had woken up and been beside themselves, so he'd stayed. She'd taken a couple of sleeping pills and gone to bed.

And then, when it turned out Annabelle was missing, well, then she no longer had the strength to throw him out.

Susanne had sworn that was the whole story. She had sworn on her father's grave that she had been home all night.

Was she telling the truth? Charlie's gut said she was, but in this case, gut instinct wasn't enough. She had felt obliged to call Anders again.

When she turned around to swim back to shore, she noticed someone sitting on the sand, not far from her pile of clothes. When she got closer, she realised it was a man in shorts and a T-shirt. She figured she would swim back and forth for a while until he left. The water no longer felt cooling, just cold. She was cold. Ten minutes later, she realised the man wasn't going to leave, that maybe he was in fact amused by the whole situation.

'Are you looking for me?' she called out. She had come in far enough to reach the bottom, but her whole body was still submerged.

'I just wanted a quick chat.'

Only then did she realise it was Johan, the journalist bastard.

'Get out of here!' she shouted.

'It's not your private beach, is it?' he shouted back.

'I would prefer to get dressed in private.'

'I can turn around.' Johan got up and walked towards the edge of the trees.

Charlie quickly walked up onto the beach and pulled her dress on over her wet skin. She just had time to put her shoes on before Johan was back.

'I didn't peep,' he said and smiled, 'so there's no reason to look so angry.'

'What the fuck are you doing here?' Charlie said. 'What do you want from me? Don't you understand what you've done?'

'What do you mean, done?'

'You got me suspended from work. Don't you think I know what you were after? I'm perfectly aware you just wanted the inside scoop on the case.'

'What do you mean?' Johan said.

'I mean exactly what I say. What you wrote about in your bloody paper, the video, after being with me. What did you think my colleague was going to think?'

'How was I supposed to know you'd tell your colleague about us?'

'He saw us. And the next day, it's in the paper that the police has secret evidence. How could you possibly think that wouldn't have consequences for me?'

'What I wrote,' Johan said, 'I got from a different source, and how was I to know that was your colleague peeping out of his room when we were on our way to yours?'

'Who's your source?'

'I can't tell you that.'

'Of course.' Charlie rolled her eyes. 'What are you people like? Are all journalists completely unethical? How can you care more about your source than ... I don't understand your kind.'

'My source might be one of your people,' Johan said, 'so don't get on some kind of ethical high horse.'

'Tell me who it is.'

'I can't.'

'Then maybe you should leave now. I've nothing more to say to you.'

'Other people's lies seem to really upset you,' Johan said, 'but you don't seem to have any scruples about lying yourself. Isn't that slightly ... contradictory?'

'You should've told me you're a journalist,' Charlie said, ignoring his question. 'Why did you lie about it?'

'Well, why do you think? Would you have gone upstairs with me if I'd been honest?'

'No.'

'There's your answer. And you, why didn't you tell me you were a police detective?'

'I honestly don't know.' Charlie started walking back towards the house.

Johan followed her up the trail. She turned around and asked what he was doing. And how had he known where to find her anyway?

'I'll tell you the truth,' Johan said, 'but I doubt you'll believe me.'

'I probably won't.'

'I wanted to see you again, but the guy at the motel said you'd checked out, so I asked around a bit about where you might have gone, and I found you here.'

'More lies,' Charlie said. 'Only two people know I'm here, and I hardly think they've talked to you about it.'

'More than two, apparently. I actually was told you might be here.'

'By whom?' Charlie turned around.

'Maybe someone who knows who you are.'

Charlie suddenly felt uneasy. Who was this unrelenting person? What did he want from her? Should she maybe run? She was fast and knew this forest like the back of her hand. That would give her a head start, but would she really be able to make it to the house and lock the door behind her before Johan caught up (if he actually decided to give chase)? She thought about the time Betty had come home with a big wolf-like dog she'd promised to look after for some friend. *Don't let him sense your fear, sweetheart, that will just provoke his hunting instinct.*

'Who the fuck are you?' Charlie said. 'Don't come any closer. I'm serious, back up.'

'My dad,' Johan said and took a step back. 'My dad lived here when I was little. It was in the house up there, Lyckebo.'

Charlie suddenly felt panic fill her chest. Her head crackled. She saw the lake, the black depths, felt that helplessness all over again, the shame.

'When?' she said, trying to control her breathing.

'Twenty years ago. His name was Mattias,' Johan said. 'Mattias Andersson.'

There and then

John-John is sitting in the sandbox outside the supermarket. No sign of stupid-head. From the bushes, Rosa whispers for him to come to them.

'Check out how easy this is going to be.'

She calls John-John, but John-John doesn't want to come.

'We have lollipops,' Rosa says. 'Come over here and I'll give you one.'

'What are you going to do?' Alice asks when John-John toddles over.

Rosa doesn't respond. She just takes John-John by the hand and Alice takes his other one, then they run away so fast John-John's feet barely touch the ground.

They only just make it out of the town centre before he starts crying for his mummy. He's already forgotten about the lollipops.

All he wants is his mummy. Mummy, Mummy, Mummy. He trips. Rosa drags him by the arm. She doesn't like cry-babies, she says. If there's one thing she hates, it's cry-babies.

'He lost his shoe,' Alice says. 'He lost his shoe.'

'Who gives a shit about his shoe,' Rosa says.

They walk along the railway tracks, John-John dangling between them. Then they meet a lady carrying a bouquet of flowers.

'Is he sad?' she asks and looks at the snot-covered toddler between them.

John-John has wet himself, his wrists are red because they've held them so tight.

'Mummy!' he screams. And the woman tilts her head and asks again if they need help with anything.

Rosa tells her they're fine, that they're bringing their little brother home to their mum.

'He's run away,' she explains. 'He's a runner.'

As they walk on, Alice can feel the woman's eyes on her back. She wants to turn around and shout that they do need help, that someone has to take this child from them before something terrible happens.

48

Charlie tried to shake Johan off, but he stubbornly followed her up the path to the house. He'd come to Gullspång to write about the case, but he'd planned to do some research as well. After all, Annabelle wasn't the first person in town to disappear. His dad had never been found either. He'd wanted to come many times before, but it had just never happened.

Charlie asked if he really hadn't known who she was that night, and Johan swore he hadn't. He'd seen her, found her attractive. It was all just a strange coincidence.

'Johan,' Charlie said. They had reached the house and she was not under any circumstances going to ask him inside. 'I believe you and all of that, but I just want to be alone now.'

'Charline,' Johan said. 'I'm so sorry I didn't tell you the truth from the beginning, about me being a journalist.'

'Me too.' Charlie put a hand on the door handle. 'You take care.'

Johan stayed where he was.

'I'm sorry,' he said. 'It's just that I ... I've thought so much about this place. When I was little, I kept waiting to move here. Dad said it was like heaven.'

'He was wrong.'

'Could I just ... could I just have a look around the house?'

Maybe it was her guilty conscience that made her let him in, offer him a glass of wine. Either way, now he was there, sitting at the kitchen table where Betty and Mattias had planned for his arrival so enthusiastically.

Johan took a sip of wine.

'Interesting taste,' he said and looked at the glass.

'It's been ageing for a long time,' Charlie replied.

They carried on talking about his dad. Johan was moved when she told him about how he had fought to get his son back. His mother hadn't exactly described his dad as someone who would fight for his child. All her life, she had stood by her claim that Mattias was a half-mad junkie. He wasn't even capable of taking care of himself, she had explained, so how was he supposed to care for a child? For a moment, Charlie considered letting Johan think his mother had lied, to show him only the part of the picture that was beautiful: the family in the countryside which would be complete with him, his sister, the cherry tree forest and the lake. But she was sick of lies.

'Your mum was right,' she said. 'Mattias was a crazy junkie. Betty, my mother, was exactly the same. They were both mad. But Mattias really did miss you. They both really wanted you to come here.'

'Is that true?'

Charlie nodded. It was the truth.

'I can't get my head around,' Johan said, 'that you used to live here with my dad.' He looked around the room as though he were trying to picture them all: Charlie, Betty and Mattias. 'What was he like to you?'

'He tried,' Charlie said. 'But I guess our relationship wasn't great. It might not have had all that much to do with him; I mostly wanted my mother to myself. I wanted things to be the way they had always been.'

'And your dad?' Johan asked.

'I don't know who he is. I actually think Mum was the only one who knew, so now there's no one left to ask.'

'When did she die?'

'Less than a year after Mattias disappeared.'

'Was she sick?'

'Yes,' Charlie said. 'She was very sick.'

They continued to talk about Mattias. Johan wanted her to tell him everything she remembered about him. Had he worked? What had his interests been? Had he still played the guitar? Was it really true he had wanted to bring him here?

Charlie nodded. They'd even set up a room for him. Johan wanted to see that room.

They went upstairs. Johan commented on the stairs. He had never seen steeper ones. Could you even survive if you fell down them?'

'A lot of people have fallen down them and lived to tell,' Charlie said. 'Intoxication apparently makes the human body relaxed and supple.' She walked over and opened the creaky door to the room right above her own. 'This is where you were going to live.'

Johan looked at the walls. Who had painted all those cars? When Charlie told him it was Betty, he said her mother, her mother had real talent.

'I tried to make her paint something else,' Charlie said. 'I told her you were probably too old for cars.'

'I think,' Johan said, running his hand over a Volvo-like car on the wall, 'I think I would have liked it here.'

Charlie said nothing. She wasn't as sure.

'What's that?' Johan pointed to an odd construction along one of the walls.

'It was going to be a bed. Mattias got it in his head he was going to custom-build it, but it didn't work out too well.'

Johan went up to what had been meant to become a bed and sat down.

'What do you think happened to him?' Johan turned to her.

'He drowned,' Charlie said.

'Sure, but why was he never found? If he did drown, shouldn't he have floated back up by now?'

'Not everyone floats back up.'

'Yes,' Johan said, 'sooner or later, they do.'

Charlie considered telling him about the undertow, the whirlpools, the turbine, but realised it would sound horrible, so she just said he might have got stuck somewhere, that they gave up on the search after a while.

'They should have kept looking,' Johan said. 'I would have liked a grave I could visit. I don't feel there's proper closure. Without a grave, I mean.'

A grave doesn't help, Charlie thought to herself.

'I was there,' she said suddenly. 'I was on the jetty when he went out in the rowing boat; I just sat there and watched him die, so I know he's in there somewhere.'

A long silence followed. Charlie thought he must be able to see her heart beating through the thin fabric of her dress. She tried to read Johan's expression. Was he sad, angry, relieved?

'It wasn't your fault,' Johan said at length.

'Feels like it was.'

'What were you supposed to have done?'

'I should have rescued him.'

'How? You were just a child.'

'I should at least have tried. But it was as if ... as if I couldn't move. I realise it sounds mental, but ...'

'It sounds more like you were in shock,' Johan said.

313

Charlie nodded, even though she knew it wasn't true.

'I understand if you can't forgive me. I understand if you ...'

'He shouldn't have gone out in the boat,' Johan said. 'He should have stayed on dry land.' He got to his feet and walked over to the window, opened it, handed Charlie a cigarette and took one himself. 'Anyway, I'm glad you told me.'

'The worst part was,' Charlie said, 'that you were about to arrive, that he was going to get you here. That he never got to experience that.'

'I don't think it would have happened,' Johan said. 'Mum would never have let me go. After Dad left me at a train station in Copenhagen once, I was never allowed to see him alone. I would never have been allowed to live with Dad.'

'It sounds like you have a smart mum.'

'Had,' Johan said. 'Sadly, she died a few years ago. Cancer.'

'Sucks.'

'Yeah. It's empty without her. I mean, I'm an only child; I'm the only one left. To be honest, sometimes, it's horrifying. Well, maybe you know what I'm talking about.'

Charlie nodded. She knew how he felt. She knew exactly.

There and then

Then John-John breaks free and starts running.

'Well, catch him, then, Alice,' Rosa's shouting. But Alice just stands there, staring. John-John only makes it a few feet before Rosa catches him. She tears at his jumper, something flashes and falls to the ground.

'His necklace.' Alice bends down and picks it up and tries to give it to John-John. He just keeps howling. Rosa curses and sticks it in her pocket.

'Rosa,' Alice says. 'I think we'd better take him home now. I think we'd better take him back.'

'It's just a joke. I just want to scare them a bit.'

'Rosa!' Alice says. 'I think I hear someone calling.'

'Just shut up,' Rosa says, 'I'm thinking.'

But John-John won't shut up. He shouts for his mummy and then he starts kicking. Rosa curses and smacks him so hard he falls over.

'He's just a little kid,' Alice says. She's crying now too.

Rosa tells them both to just be quiet, but John-John can't stop crying. Rosa straddles his stomach and puts her hands over his mouth. He whimpers and Rosa lets go of his mouth and wraps her fingers around his neck. John-John's hands flail in the air.

And Alice just wants to scream at her to let him go, that she has to let him go before he ... but she just stands there.

When Rosa finally lets go, the child is still and quiet. His little face is no longer red. Rosa shakes his shoulders.

'Wake up,' she says, 'wake up, you stupid brat.'

But John-John doesn't wake up.

49

Fredrik got out of the armchair and went out into the kitchen. He stood next to the sink for a while, turned the water on, but forgot to take a drink. Then he went back to the living room.

Nora had been taken to the psychiatric emergency ward. She had refused, but an urgent care doctor had insisted and Fredrik had not objected. There was nothing he could do to help her. At least in the hospital, she'd be given something strong enough to blur reality.

In front of him on the coffee table was a brown wooden trunk with a broken lock that he had carried down from the attic. Before Nora left, she had mumbled something about a trunk in the attic, saying he might as well read what was in it, that she no longer cared. You might not forgive, she had whispered, you might not even understand.

There was something in Fredrik that wanted to know and understand. He sensed that whatever that trunk contained, it might break him. There are limits to how much a person can bear.

He took a big sip of whisky from the glass he had filled to the brim, leaned his head against the back of the sofa and closed his eyes. The picture of Nora's hopeful face when they moved into the house came back to him. *I think I can be happy here.*

But she has never been happy, he thought. She's just been more or less unhappy.

He leaned forward and took another sip of whisky, then he opened the lid. In the trunk were notebooks, newspaper clippings and a handful of letters. He started reading the articles. They were on the same theme as the one he'd glimpsed in Annabelle's closet. And the notebook he'd found there as well, which he'd understood to be a diary, was continued here. Since Nora had deteriorated rapidly, he hadn't had a chance to give it a closer look. And since the diary seemed to belong to a girl he didn't know, he hadn't thought much of it. But now he had the rest of the story. He went cold as it started dawning on him who had written the diaries. Who Alice was.

Three hours and two glasses of whisky later, he stood up, went to fetch his phone and called Charlie Lager.

That evening

'Annabelle!' Svante Linder shouted when she entered the kitchen. He was sitting at the kitchen table with Jonas, smoking. 'We thought you'd left, that you were too busy fucking some old geezer.'

'What the fuck are you on about?' Annabelle said. She glared at him.

'Calm down.' He put his hands up. 'Don't get excited now. I'm just telling you what I've heard.'

'And what the fuck have you heard?'

'That you fuck old men, that you don't have time to party any more, because you're so busy fucking.'

'Maybe I prefer fucking old men to fucking children.'

'What are you implying?'

'I think you know.'

Svante's eyes went black. He looked like he wanted to hit her, but his voice was deceptively soft when he asked if he could offer her some weed, for old times' sake.

Annabelle shrugged. She wanted a smoke, but at the same time she loathed taking anything from Svante. There was something about him that made her skin crawl.

'Where's William?' she said without answering his question.

'The Fucking Room. He's banging Rebecka instead since you ...'

'Oh, come off it, will you.'

'Come on,' Svante said. He pulled out the chair next to his and waved a rolled joint at her. 'I'm sure you'll be happier after smoking this.'

Annabelle sat down next to him, hoping he was right.

50

Johan had left. He might be back, he'd told her. Charlie sort of wished he hadn't meant it, but at the same time she already missed him. They had kissed at the door. He had stroked her hair and told her he was happy to finally have had some answers.

Then she went to bed, and for the first time in a long time her dreams were peaceful. When she woke up, the sun had disappeared from her window and evening mist had started rolling into the garden. It was eleven o'clock. She had just pulled out her phone when it rang. It was Fredrik Roos. Could she come over? He had something for her, something she might want to read.

Half an hour later, Charlie was outside his front door.

'I've found some things,' Fredrik said. He handed over a bag with a stack of newspaper clippings, a few black notebooks and a pile of letters. 'I think Annabelle might have seen some of this.'

Charlie took the bag.

'Don't show them to anyone else,' he said.

Charlie opened her mouth to say something, but Fredrik backed away and closed the door in her face.

*

When she got back to Lyckebo, she sat down in the kitchen and started flipping through the clippings. They were all from the seventies and were about the murder of a young boy. Two-year-old John-John Larsson had disappeared in the middle of the day from a car park by a supermarket.

In one article, there was a photograph of the murdered boy's family, mother, father, brother, with their arms around each other. Further down the page was a picture of the child they had lost, a smiling, curly-haired toddler. Charlie's brain was racing. Her fingers were damp with sweat when she flipped through the newspaper articles. What did this case have to do with Annabelle's disappearance and why did Fredrik want her to read about it? Especially since he knew she'd been suspended.

Satan's children? The next headline read. It was a quote from one of the murdered boy's relatives. In this article, the police confirmed that the main suspects were two children.

Charlie stood up and walked over to the kitchen counter to top up her wine glass. The bottle was empty. She stepped into Betty's clogs and went down to the basement to fetch another one. When she got back up to the kitchen, she opened one of the many black notebooks. It contained diary entries written by a girl called Alice. Something about her life was not right, that much became clear fairly quickly. She described her mother's claw-like hands, the longing for an absent father, her fear of the boys who harassed her on her way home from school. But after a few pages, there was suddenly a measure of joy in the elaborate, childish hand. There was a new friend.

I just can't understand that she, Rosa Manner, wants to be with me, that we're best friends now. Then followed long, rapturous descriptions of visits to Rosa's house. They were allowed to do whatever they wanted there, Alice wrote, bake, stay up all night, order pizza on a school night. *I'm the happiest person in the world.*

The rest of the first diary was all about Rosa, about going swimming in the lake, the games they played and their run-ins with someone called 'stupid-head'.

As soon as she finished the first diary, Charlie picked up the next one. The tone was more serious now, she noted. Alice was no longer as positive about everything Rosa did. *She scares me when she's angry. I don't understand why she's so angry. And her mum ... there's something weird about her.*

When Charlie got to the third diary, it was as if time and space dissolved. She longer bothered about why she was supposed to read an unknown girl's diary, why Fredrik had given her all of this. She read about the games that went wrong, the threats, all the encounters with shady men at Rosa's house. She read about the assault on Rosa's pregnant mother, the man who had kicked and the little stillborn girl, about Alice's confusion and fear. *Sometimes I think we must have summoned the devil, no matter what Rosa says.*

And just when Charlie thought it couldn't get any worse, it got more intense. She shuddered to read about the cat in the rain barrel, about Rosa haranguing Alice about how she should do anything for her if she really was her best friend.

The final book was the least coherent. Clearly, something horrible had happened.

Rosa was the one who said we should do it. She said she just wanted to scare him. But now ... what have we done??? If there's a heaven and a hell, I know where I'm going. I told Rosa that yesterday. I said we're going to hell for this. She said it would be hell long before we died if anyone found out what had happened. Because no one would believe us, no one would believe we hadn't meant to, that it was an accident. Rosa had just wanted to give that braggy family a scare. It wasn't her fault the kid stopped breathing all of a sudden. How was she supposed to know it would happen so quickly? But maybe the world wasn't so unfair after all, she figured, because if anyone should find out what it feels like when a child dies, it was John-John's dad.

That was when I finally realised who that man had been, that he was the reason why Rosa's sister had never drawn a single breath.

After finishing the final diary, Charlie stood up and lit a cigarette. She had been so engrossed in the story about the girls, the boy and the murder that she had forgotten to put the events into a bigger perspective. Do I even want to know more, she wondered. All that remained now were the letters. Charlie's hands trembled slightly when she pulled the first one out of its envelope. The letters had no sender on them and contained only a few brief lines. *Have you forgotten who saved you?* In some, there was just desperation about the lack of response: *Why won't you write back?*

It wasn't until she got to the last letter that all the pieces fell into place. It was the only one that had both the sender and the recipient's names in it. Sharp knives stabbed at Charlie's brain; she had to lie down on the kitchen bench for a while. Then she sat up and read the last letter again.

Darling Nora, it feels strange to call you anything other than Alice, but maybe I shouldn't worry about it since you don't want to be in touch.

What you tell me is probably true, that some people don't deserve a second chance. But I want you to at least know that I didn't move here to make life hard for you. I did it because I missed you, because I've kept the promise we once made to each other. I thought you'd be happy I'd found you. It wasn't easy, but I finally succeeded. I suppose I should move away from here now, but my little girl's already settled and I have a job. But you don't have to worry. I'm going to leave you alone. You know where to find me if you ever change your mind.

Your friend forever
Rosa 'Betty'

Charlie looked around the kitchen, the old clock on the wall, the copper pots, the bread-drying stick under the roof. It was as though everything was coming at her, talking to her, as though she was losing her grasp on reality. I should call Anders, she thought. Annabelle's disappearance might have something to do with Nora's past, there might be someone looking for revenge, who wants to do the same thing to her child that she was part of doing to someone else's. I'm going to call Anders, I just have to … close my eyes for a bit first. She put her head down on her arms on the kitchen table. Pictures of Betty danced around in her head. Betty in her white nightgown in the cherry forest, her hair loose and her eyes staring skyward. Charlie herself was a child again, sitting in the open kitchen window, singing along to the music playing.

That night

They had moved up to the living room and were sitting in a circle on the floor. A cigarette was being passed around; whomever the ash fell on had to answer any question honestly.

The secondary school kid from the front steps, the one whose name Annabelle couldn't remember, was too wasted to understand the rules. She answered other people's questions, laughed at nothing and was unable to sit still.

'Aren't you going to ask me something, Svante?' she giggled when she dropped still-glowing ash in her lap. 'Aren't you going to ask what happened in the barn ...?'

'I don't know what you're talking about,' Svante said. 'Are you even allowed out this late, Sandra?'

The girl glared at him defiantly and said her name was Sara and she was allowed to stay out as long as she liked. She was thirteen years old, after all.

A guy in the year above Annabelle looked at Svante and said that if that was the case, what Svante was doing was illegal.

'Cut it out,' Svante said. 'I don't know what she's on about. Hey, Sandra,' he said. 'Maybe you should go feed Turtle. I think he's hungry.'

Sara stood up and staggered off. They heard her call out something about turtle food, but then there was only silence.

The cigarette resumed its journey and the next time, the ash ended up in Annabelle's lap. She managed to brush it off before it burned a hole in her dress.

'Unlucky,' Svante said. 'Now everyone gets to ask Annabelle.'

Annabelle sighed and said the whole cigarette thing was just a stupid game, that she didn't have to answer anything.

'Don't be a poor sport,' Jonas said.

'You could always choose to do something,' Svante said. 'You could choose dare.'

Annabelle burst out laughing. So the cigarette game was just a disguised truth or dare. How old were they? Five?

'Fine, I guess I'll do a dare then. But don't give me any bullshit about jumping around the house on one leg or whatever.'

'Suck my cock,' Svante said and pointed to his crotch. 'I've heard you're good at blowjobs.'

'Are you serious?' Annabelle stared at him.

Svante nodded. If there was one thing he never joked about, it was blowjobs.

'Give over, will you, Svante,' Jonas said.

'What?' Svante said. 'Didn't you just tell her not to be a bad sport?'

'Sure, but ...'

'Drop your pants then,' Annabelle broke in. She gave Svante a level look. 'I can't very well do it if you're dressed. Or are you chicken? Are you scared?'

Svante said scared was the last thing he was. He put his glass down and unbuttoned his jeans.

Annabelle started crawling across the floor on all fours. Svante sat there grinning in his white boxers.

'Take them off,' she whispered when she reached him. 'Take it all off.'

Svante stood up and pulled his pants down. He grabbed her hair and pulled her towards him.

Jonas got up and told them they were both sick.

Annabelle opened her mouth, moved closer, but then, just inches away, she tore free of Svante's grasp.

'You didn't think I was going to do it, did you?' she said. She rolled around on the floor. 'Idiots,' she laughed. 'I'm so fucking sick of being surrounded by idiots.'

51

Her phone buzzed. Charlie picked up. It was Johan.

'I just wanted to call to see how you're feeling?'

'I'm a bit tired,' Charlie said. She checked her watch and saw it was nine, that it was morning, a new day. She must have lain down on the kitchen bench and fallen asleep in the middle of everything.

'Can I come in? I'm standing down by the gate.'

'I don't think now's such a good time,' Charlie said.

Johan was the kind of person who didn't understand the meaning of no, as Charlie discovered a minute later when he knocked on her door. She didn't have the energy to get up, and prayed she had locked it.

She hadn't, because seconds later he appeared in the kitchen. She saw him eye the mess around her, the newspaper clippings, the notebooks, the envelopes, the bottles and the ashtray.

'What do you want?' she said.

'I don't know. I just had this feeling you weren't doing well.'

'I guess you were right about that. But unfortunately I don't think you can help me.'

'Does it have anything to do with this?' Johan pointed at the things strewn across the kitchen table.

Charlie nodded.

'Can I read it?'

'Be my guest. Is it all right if I lie down for a bit? I think I need some more sleep.'

'Go ahead,' Johan said.

Charlie went to her room and lay down on her bed. She thought about all the evenings and nights she had lain there, trying to figure Betty out. Was this the reason behind the drinking, the darkness, the lack of personal history? No, she realised, this new, revolting knowledge was just the start of an even bigger *why*? Why did you do it, Mummy?

The pictures of the murdered little boy followed her into a restless, sweaty sleep.

When she woke up, she didn't know if she'd been asleep for ten minutes or ten hours, if it was morning or evening.

Johan was still in the kitchen.

'What time is it?' she asked.

'Four.'

'P.m.?'

'Yes.'

'You've been reading, I see,' Charlie said, nodding at the clippings.

'Yes, but it took me a while to get it.'

'I'm still not sure I get it, if I even want to get it.'

'Did you know anything about this, I mean ... did you have any idea they knew each other, your mum and Nora?'

'No, I had no idea.'

'It's a pretty gruesome story.'

'If you write about this in your fucking paper, I'm going to kill you.'

'What kind of person do you think I am?'

'I don't know you,' Charlie said. She looked at the papers

and notebooks on the kitchen table and suddenly had an urge to burn it all, forget she'd ever read it.

'Do you think it might have anything to do with the disappearance?' Johan looked at her.

'I don't know.'

'But have you talked to any of your colleagues?'

'I will.'

'I don't understand how they could do it,' Johan said. 'I don't understand how you can do that to a small child.'

'I assume,' Charlie said, 'there was something seriously wrong with them.'

'According to the diaries, your mother was the driving force.'

'Yes, but what do we really know about that? Seeing how Nora wrote it. Either way, it doesn't matter, because surely it's as bad to just stand there and watch?'

'Not as bad as strangling a two-year-old,' Johan said. 'Nothing's as bad as that. That would be like saying you drowned my dad because you didn't save him. I'm sorry,' he said when he noticed the look on Charlie's face. 'I didn't mean to ... it's really not the same thing ...'

'I think it's time for you to leave now.'

'I'm sorry,' Johan repeated. 'It's just so hard to understand. I really didn't mean to ...'

'It's fine, but I would prefer to be alone now.'

Johan got to his feet, but instead of leaving, he opened the window and pulled out his cigarettes. He took a few deep drags and gazed out across the garden.

Charlie thought maybe he was grateful now, grateful not to have been put in his father's care, not to have grown up with these lunatics. What did it matter that the garden was big, that there was a lake nearby and that the forest was enchantingly beautiful? What did any of it matter when the woman who was supposed to have become his stepmother was … Well, what was she?

Charlie walked over to the window as well. Johan wordlessly handed her a cigarette and lit it.

'The child, the one who died in the womb after the assault,' Charlie said. 'Did you get who it was that did that to my grandmother?'

Johan shook his head; he'd missed that.

'The father,' Charlie said, 'the two-year-old's father.'

Johan frowned and was quiet for so long Charlie felt compelled to clarify: 'He was the one who assaulted my grandmother. It happened before …'

'So it was revenge?' Johan looked at her searchingly.

'I don't know what it was. An accident, I hope.'

'If the boy's father was the one who did that, the revenge theory sounds more plausible,' Johan said.

'It might have been both. A revenge that wasn't all that seriously intended, a revenge that went off the rails.'

'I suppose we'll never know,' Johan said.

That night

Svante had more stuff in the gazebo, he said, stronger stuff, the kind that could take her to the moon if she wanted.

But Annabelle said the only thing she wanted was to get away from herself. She wanted something that could silence every last bloody thought.

Svante said he could sort her out no problem. He said if she came with him to the gazebo, he'd definitely be able to help her. Annabelle hesitated for a split second. She didn't like being alone with Svante. She had seen his eyes turn black when they were playing earlier, but he didn't seem angry now.

'Can't we do it here?' she said.

Svante shook his head. This stuff wasn't something he wanted to share around.

They went down to the hallway.

'You don't need shoes,' he said, 'we're only going to the gazebo.'

'This garden,' Annabelle said when they exited into the backyard, 'is like a fucking jungle. And the trees' – she pointed to the fruit trees – 'are they sinking into the ground or is the ground rising around them?'

'Wouldn't that be the same thing?' Svante said. 'Fuck,' he exclaimed and stopped dead.

'What?' Annabelle said.

'I thought I saw a snake.'

'Are you scared?' She shot him a teasing smile. 'If you're so scared of snakes, you should have put shoes on.'

Svante strode away without a word. When they reached the gazebo, they sat down across from each other on the bench seats. Svante pulled a tin of hand-rolled joints from his pocket, took one out and lit it.

'What's the difference between those and the ones we smoked earlier?' Annabelle asked.

'These are stronger,' Svante said, 'hit harder.' He handed her the joint. 'Let it sit in your lungs before you exhale. It gives it more of a kick.'

Annabelle took a deep drag and waited as long as she could before letting the smoke out.

'Good?' Svante asked.

'Fucking marvellous,' Annabelle replied.

'Thirsty?'

Annabelle nodded. She was very thirsty.

Svante bent down and fumbled around under the bench.

'Well, well, what do you know,' he said when his hands found a bottle. 'How convenient that this was still there.'

He unscrewed the top and took a long swig before handing the bottle to Annabelle. She took three quick sips before the burning sensation overwhelmed her and she started to cough.

Svante laughed and said this was the strongest moonshine he'd ever come across.

'How strong?' Annabelle said and handed the bottle back.

'Really fucking strong,' Svante said with a smile. 'Here, have some more.'

Annabelle wanted to say no; she'd already had too much of everything, and yet she drank more, sip after sip.

334

'So, how's your love life?' Svante said.

'What love life?'

'That guy you fucked out on the island. Was it good?'

'Yeah, I suppose it was.' Annabelle started laughing. She was surprised at herself, because there really wasn't anything to laugh about, but hard as she tried, she couldn't hold it back. There was something about Svante's face, it was changing shape, dissolving, growing and shrinking and growing again.

'What's the matter with you?' Svante said. 'Have you completely lost your shit?'

Annabelle tried to reply, but she couldn't quite make her lips form words and her tongue felt big and limp in her mouth. I need to get back to the others, she thought and yanked open the gazebo door. The ground was covered in a cotton-like fog. Svante called after her to wait, but she kept walking. It was impossible to keep to the small path winding its way through the grass, because it kept swaying, splitting and disappearing. She stopped to focus on where she was going. That's when she was pushed from behind.

'What are you doing?' she slurred. A moment later, she was on the ground with Svante on top of her.

'Lie still,' he hissed when she started waving her hands in his face. 'Lie still and shut up before I shut you up permanently.'

52

Johan was just about to leave when his phone dinged. Charlie had walked him to the door to lock it behind him. She couldn't take any more unexpected visitors right now.

'Fuck,' he said after reading the message.

'What?'

'They found her.'

'Where?' Charlie said.

'In the river, by the village shop. By the inlet gates. I have to go.'

'I'll come with you.'

Johan opened his mouth as if to object, but she'd already put her shoes on.

In the car on their way to Vall's village shop, Charlie thought about Fredrik's bloodshot eyes, Nora's flapping hands, the lawnmower in their garden, Annabelle's pink bedroom. The pain. She thought about the tattoo on Annabelle's arm, *Becka and Bella forever*, on the little semicolon on Annabelle's wrist, that there would never be more to come now. Her story would end here.

They parked near the beginning of the bridge. They were still a few hundred yards from the inlet gates, but it was as far as the car could take them. Several other cars were already parked along the road. Charlie's eye was caught by an old yellow Volvo with a sticker in its rear window. *Jesus is the life, the truth and the way.* In the dust next to it, someone had written *Hell no!*

Johan took out his camera from the back seat.

'Are you coming?' he said. 'I don't know where to go.'

'I think there's a footpath further on,' Charlie said.

The path was no longer a path. Brambly undergrowth made the going difficult. But after a few minutes, they reached the police cordon. They were not alone. Around twenty people had already gathered there. Most of them looked like they had dropped whatever they were doing to witness the denouement of the drama. The divers could be heard talking about how she was stuck, that they had to be careful. Charlie and Johan tried to get closer, but Micke was guarding the blue-and-white tape and stopped them when they tried to pass.

'No journalists,' he said and looked at Johan. Then, when Charlie tried to go on alone, he put a hand on her shoulder and said the cordon was there for a reason. No unauthorised access.

Charlie opened her mouth to say something prickly, but then decided she didn't want to give Micke the satisfaction. So she backed up, turned around and started walking away at a brisk pace.

'Let's go over to those trees,' she said to Johan and pointed. 'There's a cliff there.'

They ran into the stand of trees and reached the cliff where they had a view of the sun-bleached green inlet gates and the waterfall.

'Look,' Johan said. 'They're bringing her up now.'

Charlie wanted to shut her eyes but forced herself to keep them open. Even at this distance, she could see it all clearly: the blue dress in tatters along her pale body, leaves and weeds in her dark hair. Her thin white arms.

It was as if the sounds and the world around Charlie faded away. She was no longer a grown woman, she was a young girl, a girl who had been out half the night and who had come home and opened the door to her mother's bedroom. She was the girl who sat motionless on the beach, watching Mattias vanish into the dark waters of the Skagen.

Why are you here now, Charline? Why are you showing up now, when it's already too late?

Eventually, you'll return to the sea. Sooner or later, we all do.

Charlie turned around and slipped down the side of the cliff. Then she broke into a run.

'Wait!' Johan called after her. 'Charlie, stop!'

But she kept running, just like she had that night nineteen years ago, ran without protecting her face from the branches whipping at her face, without looking up. And then she fell, fell and had the air knocked out of her. I should get up, she thought, once her breathing had returned to normal, but she didn't have the strength.

'Are you okay?' Johan had caught up with her.

Charlie shook her head. She wasn't okay. She was very far from okay.

'You can't just lie there,' Johan said and held out his hand.

Charlie was about to protest and tell him she absolutely could. The way she was feeling, it was a tempting alternative, to just let it all go, stay down and never get up again. Because what was the point of getting back up and fighting in a world where young girls were dragged up from the bottom of a river, a world where teenagers had to numb themselves with drugs to survive, a world where she couldn't save anyone, not even herself?

She rested her head on the heather and closed her eyes, as though everything around her would go away if she could just shut her eyes tightly enough.

That night

Fog had settled across the fields and crickets were chirping from the grass verge. Annabelle was staggering down the gravel road. There was a throbbing between her legs; something was seeping out of her. She thought to herself she should be crying, but no tears came.

What time was it? Eleven? Twelve? She pulled her phone out of her purse. Almost half twelve. Her mum was going to have a fit. She was going to meet her at the front door, shake her shoulders and furiously demand to know where she had been, and then she would notice the rips, the blood, the torn dress. And how was she going to explain those things?

Her eyes weren't working right; the world around her seemed to be slipping. It was as though everything was coming loose, as though she was on her way into something that was only real to her.

She gazed out across the fields and tried to calm herself with what her dad had used to tell her when she was little, that fog was actually dancing elves. She had never been able to spot any dancing girls in the billowing whiteness, but now she saw them, girls with sweeping arms in the meadow and further up among the trees.

She was so preoccupied she didn't notice the figure in front of her until it was no more than a few feet away. A yelp escaped her at first, but when she recognised his face, she relaxed.

'Oh, it's just you?' she slurred. 'You scared me half to death. What the fuck are you doing here?'

'I wanted to talk to you.'

'And what does your crazy wife have to say about that, Mr Rochester? Or have you locked her in the attic?' Annabelle burst out laughing.

'Is it true?' Isak said.

'What?'

'Well, what do you think ... the message you sent, the picture. Why are you laughing? What are you on? And what did you do to your hand?'

'Don't touch me,' Annabelle said when he took her hand. 'You're never touching me again.'

'We have to talk, Bella, I can help you. I mean ... with ...'

'With getting rid of, right?' Annabelle staggered towards him, moving in close. 'And if I don't want to? If I want to keep it?'

'Think about your future,' Isak said. 'Think about all the things you dream of doing.'

'Go fuck yourself.' She shoved him in the chest. Isak grabbed her arms and held her still.

'And now what?' Annabelle laughed. 'What were you planning to do with me now?'

53

On their way back to Lyckebo, Charlie started feeling cold. Johan took off his jumper and demanded she put it on.

'As I said before, I think we need to talk to your colleagues about what we read about Nora.'

'We don't,' Charlie said, 'I do.'

She regretted having read any of it, regretted not obeying Challe's order to stay clear of the investigation, regretted having come to Gullspång at all.

'Do you want me to come in with you?' Johan said when they reached the house.

Charlie shook her head. Right now, all she needed was sleep.

'Keep the jumper,' Johan said. 'We'll sort it out some other time.'

When she got inside, she took two Imovane that Susanne had given her. Then she got in her bed and hoped the pills would plunge her into a sleep too deep for dreams.

The first thing she did when she woke up the next morning was call Anders.

'How's it going?' she said.

Anders made an awkward attempt at explaining that he couldn't tell her anything.

'The fact that you can't tell me is ludicrous.'

'Nevertheless, it's how it usually goes,' Anders said, 'when a person gets suspended from an investigation.'

'I gave you Isak,' Charlie said, 'I ...'

'But you're still suspended.'

'Was it him? Was it Isak?'

'You just don't give up, do you?' Anders said. 'Isak has admitted to being in a relationship with Annabelle, saying he ended it and then found out she was pregnant. He says he saw her that night and tried to talk to her, but that she was sad, angry and hurt. And when he tried to help her get back home, she just shouted at him to leave her alone.'

'Is he credible?' Charlie said.

'He's saying he kept it to himself for his family's sake. That either way, he didn't know more than anyone else. Annabelle had already been spotted on the road by the village shop, and the fact that he had seen her too wouldn't have changed any-thing. For what it's worth, he did seem genuinely sad.'

'And his wife,' Charlie said. 'How's Susanne doing?'

'We've interviewed her. She told us about her meeting with Annabelle that day, about the phone and the message about the pregnancy. We're obviously going to conduct more interviews, but unless the post-mortem reveals more than drowning and traces of the rape, I don't think we're going to be able to tie anyone to this.'

Charlie said nothing.

'Are you still there?'

'Yes.'

'Can I call you back later?'

'Sure.' Charlie hung up. She had planned to tell Anders about her recent discoveries, but why should she? It didn't seem to have anything to do with the investigation. It was bad enough that she knew.

54

The next day brought rain. For the first time in a long time, Charlie woke up and felt properly rested. She lay listening to the soothing sound of the rain pattering against the roof above her. Today, she thought, I'll go and see Betty.

The cemetery was completely deserted. The rain had stopped as suddenly as it had begun. The air felt clear and fresh. Charlie walked along the well-tended gravel paths, reading the headstones. She remembered the graves that had interested her as a child. The small, white children's crosses by the south wall of the church, the family grave with the Nils Ferlin poem.

> Not even a little grey sparrow
> that sings in the greenwood tree
> exists over there, on the other side,
> and how sad such a place must be.

Charlie couldn't stop herself from scraping off a piece of grey moss that concealed the last word of the poem. But now she was on her way to the chestnut tree by the wall, the place where Betty Lager was buried.

She studied the pecking dove on the headstone for a while. It was covered in white bird shit. Betty hadn't wanted a dove, or a headstone; no words about missing her. She was supposed to be scattered 'at sea'. And yet there it all was: the stone, the dove and birth and death dates, under the inscription, *Betty Lager, loved, missed*. Who had actually seen to the funeral arrangements? Charlie couldn't remember. She remembered almost nothing from the time right after Betty died.

There were no flowers or candles in front of the headstone, just a green, shrub-like plant, the same kind that seemed to have been planted on all graves that were not actively looked after by loved ones. Charlie climbed over the cemetery wall and picked a large bouquet of pink and purple lupins. Then she walked over to the tap and filled a pointed vase designed to be planted into the ground. Having set up the vase, she sat down next to the grave, tracing the ornate letters of Betty's name with her index finger. Betty Lager, she thought. You should have told me the truth. Maybe I would have understood you better if you had just told me. Then she realised that wasn't true, because if Betty had told her the truth, it would probably have made things worse. Because how was she, a child herself, supposed to be able to handle the knowledge that her mother had killed a child? It was impossible to fathom even as an adult.

Who were you, Betty Lager? Who were you really, Rosa Manner? She pondered the revenge angle. Was that enough to explain it? One of the newspaper articles had talked about the young perpetrators' tragic backgrounds, about substance abuse, prostitution and illness, society's neglect. But it was all too simplistic, Charlie mused. Millions of children were let down by their parents and society and didn't end up murderers. There must have been some intrinsic darkness in Betty. Is it in me too, she couldn't help asking herself. Am I like Betty?

No, she thought, no, no, no. I'm not Betty Lager. I'm not like her.

*

Charlie got back to Lyckebo a few hours later to find Johan on the patio. He was sitting by the wall, eyes closed in the sun. He hadn't heard her coming. She stood still for a moment, watching him. His tanned legs in those shorts, his curly hair. He looked relaxed, like it was his house, his wild, flowering garden and patio. She moved closer. Johan opened his eyes, looked at her and smiled.

'Stopping by uninvited seems to be your thing,' she said.

'I'm sorry to bother you. It's just that this place ... it makes me feel calm somehow.'

Charlie sat down on the chair next to him.

'What happens now?' Johan said.

Charlie shrugged, because she wasn't sure what he was referring to.

'Maybe we could meet up,' he went on. 'I mean, when we're back in Stockholm, just for a coffee or something.'

'Sure,' Charlie said. 'Maybe we can, like the siblings we should have been.'

'I'm glad we're not siblings.'

Charlie smiled at him and thought she should say something similar back, but felt that might be a bit too ... predictable.

55

Their work in Gullspång was done. Charlie had thought she'd
be relieved to be leaving, but something inside her had changed.
I'll be back, she thought. This goodbye is only temporary.

'My God, you're driving like a maniac.' Anders said.

'You're just jealous,' Charlie replied.

'Of what? Because I don't drive like a teenage boy with a
death wish?'

'Because you're too scared to overtake, because you're always
thinking better safe than sorry, because you can't keep a steady
pace and ...'

'You're still angry with me, aren't you?'

'Not with you,' Charlie said. 'I'm mostly angry at myself.'

'Forgive yourself,' Anders said.

'Gardell?'

'What?'

'What you just said, forgive yourself. That used to be my
mantra when I was younger, to calm my nerves when I ... felt
like a bad person: *For all the things you hate about yourself – forgive yourself*. I think Jonas Gardell wrote it.'

'I didn't know he wrote things, I thought he was just a com-
edian.'

'Oh my God,' Charlie said.

'So, did it help, the motto?' Anders smiled at her.

'No,' she replied, 'I've always had a hard time forgiving.'

'Yourself or others?'

'Both.'

There was a meow from the back seat.

'Challe's not going to like the cat thing,' Anders said. 'You do realise he has a pet allergy?'

'I wasn't planning on taking it to his house.'

'But if he drives this car, he'll get sick.'

'I suppose I'm going to have to clean it, then,' Charlie said. She called to the cat, who joined them in the front and lay down on her lap.

'It really doesn't look like it's doing too well. It looks more dead than alive.'

'It'll get better,' Charlie said.

Anders's phone rang.

'Yes,' he said. 'Yes, we're on our way. Two hours maybe, yes, but we probably have to stop for a bit of something along the way. No, but I'm hungry now.'

'Did you just hang up?' Charlie looked at him.

'Well, yes, she can't bloody well be in charge of whether I eat or not.'

'You don't have to justify yourself to me,' Charlie said. 'I completely agree.'

They stopped at a fast food restaurant. Anders ordered a whole burger menu. They ate in silence.

Charlie's thoughts wandered back to what the papers had written about Betty and Nora. Everyone seemed to have disagreed about what had really happened. The work of two little psychopaths? A game gone awry? A natural consequence of what can happen when children are forced to live on the margins

349

of society? Charlie thought about the baby her grandmother had lost, Betty's sister, her aunt. She wished the journalists had known about that. Maybe that would have mitigated the image of her mother as a cold-blooded murderer, created an ounce of understanding for the tragedy. Or maybe it wouldn't have mattered. A two-year-old boy had been killed, abducted, strangled and hidden.

Charlie thought about her grandmother. Cecilia Manner. Who had she been? A junkie prostitute, if what she'd read about her was to be believed, a woman who had driven her own child to ruin. But Betty had never said a bad word about her mother. And even if Cecilia had been the worst person in the world, who was to say the blame started and ended with her?

One of the papers had said there were no perpetrators in the case of the dead little boy, that everyone involved was a victim.

That's true, Charlie thought. In this story, there are only victims.

That night

Annabelle heard Isak calling behind her.

'Didn't I tell you to go fuck yourself?' she shouted without turning around. 'Didn't I tell you to leave me alone?'

'I'll walk you home,' Isak shouted back. 'I think you should go home.'

'I'm not going home. Go away.'

And yet she hoped he would follow her, that he would grab her again, say he loved her, that everything was going to be okay, but when she turned around, he was gone.

She stood motionless for a long time, pondering what to do next. Going home wasn't an option. So instead of continuing down the gravel road, she turned off towards the bridge. Half-way across, she stepped up to the railing and gazed into the black current.

The inlet gates must be wide open, she realised, because the water was swirling and churning violently beneath her. She suddenly felt an urge to climb over the railing. She hiked up her dress and then she was suddenly on the other side. The wind snatched at her hair; her head was spinning. If you're dizzy, her dad always said, if you're dizzy, you should find a single point to look at. She looked down, tried to find a fixed point among the eddies. But everything was moving.

When she attempted to climb back, she fell, just a small slip and then ... she was soaring through the air.

Am I flying, she had time to think before her body broke the surface and she was pulled under.

Don't miss *For The Dead* - the thrilling new novel featuring Detective Inspector Charlie Lager, from Lina Bengtsdotter

Keep reading for an exclusive preview . . .

I

Charlie tried to make herself comfortable in the reclined chair. Eva, the psychologist, was sitting across from her.

Eva had just gone over the guidelines for their conversations. It was important to start and stop sessions on time, important to be honest if something didn't feel good; important that Charlie knew everything she said in this room would stay in this room.

Eva's tone was friendly, but her eyes revealed she could be stern if the need arose. Charlie had looked her up and knew she was a member of the Swedish Psychologists' Association and had fifteen years of professional experience. That had been Charlie's first demand when Challe ordered her to see a therapist, that it had to be someone with a proper education, not some smug git with an eight-week diploma in personal development. She didn't want to waste her time on someone who spouted banalities or talked too much about their own life. More than anything, she wanted not to do it at all, which is why she had postponed this meeting for as long as she could. She'd tried to show Challe she was doing fine, that she was completely capable of taking care of herself and doing her job, but after what had happened the previous summer, she didn't exactly enjoy her boss's full confidence.

Either way, here she was, in a strange chair in Eva's office.

Outside, the leaves of an enormous oak tree glistened gold and orange and rain trickled down the window pane in tiny rivulets.

'Tell me why you're here, Charline,' Eva said.

'You can call me Charlie.'

'What brings you here, Charlie?'

'My boss. It was an ultimatum. He feels I need help.'

'I see.' Eva gave Charlie a probing look; Charlie figured she was making a mental note: . 'Do you agree with him?'

'About needing help?'

'Yes.'

'I guess so, but I might not have come if it weren't for the fact that I want to keep my job.'

'Can you tell me a bit about yourself, in general terms. I know what you do for a living but that's about it.'

'What more do you need to know?' Charlie said.

Eva smiled and said a person is more than just their job. Perhaps Charlie could just give a brief description of herself.

'Sure,' Charlie said. 'I like to … ' She paused. What did she like? Reading, drinking, being alone. She couldn't think of anything that didn't sound depressing off the top of her head. 'I like to read.'

When she realised Eva was waiting for more, she had an urge to add she loved working out as well, but what was the point of lying about that?

'Have you had therapy before?' Eva said after a while.

'Yes, a handful of sessions as an adult and a longer period of counselling as a teenager. My mother died when I was fourteen.'

'That's a difficult age to lose a parent.'

Charlie nodded.

'And your father?'

'Unknown.'

'I see.'

'What was your relationship with your mother like?'

'It was …' Charlie didn't know what to say. Complicated? 'My mother was unique.'

'In what way?'

'I suppose she wasn't like other mothers. I guess you might say I'm fighting hard not to become her.'

'That's natural, though, isn't it?' Eva said. 'Wanting to avoid repeating your parents' mistakes? But even if you're trying to be different from your mother, you are still using her as your reference point. You may not be able to step out of her shadow until you start acting without reference to her.'

'Sure.'

'We can come back to that. But first I want you to talk a bit about why your boss made his ultimatum. Requiring you to see a therapist.'

Betty's voice began echoing in Charlie's head. That thing she used to say when she hit a rough patch: '

'It's probably because of my drinking,' Charlie says. 'Sometimes I drink a bit too much. And the reason I'm here now is that, until recently, I was able to keep it under control. Drinking only when I was off-duty and not even the day before work, at least not in any significant quantities. But these days I find myself having a few drinks even if I'm working the next day, so I guess there must have been alcohol on my breath. Challe, my boss, has an incredible sense of smell.'

'Maybe that's lucky for you,' Eva said. 'I mean, because it had led you to seek professional help while there's still time.'

'How do you know there's still time?' Charlie had to ask.

'You're aware and open about your problem. That's a pretty good place to start.'

'I've been aware of it for a long time, but that hasn't meant I've been able to do anything about it, so I don't know if that's true.'

'I thought you just told me you've been able to keep it under control?'

'There have been times when I lost control,' Charlie said.

'But now you're here.'

'Yes, now I'm here.'

A few minutes of superficial chitchat followed, then silence fell. Charlie studied the paintings behind Eva. Framed pictures that looked like Rorschach tests, Charlie suddenly realised ... She tried to see patterns in the blots to gauge her mental health, but was interrupted by Eva who wanted to know more about her duties at work.

Charlie told her about what she did as a detective working for the National Operations department; about how she and her colleagues were brought in to assist local law enforcement with difficult cases all over the country.

'And what does the rest of your life look like?' Eva asked.

'Single, no children.' Charlie replied.

'And if we go back to your drinking,' Eva said, without commenting on the lack of partner, 'How long has it been a problem?'

'I'm not sure. I suppose it depends on who you ask.'

'I'm asking you.'

'Ever since I had my first drink, I liked it a lot, and I've always drunk more than the people around me. I've never been able to comprehend that one-glass-only mentality. But I wouldn't call myself an alcoholic just because I drink more than other people. I suppose I drink more sometimes, but then there are calmer periods too.'

'And the uptick that led to this meeting, when did it start?'

'I honestly don't remember exactly, but I went back to Gullspång – the town I grew up in – a few months ago. It's a small town in Västergötland.' She added when Eva looked nonplussed. 'I lived there until my mum died. That's when I moved to Stockholm.'

'Did you have family here?'

'No, I ended up in foster care.'

'What was that like?'

Charlie didn't know how to respond. What was there really to say about her life in the small terraced house in Huddinge? She pictured the garden, the raked gravel path, the flowerbeds where everything grew in neat rows and the tiny apple tree that never bore fruit. She thought about her first meeting with her foster parents Bengt and Lena and their daughter, Lisen, how the three of them had stiffly welcomed her into their clinically clean house. On the surface, her new family was exactly the kind she'd wished for whenever Betty went off the rails: calm, orderly people with regular sleep schedules, sit-down family meals and a mother who packed gym bags and cooked traditional food and didn't have mental breakdowns. Lena never ended up slumped on a sofa, begging to be away from all light and sound. She never threw parties and invited people she didn't know. Charlie thought about her room in the terraced house, the laundered sheets on her bed, the smell of soap and roses. , Lena had told her that first night.

But Charlie had never felt at home in the house in Huddinge, and she and Lisen had never become anything like sisters.

Eva cleared her throat.

'It was functional,' Charlie said, 'my foster family. Everything was neat and orderly and I was able to focus on school.'

'That's good,' Eva said, 'but back to when this period started. You went to Gullspång at the start of the summer. How come?'

'It was for work; a young girl had disappeared. Annabelle Roos. You might have read about it in the papers.'

'Yes, I remember.'

'We went down there to help the local police and it turned out being back was pretty rough. Much worse than I'd thought it'd be.'

'In what way?'

'It stirred up a lot of memories and I was ...'

Charlie saw Annabelle's thin body being pulled out of the black waters of the Gullspång River, saw Betty's boyfriend, Mattias, disappear into the same black depths two decades earlier, saw two little girls with a crying toddler between them, even further back in time, long before she was born.

'You were what?' Eva asked, leaning forward in her chair.

'I suppose you might say I got personally involved in the case, to some degree. And I made a mistake down there and was suspended and that obviously affected me as well. When I returned to Stockholm, I thought everything would go back to normal, but it didn't. It actually got worse.'

'What got worse?'

'My anxiety, the futility of it all, my sleeping problems. I have a hard time falling asleep and once I do, I have bad dreams.'

'Describe them.'

'My dreams?'

'Yes.'

'They started when I got back from Gullspång. They were slowly going away, but I'm working on a case now that's getting to me more than I'd like to admit.'

Eva asked what kind of case it was and Charlie told her about the two young women from Estonia, the ones who had been found murdered and dumped in a patch of forest in the suburbs. One of them had a three-year-old daughter, a hollow-eyed, hungry girl who had been locked alone in a flat for at least two days. The daughter still hadn't said a word, even though it had been two weeks since they found her.

Eva said she wasn't surprised Charlie felt affected by it, that an abandoned child would make most people feel the same way. But the little girl was okay, wasn't she?

'She's alive,' Charlie said. 'But that's about it. Last night, I dreamt she was my child, that I was her mother. I wanted to run home and rescue her, but I couldn't, because I was dead. And then, in my next dream, I was the child and ... well ... you get it.'

'Are you on any kind of medication?' Eva asked, without commenting on the dreams.

'Sertraline,' Charlie said, 'one hundred milligrams.' She didn't mention that she sometimes complemented the sertraline with oxazepam or sleeping pills or both.

'Nothing else?' Eva asked.

Charlie shook her head.

'Are you aware nightmares are a common side effect when you're on sertraline?'

Charlie nodded. She knew that, but since she'd been on sertraline for years, it was unlikely to be related.

Eva folded her hands around her knee.

'This mistake you mentioned,' she continued, 'I would like to talk some more about that.'

Charlie thought about that night at the pub for a minute. The liquorice shots, the wine, the beer, Johan. She'd been foolish to go rooting through his life when she got back to Stockholm. If you wanted to move on, you had to put the lid on things and leave them well enough alone, she knew that, but instead, she'd left no rock unturned. It had started with her wanting to find out where he lived, to check if he was married, if everything he'd said about being Betty's boyfriend's son was really true. It seemed to be.

'Charlie?' Eva was looking at her.

'I'm sorry, what were you saying?'

'I asked you to tell me about that mistake you mentioned.'

'Right. I actually don't remember everything, but I had too much to drink and brought a journalist back to my room. The next day, privileged information was printed in the papers. But I wasn't the leak, even though everyone obviously thought I was. And, well, it was a problem, to put it mildly.'

Eva said nothing for a minute, as if waiting for Charlie to continue. Then she asked, 'Do you think you would've spent the night with this man if you'd been sober?'

'God, no!'

'Why not?'

Charlie didn't quite know how to answer that, so she told it like it was: she couldn't really remember the last time she'd gone to bed with a man sober. And was there something wrong with that?

'What do you think?' Eva retorted.

'I obviously think that particular instance was lunacy, but in other contexts, I mean, when I'm not working? Do you think one-night stands are wrong?'

'Is what I think important to you?'

Charlie said it wasn't, but that was a lie, because if there was one thing she despised, it was judgemental people.

'Either way, that's not for me to say,' Eva said. 'But I will tell you that using sex to feel better might not be entirely constructive.'

'It's better than alcohol, though, right?'

'As far as I understand, you do both.'

Charlie sighed and looked out the window, watching a blackbird fly past.

'I'm not saying it's wrong to have sex with strangers. I'm just saying you should think about why you do it. What you hope to achieve by it.'

'Isn't it enough that it makes me feel better? Does there have to be a deeper purpose? Why can't people just do what makes them feel good?'

'I suppose they can. But maybe what makes you feel good in the moment isn't what makes you feel good in the long run.'

Charlie nodded. Sad, but true.

'I mean, a drug addict feels good getting high,' Eva continued, 'but that doesn't mean ...'

'Yeah, I get it.'

Charlie was starting to regret demanding a trained psychologist. It would have been easier to see a happy-go-lucky life coach who'd tell her about new kinds of yoga and meditation. If she was serious about wanting help, she was going to have to dig deep, and she didn't know if she was up for it. She was so tired.

'Going back to your mother,' Eva said. 'What was she like?'

'She was ... different.'

Charlie glanced at the clock. Not that it mattered how much time was left, she wouldn't be able to describe Betty if she had a lifetime. Because Betty was so full of contradictions and contrasts, of darkness and light, drive and apathy. When Charlie studied psychology, she'd tried to find a diagnosis that fit, but none of them had felt exactly right. It was as though all descriptors were too narrow to encompass Betty Lager.